The Nymph of
Syracuse

Alexander Lucie-Smith

Chapter One

It was January, and the new decade had just begun. It was cold, and he stood on the steps of the Church of the Holy Souls in Purgatory, which faced the warming sun. He was wearing one of the suits his wife had bought him on her most recent trip to Milan; and a light unbuttoned overcoat, which, though hardly necessary in Catania even in the depths of winter, he had grown to like. The figure he cut advertised the power he wielded, and the wealth that it brought. That was why he tried his very best to rein in his appetite for food. It would not do to get fat, and to look old. After all, he was only twenty-five years old, though he projected the gravitas of a much older man. His eldest daughter, Isabella, was seven, his younger, Natalia, was three; his long-awaited son was less than one month old. The son was called Renato, and named after his paternal grandfather, the notorious bombmaker, a man known to all by his posthumous nickname of the Chemist. But there would come a time, and soon, Calogero di Rienzi hoped, when his father, now dead nearly ten years, would no longer overshadow the family; his hope was that Renato would grow up in a world where the Chemist, and the origin of the family fortune, would be forgotten.

In his hand he held a piece of paper, which, some ten minutes previously, one of the small boys of the quarter had handed him. This boy, no more than about ten years old, had shyly approached him, and said that he had been asked to give him the envelope. Calogero had smiled at the boy, asked him his name (it was Tonino, Tonino Grassi) and given him a five euro note for his pains, and then looked at the message; before the boy ran off, he asked him if he knew Traiano. The boy nodded.

'Tell him I am here and I am waiting for him,' said Calogero.

The boy went to do the errand. As he waited, Calogero once more looked at the note in his hand. It was very simple. It said: 'Under the reconstructed dome.' He knew exactly where that meant. But there was no time, no date. The last time he had been summoned – and that was in fact the first and only time he had been summoned - it had been to hear the lion roar in Messina on Sunday at noon. But the current message, which could hardly be a hoax – he remembered what he had been told – you could not ask to see them, they asked to see you – the current message could not be ignored. Five years almost exactly had passed since the summons to Messina and the subsequent murder of Carmine del Monaco. For five years he had had their blessing to do as he pleased in the Purgatory quarter of Catania. For five years he had received money from them, laundered through the Confraternity of the Holy Souls, and for five years he had paid them their cut of what he earned through the same channel. Now, it seemed, they wanted something more. What? Was this some terrible crisis that was about to engulf him? Or was it some wonderful new opportunity?

Everything he did was legal, and everything he did was hugely profitable. He owned numerous properties in the quarter, and these had risen in value, as Purgatory had ceased to be a slum and had become almost a fashionable place of entertainment. He had invested the money he made wisely, and at the age of twenty-five had paid off the bank loans he had taken out to help him expand, and now had a net worth of several million euros, and many diversified holdings throughout the city, though the concentration was in Purgatory. As for the illegal things, those had been franchised out to the

4

late Turiddu, now ten months dead, and were now in the hands of Traiano, who controlled the prostitution and the drugs in the quarter, and who handed out the punishment beatings, increasingly rare, to difficult customers. Traiano was still only a teenager, but he was feared, and that was what counted. That was why punishment beatings were very rare; the fearful reputation was enough to maintain order. But he knew that power and wealth brought with them jealousy. There were other men in Catania who might look upon what he had inherited from his father and what he had built up, and want what he had. They might apply to others, and have him removed, just as Carmine del Monaco had been removed. The more successful you were, the more perilous your position. You became like that Roman Emperor who had his corridors lined with mirrors so he could see whoever might be creeping up behind him with a dagger. He had seen those corridors under the Palatine Hill, when he had accompanied his wife to Rome and seen the sights. It had availed Domitian nothing. They had stabbed him, not in the back, but in the front, in the groin. There were always novel ways of killing people, he supposed, but the knife was best. There was a certain neatness and panache to the use of a knife. He had stabbed Vitale to death, with one clean cut, then burned his shop down about him; Turiddu had disposed of Carmine del Monaco with two movements of the knife, which he had demonstrated to him. As for Turiddu himself, he had been strangled with a belt and then hung up to make it look as if he had done it himself. His death had been a humiliation.

The deliverer of that death now approached the one who had decreed it. Traiano was crossing the square. He came and stood before Calogero.

'You look smart,' he said, taking in the overcoat.

5

Calogero looked at Traiano. He had inherited his mother's good looks, he supposed. He remembered Anna. Some things you never forgot: her hair spread against a dirty pillow case, her indifferent stare fixed on the cracked ceiling on the dingy ground floor room, her skirt pulled up, her legs open, while he climbed on top of her. He hadn't seen her for over six months, but that was the image that haunted him, that picture of his thirteen-year-old self. And if Traiano recalled Anna in some ways, he must have recalled his unknown father in others: broad shouldered, strong, tall. His father was doing time in Bucharest for grievous bodily harm. Not that Traiano remembered his father at all. But the genes were there.

He took in Traiano's clothes, the trainers, the jeans, the black leather jacket, the shiny shirt. He saw the long curly hair, the unshaven chin.

'You look like a pimp,' he said.

'You made me one, boss,' he answered with a laugh.

'Have you been to Noto?' asked Calogero.

'No.'

'Well, we are going. I need to go, and I want you to come with me. We will set off after lunch. We may be some time there, so pack a few things and meet me below my flat at three. And make sure you are prepared. And tell no one where you are going.'

6

Traiano understood.

Calogero did not tell his wife where he was going; he merely told her he would be away, perhaps for a couple of nights. She did not ask for any further elucidation. She knew if he was going away it was for some purpose which it were better she did not know. It might be important. She could not imagine him taking a pleasure trip without warning. He would presumably come back. She sometimes wondered about the possibility of him never coming back, of going out, and never returning; of his body being found in the sea, or on the lava fields of Mount Etna, or between rubbish bins in some narrow street in Purgatory. One day, she thought, it would end that way; but perhaps not this time. He was good for a few years yet. But the thought of her husband's death haunted her. She wondered if her mother-in-law had ever felt the same: her husband, the Chemist, had left for unexplained trips abroad, and one day never returned, after that fatal explosion in the Milan hotel room. The Chemist had practised the art of murder the length of the peninsula and beyond. She wondered what Calogero was going to do.

Calogero too had a sense of death as he packed his case, for he remembered his father doing something similar. And he remembered how he himself, in childhood, would go through the contents of his father's case in the search for clues to that enigmatic man's activities. One day his father had packed and left and never returned, and perhaps one day he too would leave the house and never return. He wondered if he were being summoned to Noto to meet his death. Had he offended someone? Had someone decided as a favour to someone else, that he was to be rubbed out? Or had they got something for him? Whichever way, good or bad, one had to take

7

precautions, and his precaution was to take Traiano with him. He would be a useful pair of eyes, and he was handy with a knife. He had known him from infancy and he trusted him.

As he walked downstairs after lunch, with his bag, he met his brother going upstairs.

'You were coming to see me?' he asked. 'In the middle of the day? What could be so important?'

'I had a few moments. It was about the wedding.' (Their elder sister, Assunta, was getting married.) 'In fact, I wanted to speak to Stefania more than you. About my suit. Are you going away? I saw that Traiano was waiting by your car.'

'Yes, I am going away,' he said shortly. 'But not for long.'

'Where will you be, in case we need you?' asked Rosario.

'You won't need me. And if I need you, I know how to get hold of you.'

He passed his brother on the stairs.

'Have a good trip,' called Rosario towards his retreating back.

Traiano was waiting for him. Very soon they were heading through the city towards the ring road, and then turning south.

'This is the way to Syracuse,' observed Traiano.

'It's past Syracuse,' said Calogero. 'But it is motorway the entire way. We will be there in an hour or so. Have you heard from your mother recently?'

Traiano wanted to discuss his mother, much as he disliked her even being mentioned, but had not been sure how to bring the subject up. He noted that the boss used to word 'heard', which surely indicated that he knew he had not seen her ever since she went to live in Syracuse, to manage the small bed and breakfast that the boss had given her to look after. He was embarrassed by his mother. He himself could take the joke that he was a pimp; but the fact that his mother had been a prostitute was a different matter.

'I have heard from her,' he conceded at last. 'Have you heard from her?'

'No. The place she looks after she rents from me, but it is her responsibility. I would only hear if something went wrong, I suppose.'

'Then you may hear sooner or later. You know how these Romanians talk...'

'These Romanians?'

'I am Sicilian by upbringing,' said Traiano. 'I do not consider myself Romanian. I was three when I left. Anyway, they have heard that she has this place in Syracuse. Wherever there are Romanians there are channels of communication. Someone told my father's mother about it in Iasi, and my

9

father has been in touch with her demanding that she send him more money. She has sent him or his mother something every month for years. Mainly to keep him away.'

'Even when he was in jail?'

'Particularly when he was in jail. She does not want to pay him anything at all any more, let alone pay any more, and he has sent some guy round to tell her that she has to. This guy made a few threats. The worst threat being that if she did not pay up, then my father would come over in person, when he gets out. That is just what she does not want. And this man, this Romanian, this chancer, has found out that she is back to her old ways and that when my father knows this, he will be very annoyed.'

'Does this man know that you are her son?'

'He claims not to be frightened of anyone.'

'I don't like him threatening my tenants,' said Calogero. 'When we have finished in Noto, we can call in in Syracuse perhaps. Take your mother by surprise. Take this Romanian by surprise too. This is a business trip, but we can add on a little pleasure.'

'What is our business in Noto?' he asked.

'Your business is to keep your eyes open. My business will be apparent in due course. Let's be patient.'

Traiano had spent all his formative years in Catania, noisy, dirty and beautiful Catania, and was surprised by how small, clean and quiet Noto was, particularly in January. Calogero parked the car in the road that bisected the public garden, in view of the triumphal arch that led into the town. He waited while Traiano took the gun out of the bag at his feet and placed it in its usual position, tucked into his belt and covered with his jacket. He himself had a knife within easy reach, and Traiano was also carrying a knife in his breast pocket, he knew. They both had similar weapons with small retractable but deadly blades.

'Are we expecting trouble, boss?' asked Traiano.

'No, but it is best to be prepared for anything that might happen,' said Calogero.

And what might happen? A knife in the guts, a bullet in the head? Both were possible. A belt tightened round one's neck? Did what one gave out to people inevitably return to you, somehow or another? Now he had a son, he wanted to stay alive for him. So, one took precautions, added precautions. Life was a gamble, and perhaps one day one would lose; but there was no point rushing to meet that which one should most avoid; there was no point in dwelling on it. And as far as he knew, he was not in danger. The idea that he had been summoned to Noto to be assassinated seemed far-fetched. But the idea that this walk into the town could be his last on earth made him tingle. It gave an added dimension to existence, this realisation that one was gambling with life itself.

11

The town lay all before them, one single road, it seemed, lined with the most extravagant baroque architecture, a little like a stage set, and no people around, even though it was not yet five on a winter afternoon. A short walk brought them to the central square and the monumental staircase that led up to the cathedral. This, he had heard, was the cathedral whose dome had collapsed back in 1996. Its reconstruction had taken eleven long years, and been completed only three years previously. They climbed the steps towards the bright stone façade, and entered the bare undecorated nave. Whoever had summoned him to a meeting here, clearly understood that the one hobby Calogero had was an interest in art, something that had led him, as a little boy, into his second career after stealing car radios, namely stealing precious objects from churches, a career that had culminated in stealing the Spanish Madonna, the Velasquez altarpiece, from the Church of the Holy Souls in Purgatory. His eye was immediately drawn to the modern works of art in this reconstructed cathedral. There were frescoes in the dome, and along the walls of the nave were dramatic stations of the cross, executed with Caravaggesque realism. They struck him as masterpieces of composition and draughtsmanship.

'I wonder who did these,' he said. 'I must look it up.'

The viewer was not spared the graphic nature of the Lord's suffering; each wound stood out with photographic clarity. Suddenly he was struck with the intensity of human suffering, and with the realisation that it must never ever happen to him or to his children, and in particular, his son. Let it happen, rather, to other people. Of course, he understood the lesson of the sufferings of the Cross, but it was a lesson he rejected: namely that one should suffer voluntarily for others. Why? Who were these others, except a

12

group of people who did not have your interests at heart? Only you could look out for yourself: the mercy of the crowd was not to be trusted. The mercy of God was illusory. What had He ever done to protect His friends or reward good people?

Traiano was also studying the canvases, these scenes of torture and death. He wondered if this was what they had come for, to see these pictures. But being in church his mind was drawn to something that had been preoccupying him.

'Don Giorgio is a most unreasonable man,' he said, speaking of the priest of the Church of the Holy Souls in Purgatory. 'He refuses even to discuss Ceccina and me getting married. He says we are too young. Well, that does not bother me too much. I told Ceccina, and I told her father, and the fact that I have asked the priest about it is enough for them. And the fact that the family get a free flat thanks to your generosity, boss.'

'That was your payment for what you have done for me,' said Calogero.

'I know. So, the marriage thing can wait. But the child has to be baptised, and even here don Giorgio is making difficulties. About how many we can invite, about when we can have it, about who can be godparents. I told him that the child was innocent. Never mind who the father is. Or that the parents aren't married; though he can hardly complain about that, as he himself has refused to marry us. I am a little disappointed. I used to be his altar server. When I was a child, I thought he liked me. My mother used to know him well. Ceccina's parents go to church every Sunday. Yet he has been so difficult, and Cristoforo is, well you know how old he is.'

'Exactly the same age as my Renato,' said Calogero, now staring up at the reconstructed dome. 'Born the very same day. Conceived the very same night, more or less.'

'When is Renato being baptised?'

'Soon, soon,' said Calogero. 'My elder sister is getting married after Easter. So, we may do it before. Stefania has been speaking to don Giorgio. I do not bother. I just provoke him, I think. He remembers my father and his funeral. We are having Rosario as the godfather. He is so good and holy, bless him. Don Giorgio would find it hard to object to him.'

'I was thinking of asking him as well,' said Traiano, 'for my little boy. I have known him a long time, and he is your brother. Would that be OK with you, boss?'

'I'd not like that at all,' said Calogero, taking his eyes off the dome, and turning to look at Traiano. 'I was looking forward to being his godfather myself.'

'I hardly dared ask,' said Traiano.

'After what you did for me with Turiddu, you can ask anything,' said Calogero. 'Mind you, don Giorgio may object to me.'

'He would not dare,' said Traiano happily. 'After all, the Confraternity pays him, does it not? And you are a member of the Confraternity. And the

14

lawyer Petrocchi, who is the only one in the Confraternity that counts, defers to you, doesn't he?'

'I am not sure if he does, but he will do in future,' said Calogero. The Cathedral was now empty, he saw looking around them. 'But don Giorgio is less clever than he thinks he is. Look at the matter of Ino's funeral. He thought that it would embarrass us, embarrass me, a huge funeral for poor dead Ino. But as it turned out, no one went. A party without guests. It was ignored. It made him look a little foolish, I think, and it made us look, well, it made us look, well, vindicated, if that is the word.'

'I thought you had forgotten about Ino,' said Traiano carefully.

'Why? Because I had not mentioned him? I have not forgotten about him. Ino's case proves I forget nothing, if it proves anything at all. Let us go and have a drink, then find a place to stay the night, and then have dinner. We may be here some time,' he added. 'But it is a nice place.'

In the Cathedral in Catania, Rosario di Rienzi knelt in front of the metal gates that protected the relics of Saint Agatha, virgin and martyr. The Cathedral was always dark, particularly so on a winter afternoon. It was six o'clock, and on the opposite side of the vast church, the daily Mass was in progress at one of the brightly lit side altars, in front of which a little crowd had gathered. By contrast the side where Saint Agatha's shrine was, was dark and deserted, the perfect spot for an assignation. At six o'clock the Angelus bell tolled, and as it did so, a person came in, genuflected, and sat

15

down immediately in front of him. It was Fabio Volta, who earlier that afternoon had received a missed call from the number that meant that he ought to keep this meeting.

'You have found something out?' said Fabio.

'Not really. He has gone away for a couple of days. I found out by accident. He was leaving just as I was going up the stairs to his flat to speak to my sister-in-law about something else entirely. He has gone by car and he has taken Traiano with him. I asked Stefania where he had gone, and she did not know, and she did not know when he would be back. I have this feeling that it is important.'

'If he is being secretive, then that could be a sign that it is,' said Fabio.

'If there was a tracker on his car or a listening device in his car, then we would know a great deal more. This could be what we have been waiting for.'

'If he had a mobile phone, we could track him too,' said Fabio. 'But we will find out later where he has been. You can bet on that.' He paused. 'Did you go to the funeral?'

'Of course,' said Rosario. 'You asked me to. Don Giorgio asked me to as well, to serve, so the fact that I was there looked very natural.'

'You are getting good at this. What did you notice?'

'Well, there was no one there to speak of, no one at all. Ino had been at school with my brother. I remember him vaguely. They were not friends, not close friends, but they knew each other. Alfio would have known him as well, but he was not there either. It was just the parents and a few relations, no contemporaries. It was like the burial of an infectious body. People were keeping away. It was a bit sad. The mother said one thing that stood out; she said it to don Giorgio, and he repeated it to me. That Ino should never have come back. That if he had stayed away, if he had heeded the warning, he would still be alive. Of course he did stay away, and stay away for seven years. He was in Milan. But he came back, and someone killed him because he came back.'

'Someone killed him because he came back,' echoed Volta. 'Seven years was not long enough. In Catania, grudges are eternal, nothing is ever forgotten, no offence, however slight. That is the message. But the news reports took the view that it was a territory dispute between drug dealers, but the truth is that he was back just to see his parents, because the father had been ill. The news reports reflect the general line designed not to alarm people. A drug dealer is murdered, and no one cares. A man coming to visit his father after an absence from Sicily of seven years, a good boy, which incidentally I am sure he was not, but someone who can be portrayed as a good boy, murdered outside the hospital, that is alarming. Outside the very hospital, having just visited his father. I saw the autopsy report.'

'And?' asked Rosario, with trepidation.

'Very nasty. A stab to the back of the leg, to make the victim turn round and then a very big cut across the lower guts. Designed to be deadly but not quick, designed to frighten, designed to be a spectacle, designed to be a warning. Where was your brother on the evening it happened?'

'He was having dinner with me, his wife and his children,' said Rosario.

'Almost as if he set it up. I am not surprised. But he would have used one of his men to do the job.'

'You are sure he did it?'

'Of course. But there is no proof. There can be no proof. A man is stabbed in a dark street outside the hospital and the murderer walks away into the crowd. How the hell do you catch someone like that? But anyone who knows the history of Ino, will know who did it, and will take note. It is clever, very clever. But for the police it is a footnote, yesterday's news. What he is doing today is much more important. Perhaps.'

Fabio Volta got up, genuflected, and left him to his devotions.

It being late January, there was only one hotel open in Noto, and only a couple of restaurants. The hotel overlooked the public gardens, where they had parked the car, and was a simple, unpretentious place. They were, Calogero explained, unexpectedly detained in Noto and wanted a room for the night. When asked for their identity documents, Calogero simply passed over a twenty euro note, and the matter was not mentioned again. He insisted on a double room, with bathroom, but no balcony, two single beds. The man who took their booking, who owned the place, understood.

'You are not the only visitors,' he said. 'In case you hear noises from the other rooms.'

'Who else is staying?'

'The name escapes me,' said the man trying to keep all expression from his voice.

'Could you recommend a restaurant, and perhaps tell them to keep a table for us for eight o'clock?' asked Calogero.

'Yes, of course, I will book a table for two for 8pm at the trattoria just round the corner, second on the left along Corso Vittorio Emanuele.'

'Is the food good?'

'Excellent. Satisfaction guaranteed.'

The restaurant was deserted, as he had expected, apart from a couple at another table, who seemed to him, at first glance, to be mother and son. But maybe not: the woman was mature in years, fortyish, attractive, smartly dressed. The man was about thirty, clearly from a different social class, hard, tough, and, judging from the way he sat, carrying either a gun or a knife. What on earth could the relationship between them be?

Calogero studied the woman, and felt a slight tingling as he did so. The woman, he could almost swear, without looking at him, knew she was being looked at, and enjoyed the experience. Traiano paid the woman no attention at all, but looked at the ugly bastard with her; he stopped himself, as he felt an instinctive desire to check his gun was still there, where he had placed it, before coming out.

The food, as he had been promised, was excellent. They had a long discussion with the owner of the restaurant, who told them what they should eat, and to whose suggestions they readily agreed. Traiano's view, often expressed, was that no one cooked better than Ceccina, her mother, or her grandmother, but on this occasion he was prepared to admit that this food was as good as what he ate at home.

'Are you missing Ceccina?' asked Calogero with the sadistic playfulness that Traiano knew so well.

'Of course I am,' said Traiano, who knew that the boss loved honesty. 'We have never been apart since we met, well, since we got together. We see each other every day. I have never been away from the quarter until now.'

Calogero nodded. People like them did not travel. He himself remembered the very first time he had left the quarter, to go on honeymoon, to stay in the luxury hotel in Taormina. Since then there had been a trip to Rome. But a man was never entirely at ease outside his own quarter, his own territory, though his confidence was building. He was very pleased with the beauty of Noto, and wondered why he had never been here before. Perhaps the time was coming when he would go to all those other places had never been to, Florence, Venice, Naples. He had, he realised now, a great desire to see Pompeii and Herculaneum. And here was Noto, on their doorstep, long unexplored, with all the other towns one heard about: Scicli, Ragusa, Modica, and of course Syracuse, which he had visited to buy the property now being run by Anna. Perhaps one should go there more often, particularly as Anna was having trouble. But Anna was a hard case to deal with, women always were. What a relief, he now realised, to be away from Stefania. He really ought to go away more often.

'Did Ceccina ask where you were going?' asked Calogero.

'Of course not,' said Traiano. 'She never asks about things like that. She is not interested. Or perhaps it is that she realises that not being interested is the best way to be. She never acknowledges anything I do outside the house. Does Stefania?'

'No, never,' said Calogero.

They both acknowledged, without mentioning it, that this was the way things were, this was the unspoken pact between them and their women. They said nothing, asked nothing, and in return, they received everything they could possibly need, within reason. Ceccina was not greedy, not at all, and Traiano gave her everything she needed for the child, for herself, and for her family, her parents, her sister, and all the uncles, aunts and cousins. He paid out a considerable amount every month, but saw this as his side of the bargain. They ignored his work, and he rewarded them for this. And they also overlooked the fact that he had seduced her, impregnated her and not, at least not yet, married her. Of course, he was very young, which

21

made the sin excusable, and at the same time more damning. But he was besotted with her, and she with him, and he was desperate to marry her, to legitimise the child, and to be with her forever, and to have more children. This was something he had told Calogero, but not explained to him in depth. He thought that Calogero did not understand his love for Ceccina, that Calogero was not really interested in it, and that perhaps Calogero was incapable of understanding it.

A deep commitment to another person was indeed not something that was familiar to Calogero. Stefania, despite seven or eight years of marriage, despite everything he had given her, and goodness she knew how to bleed him dry with her spending, Stefania disliked him. The mother of his son, and of his two daughters, did not like him. This was not only disappointing, it was strange, for it struck him as ingratitude, and most people were grateful for what he did for them, and feared losing his friendship. But not Stefania. Not that he cared. They now had a son, and that was that, the purpose of the marriage was fulfilled. He had no intention of making love to her ever again. It had been hard enough in the past. Now he could no longer be bothered.

'You will get tired of Ceccina,' he now said. 'Perhaps before you marry her. Maybe don Giorgio is not so stupid after all. Maybe he should have stopped me marrying Stefania. We were both very young.'

'Are you tired of Stefania, boss?' asked Traiano.

'You know I am,' said Calogero. 'You have seen. You are not stupid.' He sighed. 'She is clever, she is intelligent, she is elegant, she in confident, she is a good mother and a good cook and she looks after the house very well. She is cultured, she has improved herself, she is an asset. If ever I get invited to Palermo, she would come with me and make a very good impression, on the people in Palermo, on their wives.' Palermo, the invitation to it, that was the summit of his ambition, and she would help with that, they both knew. 'But,' said Calogero bitterly, 'in the bedroom, it is like climbing a mountain, and when you get to the top you wonder why you made such an effort to get there. I mean, obviously, the children, and particularly having a son. But now I have a son, I can look elsewhere for my pleasures. Not that Stefania was much of a pleasure in the first place.'

This was ungallant, he knew; but he was already looking elsewhere, his eyes fixed on the woman on the other side of the restaurant. There was a look in his eyes that was unmistakable. Traiano wondered whether the lady noticed, but he could not check without turning round to look. But he understood. The boss, he realised, had been married long enough, and was looking for diversion. Indeed, he had been looking for diversion for some time. He had sought it once with Anna, Traiano's mother, the Romanian prostitute, but perhaps now he was looking for something else. Had he come here with just such an idea in mind? Surely not? Noto in January was hardly the place to find a casual sexual encounter. And if he eventually found a mistress, someone permanent, how would that affect things in the quarter? How would that alter the delicate balance of powers?

But the boss's mind was ever wide-ranging, and while keeping an eye on the beautiful lady on the other side of the restaurant, he thought of something else.

'How is my brother?' he asked.

'He is well,' answered Traiano.

'You speak?'

'All the time, every day.'

'You need to keep your ears and eyes open. Watch him. I do not trust him at all.'

'He's your brother, boss.'

'Those closest to you can pose the greatest threat,' said Calogero. 'What on earth do you talk about?'

'We are friends, boss. What do friends talk about?' asked Traiano. 'He is harmless, boss. I mean, he is a really nice person. He is not ambitious. He is happy the way he is. He likes working for the lawyer Petrocchi. He was very annoyed about me and Ceccina living in sin. Well, I told him that don Giorgio has refused to marry us, and perhaps he can speak to don Giorgio about it. Don Giorgio will give way eventually, I know he will, because he likes me really, and he always liked Anna. Of course, Rosario himself has never lived in sin with anyone, not even for five minutes, but I know he would like to, you can see it in his eyes. And there are quite a few who would like to with him. Ceccina says that all the girls in the quarter are crazy about him. Without exception. I told him this and he just looked puzzled.'

'Really? If they like him it is only because he is my brother. Look at Assunta, she is getting married, and so I have to do something for her. They look at my brother, gangly Rosario, and they think of the huge cheque he would bring with him. Greed. That is what it is. The ultimate human motivation.'

There was silence between them. Greed perhaps did motivate many people, thought Traiano, but surely not everyone. He understood the boss's implication, that woman were greedy, but while it might be true of most, and true of Ceccina's relations, but it was not true of Ceccina herself. She loved him. He knew she did. But the family perhaps thought that the money, the favours, the jobs, the chance of a better flat, all these things compensated for a prospective son-in-law who was not Sicilian but Romanian, who had no education, whose mother was a prostitute, and who was covered in scars, and who, while not having a criminal record, stank of crime.

'Everyone loves Rosario,' said Traiano. 'He was very nice to me when I was child.'

'Do you love him?'

'Of course.'

'Well, don't. One day that may get in the way of things.'

'Boss, about Ino,' said Traiano.

'He is dead. Forget about Ino, we have discussed him enough,' said Calogero easily.

'It was in the papers, and Anna saw it, and it was on the television, though very briefly,' said Traiano. 'That was why she phoned me, the last time we spoke. She wanted to ask about the circumstances of the death, the funeral. She knew him. She said it upset her to think he was dead.'

'That way of thinking,' said Calogero. 'It is not logical. It is one of the reasons, the many reasons, why women have nothing to do with our business. She rang not because she thought you had anything to do with Ino's death; she rang because she remembered that once, years ago, Ino paid her fifty euros for half an hour of her time; or she thought she remembered that. Your mother is a prostitute; is, not was; because once a prostitute, a prostitute forever. She had numerous transactions with numerous clients, but now in her memory she endows one of those passing business deals with a significance it could not possibly have had at the time. This is silly sentimentality. I know what I am speaking of. I went to bed with Anna, and I barely remember it. I mean, I know it happened, I assume it was enjoyable, but... I was little more than a child. I was thirteen or so. You were about five at the time. Why should it bother you?' asked Calogero. 'If I had known at the time that we would be discussing this now....'

'Boss, you know... I know she was a prostitute. I know she and Turiddu..... You took him up there, and you took me out for an ice-cream while they did it. But she did not object. And she had his child. I feel sorry

26

for that child. I feel sorry for Anna. I hate her, and that child of Turiddu's will hate her one day.'

'You hate her?'

'Isn't that what you wanted?' he asked. 'You made me hate her.'

'Good,' said Calogero. 'Hatred is one step towards indifference. What counts for you, or should count for you, is me and your son and my son. That is all. Anna does not count. She is someone whom we passed on the way. Ceccina and Stefania are different as they are the mothers of our children. But women like Anna… We use them and we move on. Of course, we will never mistreat them, but as women, they don't count for much. You count. And let me tell you if anyone is annoying Anna in Syracuse, we will deal with that not because of her, but because of you, your reputation.'

'Can I kill him?'

'You have gun, and now you need to prove you can use it,' said Calogero levelly. 'You have been practising?'

Traiano nodded.

'Whoever he is, you can practice on him. Just make sure he does not have any friends that can come after you, and that you do not get caught.'

The plates from the second course were now cleared away and there was a slight pause while they considered the possibility of pudding. As they scanned the menu, the couple at the other table on the far side of the room stood to leave, and as they passed their table the woman stopped to wish them good evening.

'Are you liking Noto?' she asked.

Calogero was immediately on his guard, but tried his best not to show it, though out of the corner of his eye he saw Traiano tense up.

'Very much,' he said with a charming and handsome smile. 'I am from Catania, but I have never been here before. I have been missing something really special.'

'The reconstructed dome,' she said, smiling herself.

'Yes,' he agreed. 'I think we are staying at the same hotel?'

'I imagine we are, as it is the only one open at this time of year. Did you have the suckling pig? Yes? So did we. It was excellent, as promised. And the ragu with the pasta was exquisite. Anyway, good night, for now at least.'

She smiled and passed on, the younger man with her following behind. He had played no part in the conversation, and had acted as if invisible. Similarly, the lady had treated Traiano as invisible. He understood what this meant. She was important, the man her bag carrier, and she treated

Calogero as a man of similar importance. He understood why they were there; to meet her.

'Let us have pudding,' he said. 'And coffee. And maybe a glass of limoncello as well. After all, we do not want to look as if we are in a hurry.'

'A hurry for what?'

'For meeting up with her,' said Calogero. 'Let her wait.'

'We have come to see her?' he asked innocently.

'Looks like it.'

Their hotel had a bar, and as they entered after dinner, the owner said to Calogero that the signora would like him to join her in the bar. He then proceeded to close the front door, as all the guests were now in the hotel. He went to the bar, and prepared to take their orders.

The lady extended her hand to Calogero.

'I have sent my assistant to bed,' she said. 'He wouldn't find this conversation very interesting. If you want to go upstairs, I can assure you that your friend will be perfectly safe with me,' she said, addressing Traiano.

Traiano looked at Calogero, who nodded. He left them. Two glasses of brandy were brought.

'We have never met,' she began. 'It will help you to place me if I tell you that I am the aunt of a police officer called Fabrizio Perraino; I am his mother's sister; you may remember poor Fabrizio was badly hurt by a man called Carmine del Monaco, much to my sister's distress, and indeed mine. Well, that matter was laid to rest, thanks to the kind offices of our friends in Palermo, and del Monaco troubles us no more. My name is Anna Maria Tancredi, and I work in finance. I represent several powerful but discreet interests. As you know, from your reading of the newspapers, the government is in trouble. Well, the government of Italy is always in trouble, you might think. But this time it is really in trouble. But they say that every time. One of the things that the government has planned and is still planning, is a massive programme of public works here in Sicily and elsewhere. But here in Sicily is what concerns us.'

'You mean the bridge over the straits of Messina?'

'That is part of it. That plan is supposedly active even as we speak. It has been proposed and cancelled so many times, but right now it is active. It would be the longest suspension bridge in the world and it will, or should I say would, cost billions of euros. Billions. More than anyone can compute. It means contracts galore. Because don't forget the bridge means a new rail line and it means new roads leading to the bridge and the upgrading of old roads. The idea is that the whole island will become a hive of activity, which is precisely the point. It is to create jobs and win votes, in preparation for the next election. But… before that happens, something else will happen. Next year in the spring, the European Central Bank will pull the carpet out from under Silvio Berlusconi, and the government will collapse. They will do this by refusing to lend him any money. Then a new government will come in, led by some banker approved by Brussels, and cancel all the grandiose and frankly useless schemes proposed by this current government.'

'You can't know that that will happen,' observed Calogero.

She laughed.

'We know. We have people in Brussels, and they see how worried people are, and they guarantee us that the Italian debt will hit the brick wall in spring next year. By autumn next year we will have a new Prime Minister who will rein in public spending, who is there purely to rein in public spending and bring the debt under control. Brussels does not like the debt, which is to say that Berlin does not like the debt.'

'So, this is a great opportunity,' said Calogero.

'Exactly,' said Anna Maria Tancredi. 'There is a vast fortune to be made and very quickly too. There will be a rush to invest in various construction companies which our friends own; and then these companies will go bankrupt once the contracts or the prospect of the contracts vanish. The investors will lose their money and be very very angry, and there will be an enquiry which will drag on for years and lead precisely nowhere.'

'And where do I come in?' asked Calogero.

'I am glad you want to come in,' she said. 'You are going to be one of the several strategically placed people who is going to buy up shares. But, wait, just hear me out. You are going to do this with money we give you, so that you lose nothing at all, and that way we will drive up the price of the shares. You are rich, and other people will follow your example. The price will rise, and then, it will suddenly deflate. Just at the right moment, we will sell. We will give you as much as you can reasonably pretend to spend, and you will get a kickback of ten percent.'

His mind began to work.

'How much can I spend. A million, two million….?'

'Something like that, but times ten. The more the better. Everyone knows you are a rich man. You can also let people know that you have borrowed to invest.'

'And won't the Financial Police come round asking questions?'

'They ask questions of a lot of people and make a regular nuisance of themselves,' conceded Anna Maria Tancredi. 'But there are some people they never touch. There is a list. Your name will be on the list. The list of untouchables. We can guarantee your impunity. That is quite a privilege. There are not many names on that list. But if you could see the list, you would be impressed.'

'And in return?'

32

'That will come later. When the collapse comes, and the investigation, there may be a few people who ought to keep quiet and who fail to keep quiet. The body politic may require some surgery. That is where you and your people come in. That is not my field of expertise. You have done that sort of work before, haven't you? And you did it well. So, I am assuming you would not mind doing it again. There would be a fee. Per head.'

'I am happy with that sort of work,' said Calogero. 'The boys I use will take to it like ducks to water. They need that sort of thing to keep them happy. Otherwise they get restless.'

'I am a banker,' she said. 'The other side of things does not interest me, though I see it as essential. But that sort of thing is left to people like you; and people like the young man who came with me tonight. He is my bag carrier and acts as a sort of driver and bodyguard. Do you know my nephew, Fabrizio?'

'I know of him,' said Calogero.

'Carmine del Monaco ruined his looks, poor boy. I can't tell you how pleased I was to hear that del Monaco had paid for his stupid crime. I owe you a debt of gratitude. Carmine del Monaco also changed not just Fabrizio's appearance, but also his character. He used to be so delightful. Now he is an angry young man. But he is useful to us, as you can imagine. Everything he finds out that goes on in the world of the Catania police, he passes on. Not that Catania is of great interest to our friends, you understand. The real money is not on the streets, it is in the world of finance. My world. But my world needs your world.'

'And my world needs yours,' said Calogero.

'Then we are agreed,' she said. 'Good. You will receive instructions in the following way.'

She explained. The Confraternity would make disbursements to him, which he would invest in accordance with the advice given by a financial columnist in one of the daily papers, who had been bought by Anna Maria and her friends. When the columnist said 'Buy', then he should buy. That money would go into the companies whose shares he bought, and be siphoned off to the original source. And the price would rise and buying fever would engulf the nation. He could also, if he liked, invest money of his own, borrowing to invest, using his properties as collateral.

'Well,' she said. 'That concludes the business part of this evening. Let us have some more brandy.'

Upstairs, Traino had gone into the room, locked the door, undressed and had a shower. After this, he looked at his watch which was on the bedside table, next to the gun and his knife, and wondered how long the boss would be. He did not wonder what the boss was doing with the stranger, for he knew the boss would tell him if he needed to know. He might tell him, or he might never tell him. It was best not to know some things and he knew that curiosity was a bad thing. On the bed furthest from the door was the boss's overnight bag. It was conveniently open. He looked inside, for though curiosity was bad, there was something he needed to know. There was a thick brown and unsealed envelope, full of banknotes. The thickness of the wodge of notes told him how much was there. Two thousand. This, he knew, was his payment for Ino. He was a little disappointed. He knew the boss liked to keep people waiting, well, liked to keep him waiting, just to underline who was in control. He had hoped for more; but still two thousand would be a help. The expenses of having a son were considerable. He had not realised how much babies needed and how much these things cost. But he loved his son, and did not grudge him anything; he wanted the best for him, and he thought that Ceccina would not ask for anything unreasonable. When he was presented with the two thousand, he would affect surprise and pleasure. Then a thought struck him: had the boss expected him to look?

The bag contained the usual overnight things such as an expensive leather spongebag, and a book, a history of Italy in the nineteenth century. He knew the boss liked that sort of thing, reading books. He had left school very young, but he did not like to be assumed ill-educated or ignorant, though Traiano noticed that he only read works of history and books about art. Traiano himself never read anything at all. He did not have time. Sometimes he picked up the newspaper, when he was in the bar, and scanned the pages, but that was all. One day he would start reading, but not just yet. There was also a brown folder that the boss habitually kept in the safe in his office with the cash, and which Traiano had seen many a time. He guessed what was in it. The boss had this stuff sent to him in anonymous envelopes through the post. The magazine in question was new, barely touched, indeed very new, for he checked the date. He turned the pages. The boss's tastes were completely normal, just what you would expect. Girls showing off their bottoms, their tits, their pussies; blondes, brunettes, all sweetly smiling. He could have any woman he wanted but he preferred them via the pages of a magazine. He must know, as did Traiano, that this was old-fashioned, for everyone nowadays, except them, had computers stuffed full of porn. He wondered what Stefania did: look after the house, look after the children, while her husband never went near her.

He replaced the magazine carefully, and then noticed that curled up in the case was the thick leather belt with the heavy brass buckle. He was familiar with this object, though he had never had the chance to examine it in peace and at leisure. He felt the weight of the buckle in his hands, and the smoothness of the other end of the belt as well. Both had been used with effect against his own flesh. The buckle hurt like hell: he remembered the bruises, the welts, the bleeding. He still had the scars and would have them forever. The leather of the belt was at least bearable. But you never knew which he would give you; it depended on how much he wanted to convey his displeasure, how much he wanted to make you suffer, how much he wanted to inflict pain. Well, pain there certainly was, though Traiano was philosophical about pain. It was part of life. It was something he dispensed to others and received himself. It was something you took with stoicism. But the rewards of being with the boss were great. He thought of the two thousand euros. It was a good amount, though not nearly enough, but more would surely come.

Leaving the case, he thought of Ceccina, he thought of the baby, Cristoforo. He wished he could phone her, but they would probably be asleep by now. Besides, the boss did not like phone calls, not when they were able to 'place' you. This applied even to calls from a call box; and a mobile was out of the question. No one was supposed to know where they were. He would have to be patient. But the people in the restaurant, they were presumably the ones the boss was here to meet, which meant that they perhaps would not be here too long. He lay on his bed and fell asleep thinking of his baby son and his son's mother.

As morning broke, he became gradually aware of his surroundings, and then suddenly alert. There were clothes spread on the boss's bed, which had not been slept in. There were sounds coming from the bathroom. Something had happened, something had changed. He was sitting on the side of his bed when Calogero entered, an expansive smile on his face.

'You have woken up,' he observed with mock surprise. 'See you at breakfast. Don't be long.'

He was not long, he knew he ought not to be long. As he expected they were the only two in the dining room of the hotel; the other visitors had left already, or so he assumed. Calogero smiled once more, and extended his cheek to be kissed, as was his custom.

'The others have gone?' observed Traiano.

'The lady had to get back to Palermo, to work. She cannot afford to take too much time off. Palermo or Donnafugata, that is where she has her house, her other house. It was purely business, a business meeting,' said Calogero. 'But there was pleasure as well. It is all good news. For you and for me. She is clever, this Anna Maria Tancredi. She has contacts. She is a banker. She knows everyone who matters. This is a big break for us.'

37

'The man with her was not her lover?'

'Not at all. That oaf? He was, is, her bodyguard. She's discerning.'

'Of course, if she picked you, Uncle Calogero… naturally she is discerning. As are you. She is a beautiful woman. Older, it is true, but beautiful, and as you say, useful to us.'

He had known the boss would find someone, but he had not thought it would be so soon. If indeed he had found someone, if indeed he were planning to see her again. He wondered if perhaps the boss's pleasure in Tancredi's embraces might not have warped his judgement of her usefulness in business. All this would remain secret. The boss had no need to tell him that. He was a little shocked by Tancredi's age, at least forty, maybe even forty-five, twenty years the boss's senior. But there was no accounting for taste, on either side. And the boss's sexual frustration assuaged, it turned out there was something in it for him too.

'About Ino,' said Calogero. 'When we get back to Catania, I have got something nice for you as a reward. Ten thousand.'

Traiano glowed with pleasure. Anna Maria Tancredi had unknowingly done him a favour.

'Boss,' said the youngster, knowing that this was the time to ask, and circumstances might not be so favourable for some time. 'Could you give me that ten thousand as the first payment on a flat in the quarter, a flat for me and Ceccina and the baby? I mean we cannot stay with her parents forever, and Anna's old place is too small. By this time next year there may be four of us, not three.'

'Another one?' said Calogero.

'Always possible,' said Traiano.

'You can have a flat, or ten thousand euros worth of a flat. You know the properties. Find one you like, get rid of the tenants, and then it is yours. And you can pay me the value bit by bit. But there is no hurry. Now, about today,' he said, changing the subject. 'We shall see Anna in Syracuse. I suppose we should let her know we are coming. You can phone her from a public phone, and try and find out when the Romanian visits her. We want to meet him too.'

After breakfast, there was time for a last look around Noto, a walk down the Corso and back along the Via Cavour, to admire the architecture. During the course of this he phoned Anna, and she agreed, grudgingly he thought, to expect them at around midday when she promised that the Romanian would be there as well.

'What do you think?' asked Calogero, about Noto.

'It's beautiful,' said Traiano.

As they got into the car to leave and drive to Syracuse, Calogero said:

'They brought me here for a reason, you know. That dome took eleven years to rebuild. The whole Cathedral was allowed to fall down, and some people said, well, there are enough churches in Sicily and even enough churches in Noto, leave it fallen down. But all the art lovers protested and the government decided it had to rebuild it.'

'Why did it fall down in the first place?' asked Traiano.

'It fell down because all the contractors charged with its maintenance, all of who had been very well paid, did a very poor job, if they did anything at all. And then all the contractors, different contractors, who did the rebuilding, charged a fortune. It cost millions and millions to rebuild the Cathedral, money from private donors, money from Rome, money from Brussels. You know how these projects always go over budget. This one was no exception. And where did all that money end up?'

'Did she tell you this?'

'Anna Maria Tancredi is her name. Yes, she did.'

'And next time they have a scam like this, will some of the money end up with you, boss?'

'And some will end up with you too,' said Calogero.

'The guy she was with, boss. Did you find out anything about him?'

'What is there to know?' asked Calogero with contempt. 'He is some guy provided by Palermo. Her bag carrier.'

'He was armed, I am sure,' said Traiano. 'The way he looked at me in the restaurant. We sort of recognised each other. From Palermo? So, provided to Anna Maria Tancredi by don Lorenzo Santucci?'

'Why are you interested?'

'I like to know who I am dealing with. I look ahead. He was tough-looking. I bet he has killed quite a few. Is he her lover, when she can't find anyone else?'

'His name is Muniddu,' said Calogero, refusing to be provoked. 'He is not her lover. He is her employee. She sleeps with a better class of man. He is a gun, a knife from Palermo. The Santucci family value her very highly. They need to keep her safe. Of course, she is not one of them, but without her help… They need her to process the money, to launder it, to invest it. Her father did the same thing. She is highly respectable. Muniddu keeps an eye out for her and acts as her chauffeur. Yes, I suppose he has killed quite a few. A useful man, I am sure. The silent type. You should follow his example. You only need to know what you need to know.'

'Understood, boss.'

'We need to think about this Romanian who is annoying Anna,' said Calogero, changing the subject. 'Let us see if he is amenable to sweet reason. Otherwise…'

41

'Tell me how to do it, and I will do it,' said Traiano.

'It shouldn't be hard, as he is not expecting any trouble, so we have the element of surprise. But we want to know if he has any friends, what he is doing here. Who knows he is here, how long he has been here, and if anyone will miss him? If he disappears, will people assume he has gone back to Romania? Men disappear all the time. We can shoot him, put him in the boot and then bury him somewhere in the woods. Or dump him in the sea. Pity it's not dark. But let us not do anything precipitate. We do not know who he is, who he represents. You could come back one day and take a pop at him in the street when he goes out to buy some milk. We will need to find out where he lives. But the important thing is to find out as much as we can, and to make sure that he suspects nothing. So, when we meet him, win his confidence.'

Traiano nodded.

They arrived in Syracuse, and drove through the modern town onto the island and parked by the fountain of the nymph Arethusa, the miraculous freshwater spring that rose just by the sea. The house that Anna managed was above the fountain, facing the bay, bathed in delicious southern sunlight even in January. It was a tall narrow house, consisting of about eight rooms, two per floor. He had bought it mainly for its position, and as a useful investment for the future; and he had given the management to Anna, he reflected, as they prepared to knock on the door, because he felt he owed it to her. His feelings towards Anna were complicated by something he did not often feel – guilt.

42

He had made love to her as a teenager, and then he had passed her on to Turiddu who had fathered her child; then he had disposed of Turiddu, albeit with her presumed consent. And then, the summer before Turiddu's supposed suicide, in fact murder, when it had been so hot, and they had all three of them spent the afternoon on her bed in the air-conditioned room…. That had amused him. Now it struck him as something he should not have done. But there was no undoing the past.

She opened the door to them, and greeted them with barely a smile. She was wearing a blue dress, modest, yet shapely, and her dark hair hung loose down to her shoulders. It was obvious to Calogero that she had spent some time preparing herself for this meeting: she was lightly made up, her hair was arranged in such a way that seemed to deny any arrangement had taken place, and the dress pretended to be just something chosen at random. But she was thirty-six years old, and at the height of her beauty. To look at her was to be reminded of that indelible picture of her that Calogero had in his mind; that her son had in his mind too. Calogero had spent the previous night with a very beautiful but different woman, but that experience was temporarily (or so he hoped) obliterated by the overwhelming presence of Anna, standing framed in the doorway of the house he owned and had more or less given her.

Come in,' she said, in tones of intense dislike.

This was something that was relatively unfamiliar to him. Most people feared him, rather than disliked him. If they disliked him, they did their best to hide it, and to flatter him. But here was someone who was clearly not afraid of him or of showing her feelings. They went in to a rather dark sitting room at the front of the house. He took a seat under the full glare of her disapproval. At Traiano, her own son, she did not deign to look. If Calogero was uneasy in her presence, Traiano was deeply uncomfortable and embarrassed, remembering those afternoons in the airconditioning. Well, he had only been a child, and it had not been his fault. The boss had been there and encouraged him, and if the boss thought it was alright then it was allowed, it was OK. But faced with her loathing and contempt, he felt the years fall away, and that he was a boy again. The boss was sitting in an armchair. He went and sat on the floor next to him, and let his head rest on the boss's knee. The boss would protect him, as he had always done.

'So, how is the business?' asked Calogero brightly.

She looked at him as if she did not know what he meant.

'The rentals?' he prompted.

'That is very good,' she said. 'We have excellent reviews on TripAdvisor. The place has almost always been full ever since I got here. They are out all day and I just have to clean between visitors. They really like it.'

'And your other business?' he asked levelly.

'I suppose he told you,' she said, not indicating her son. 'I see gentlemen in the afternoons when all the people upstairs are out. I see them in my own quarters,' she said with dignity. 'They are all regulars and they are all over seventy and they treat me very well. I like them. I am sick to death of young men and boys, but these old men are charming and not demanding. In fact, I enjoy seeing them. And it is profitable. One per afternoon, six days a week; six hundred euros a week. It's easy money.'

'You could charge more,' said Traiano, the pimp in him speaking. 'Two hundred even.'

'Shut up,' said his mother severely.

Calogero put a hand on the boy's head to stop him replying.

'I know you are angry,' said Calogero. 'I thought in the six months or so since I saw you last you might have got over your anger.'

'You promised Rosario that no harm would come to Turiddu,' she said. 'And you promised me too. But you killed him. You lying bastard. Not immediately, you waited, and then when you thought it was safe to do so, when you thought I had forgotten your promise, then you killed him.'

'I didn't kill him, he killed himself,' said Calogero calmly.

'You expect me to believe that?' she said.

'It is what his parents believe, it is what my brother Rosario believes, it is what the police believe. Do you think Rosario would hang around with me if I had lied to him as you say I did? Of course not. And another thing. You seem to have forgotten just how much you disliked Turiddu.'

45

'I have not forgotten that. But I remember he was the father of my son. I felt nothing for him, but he felt something for me. He did not deserve to die.'

'You should ask yourself why he killed himself. If you had been kinder to him, if you had given him something to live for, perhaps he wouldn't have hanged himself.'

She assumed a look of injured innocence.

'I was the one who was kind to him,' she said. 'Unlike you.'

'Holy Mary,' said Traiano under his breath.

She heard him, and she looked at him with venomous hatred.

'I get it,' said Calogero with a sharpness of tone that had not been heard before. 'You hate all men. You hated your husband because he almost beat you to death. You hate me, because I am a man. You hate all your clients in Catania, because they exploited you. You hate your own son because, well, enough said about that. You liked Turiddu because he was hardly a man, and you like these new clients because they are old and harmless. But me, the one who set you up here, the one who hardly charges you any rent, you think that I have to owe you a living for the rest of your life, and the moment someone gives you any trouble, it is me you turn to with your sense of entitlement.'

'Yes,' she said. 'That is entirely it. You owe me a living.'

'Jesus,' said Traiano.

She looked at him. Again, Calogero's hand cautioned him not to say anything.

'You haven't even seen your grandson or asked after him,' said Traiano.

'And you haven't asked about Salvatore,' she said.

'How is he? Where is he?' asked Traiano, softening.

'Asleep for now. But he will wake up soon.'

'You had better tell me all about this Romanian, before he turns up,' said Calogero.

The story of the Romanian was very simple. He called himself Michele, having Italianised his name. He said he knew her husband, Traiano's father, and that they had met in jail. He had discovered her here after asking around in Catania. He claimed to be in contact with her husband, to whose family she sent a monthly subvention. The husband would be getting out of jail in a year's time, perhaps two. In the meantime, he was blackmailing her, wanting money, wanting to live off her, wanting her for sex, threatening her with telling her husband.

Calogero listened to this in silence, as did Traiano. Then Calogero asked:

'Has he been here long? Has he any friends here? What was he in jail for?'

'I don't know what he was in for, but he was in for a long time. He is not old, he is my age, thirty-six at most. He is pretty tough.'

'But he wants to live off a woman,' said Calogero contemptuously. 'You've slept with him?' he asked.

'Of course she has,' said Traiano angrily.

'That makes it easy. If you want, we can deal with him. No problem,' said Calogero. 'We can try talking to him when he comes round, which is soon. He may meet us and realise that you have friends and that he should behave. If he doesn't behave, the next time he comes round, someone will be waiting for him with a knife, and we will dump his corpse in the sea. I take it that is what you want?'

'Who would do that?' asked Anna.

'We will think of someone, won't we, Traiano? Or else we can take a pop at him in the street and walk away. Another dead Romanian, who cares?'

'Why did you sleep with him?' asked Traiano.

'What do you know about anything?' she asked.

There was a ring at the door. She went to open it. The street door opened onto a small hallway, and a moment later she ushered in the man Michele. Introductions were made. Two friends from Catania, arrived unexpectedly. One was her elder son, Traiano.

Michele shook hands, announcing that it was a pleasure to meet them. Calogero and Traiano said the same, with smiles. A moment previously they had been plotting his murder. Now they were all politeness.

They all sat down. Suddenly there was complete silence in the room. Michele sat with knees wide apart. He regarded Calogero with a bold stare.

Calogero got straight to the point.

'You were inside back in Romania?' he asked. 'With Traiano's father?'

'Yes,' said Michele. 'Anna's husband, Traiano's father, was in for grievous bodily harm.'

'And you?'

'Murder.'

'Unfortunate to get caught,' said Calogero.

'I was betrayed,' said Michele. 'Unfortunate for the traitor, as when I got out, I went to find him.'

'And did you?'

'Of course.'

'And now?'

'I decided that here would be a good place to start again. You know, looking for a job.'

'You have a profession or a trade?'

'Just the one,' said Michele.

'You like it here?'

'Very much,' said Michele.

He extended a hand towards Anna and took hers.

They all heard the cry of a child.

'Salvatore,' said Anna, disengaging herself swiftly, and going into the room behind. Traiano followed her, wanting to see his half-brother.

Calogero watched them go.

'Have you got lots of experience?' he asked. 'Are there people who can recommend you?'

'The people in Bucharest spoke to the people in Palermo. They asked me to stay here and to cover this part of the island. They will send me jobs as and when they arise. It is what I did before they caught me, it's the only work I know.'

'I can ask the people in Palermo, and in the future, I may have work for you,' said Calogero.

'You speak to the people in Palermo?'

'From time to time,' said Calogero, which was not true. 'What are you calling yourself these days?'

'Michele Lotto.'

'You have been fucking Anna?'

'Yes, boss.'

'You know she is a whore?'

'I gathered, boss. I don't mind.'

'Use her as much as you like. But she is moody, you know. Try and keep her happy. I own this place and she works for me, so I am happy for you to have as much of her as you want.'

'Thanks, boss. I hope I won't have to remind her of that.'

'When I want you, I shall send a message through her,' said Calogero.

Anna and Traiano came in with the child Salvatore. It was interesting to see how taken with his eighteen-month-old half-brother Traiano seemed to be. The rest of the visit was passed in admiring the child, and in a considerably better mood than it had started. It was decided that they would all go for a walk to the fortress at the end of the island, along the sea road, to enjoy the sunshine. Calogero wondered how he had ended up being roped in to this, walking alongside a woman pushing a perambulator, something he had never ever done with his own wife and children. Traiano went ahead, carrying Salvatore, a child that thankfully looked nothing like Turiddu, on his shoulders, with Michele Lotto next to him. They were speaking in Romanian, somewhat to Calogero's surprise.

'I thought he had forgotten how to speak Romanian,' he remarked to Anna.

'I used to speak to him in Romanian so he would not forget it. One day he might want to go back there. One day he might need to go back there,' she added with meaning.

'Just like Michele Lotto needed to come here? To get away? New identity as well. He worked for them there, and now he works for them here. You knew that?'

'No,' she said.

'Obviously he read our arrival as not entirely a coincidence or a purely social visit. He's clever. We wanted to show him that you had friends, and that he should act accordingly. He wanted to show us that his friends were more important than your friends. And I think he is right. He works for the people in Palermo. He is a professional killer. An ugly customer. Not the sort one wants to cross. So, my advice to you is to give him want he wants, within reason. I think he will be reasonable. If he is not, then we can think again. But I expect him to be. Are you happy with that?'

'I always have to do what you say, don't I?' she said. 'It is my fate.'

'Yes, it is your fate. It could have been worse. I am a kind and generous master, am I not? Just keep this man on board. He could be very dangerous if offended, and he could be very useful to me later on. Right now, I stand to make lots of money.'

'I thought you had already done that?'

'I have indeed. Some years ago, thanks to the backing of the people who matter, I was able to borrow a huge amount from the bank and invest it in properties all of which have gone up in value. I am rich. You have benefitted. Look at this place. It's paradise. But what I meant was that very soon I hope to make a huge amount more. So, no complications. Remember if I go down, so do you, so you need to play your part.'

'So, if that man says open your legs, I open my legs,' she said bitterly.

'You already have done so. So it can't have been so bad. Besides it is your work. It is what you do. I didn't make you into a prostitute, did I?' He sighed. 'I know I must have been a nuisance to you when I was thirteen. But isn't it time you let go of it? Or have I to pay for that for the rest of my life? And you should realise that no one, absolutely no one, not even Stefania, talks to me the way you do. You are privileged. But you should not take it too far.'

She nodded.

'How is my grandson?' she asked.

'The one you have not seen? He is fine. Your son is devoted to him. He and his mother are being well provided for. Traiano seems to like young children,' he said. 'Look at him now.'

'Yes,' she remarked. 'He is still a child himself. I may come for the baptism.'

'Good.'

'You need to make Traiano go to church. How is don Giorgio? I miss him. He was angry with me, but I miss him.'

'I will give him your regards. That will annoy him. He does not like me at all. But he has always got on with Stefania and he adores Rosario.'

'Rosario is good, you are not.'

'Thank you for pointing that out. There is nothing quite like a moralising prostitute, is there?'

She laughed.

'When I retire, I will devote myself to morality full time,' she said. 'Then I will really come after you.'

'I look forward to the day,' he said.

When they were in the car, heading back to Catania, Calogero said:

'Your mother wants me to force you to go to Church.'

'Holy Mary,' said Traiano.

'Actually, it is a good idea. Make people think you are better than you are. Particularly with your son's baptism coming up. It would please Rosario as well. Keep him onside. You were going to ask him to be a godfather, aren't you?'

'Yes, but you said you would take the honour.'

'Indeed, I did. And I will hold to that promise. What were you talking to Michele Lotto about?'

'He's an ugly customer, boss.'

'So I found out when you and Anna were out of the room. A professional killer. That Muniddu person who accompanied signora Tancredi, might have killed a few, but Lotto will have killed several dozen.'

'He was in jail, with my father.'

'Best place for him, perhaps. But when he came out of jail, he killed whoever it was sent him there. And then came here. Bucharest and Palermo traded him. Palermo must have thought him worth having. We have to leave him alone. Palermo have him on their books.'

'But they have you on their books too, boss.'

'Yes, but the way they manage things, you never know how far you are in with them. They like to keep you guessing. You never know how important you are for them, or how much someone else counts with them. It means no one gets overconfident. But signora Tancredi has just given me a job which will net me at least a couple of million euros for doing very little, just for sitting at a desk. The harder work may come later. That is where you will help.'

He explained what Anna Maria Tancredi had explained to him.

'Tancredi trusts you, boss,' remarked Traiano. 'You have struck it lucky there. So, we are to leave Lotto alone for the moment?'

'For the moment, yes. Don't be disappointed. There will be others.' There was silence between them. 'So what did you enjoy most about our little trip?'

'I was happy to see Salvatore. I love him. Odd to think that I killed his father.'

'He never knew his father. Oh, what did Lotto say about your father?'

'That he had spoken of coming to Sicily when he got out, but Lotto would try to persuade him not to. He seemed to think this was a favour to me. I suppose it is. I never knew my father, and cannot remember him at all. I liked the dome of Noto cathedral. That was nice. Since you ask what was best about the trip.'

'Ah, the reconstructed dome,' said Calogero. 'It made many fortunes. And perhaps ours will be made under it too.'

Chapter Two

It turned out not to be hard for Rosario to find out where his brother had gone, for Traiano went to see don Giorgio the day after the trip in order to pass on his mother's greetings, which meant that they had gone to Syracuse, something that Rosario as soon as he could told Fabio Volta, who might be able to work out whether there was any further significance to the trip. Rosario was convinced there was. After all, Anna the Romanian prostitute had left Purgatory and Catania after the death of Turiddu, in order to get away from a place and people she associated with sadness and grief, or so he supposed. She had not seen Calogero or Traiano in the intervening six months, and they had not made any move to see her. So why now? His guess was that the visit to Anna was a cover for some other activity.

The opportunity to find out more soon arose. Don Giorgio had told him that Traiano had come to see him to discuss the baptism once more, and that the meeting had been somehow unsatisfactory; therefore, when Rosario received an invitation to meet up with Traiano, he guessed that the youngster wanted him to intercede with don Giorgio, and that he would use the occasion to see what he could find out.

He found Traiano as arranged, after his work in Petrocchi's office was over, in one of the bars that Calogero owned. This large establishment was one of the newly popular places in Catania, and quite a few people ventured the ten minute or so walk from the Via Etnea to come here. One of its gimmicks was that it was open twenty-four hours a day. From very early in the morning it served coffee and pastries; in fact, its boast, which was recorded in the latest tourist guides, was that this was the place where those returning from night clubs could mingle with early morning workers, such as street sweepers, over cappuccino and cornetto. Coffee was served in the day, and so was food. By six, the place devoted itself to cocktails, beer and wine, which went on till late. After midnight, in the small hours, it was the place to come and meet prostitutes of the more respectable type, who would entertain clients in the upstairs rooms. Anna had managed the place before she decamped to Syracuse, and left it to her son. There was a manager who did the actual work: Traiano kept an eye on this place and others for Calogero.

It was six in the evening when Rosario entered, in his suit, and joined Traiano at his usual table where he sat with a glass of Cinzano. Traiano stood, and smiled, for he had known Rosario for as long as he had known Calogero, namely all his life, and Rosario was closer to him in age too, and they had spent some years together as altar boys for don Giorgio. He kissed his cheek which was his usual way of greeting.

'It's nice to see you,' said Traiano.

'And you, Traiano,' said Rosario.

He accepted a Peroni and a bowl of crisps. Traiano, who did not like alcohol much, at least not yet, carried on with his nearly exhausted Cinzano.

'Don Giorgio told me you saw Anna,' said Rosario conversationally. 'How is she?'

59

'She is fine, really, I think,' said Traiano. 'The place Uncle Caloriu gave her to look after is really nice. It overlooks the sea, faces south, by the fountain of Arethusa. Who was Arethusa? I have no idea.'

'She was a nymph,' said Rosario. 'You know, a goddess. She turned herself into a fountain, a spring, because she was being chased by some god. She wanted to preserve her virginity.'

'You know everything,' said Traiano, admiringly. 'The place is a real beauty spot, so it is full of tourists. Eight rooms, I think, and they are never empty. But… she has found her way back to selling herself. Every afternoon, she sees a bunch of regulars, all very respectable and all over seventy. Or so she says.'

Rosario knew that this was a sensitive subject, and that Traiano had been branded the son of a whore from an early age.

'Mothers are difficult,' said Rosario. 'Mine…. Well, now my elder sister is getting married, she is more dominant than ever.'

'Dominant? I thought she was the retiring type?'

'She is. That's her way of being dominant. She makes us all feel guilty, even Caloriu. Perhaps Anna wants you to feel guilty.'

'Not me. It is Uncle Caloriu she hates. She is indifferent to me, really. But with Uncle Caloriu… hatred is a love gone wrong, don't they say? She blames him for everything. And now she has found a new lover. He is terrible. A real ugly customer. He is a Romanian and he tracked her down because he was with my father in prison in Bucharest. He calls himself Michele Lotto, but his real name is something different. He came here and changed his identity to get away from his crimes there. Even your brother does not like him.'

'And Anna does?'

'Who knows what she likes?' said Traiano gloomily. 'She now says she liked Turiddu a lot. But that wasn't the case when he was alive, I seem to remember. She has the privilege of changing her mind with no regard to the facts. We saw little Salvatore.'

'How is he?'

'Very sweet. Not like his father. He doesn't look like his father either. Thank God. He is sweet and healthy and very pretty. Turiddu was none of those.'

'Are we sure he is Turiddu's child?' asked Rosario curiously.

'Yes, sure. During that time she wasn't working at all. Turiddu lived with us and most nights he would sleep in my room, but sometimes he would go to her room, and sleep in her bed, and just sleep. But on one or two occasions he would go a bit further. That is the story she told, and that is the story he told.'

'Very curious behaviour,' said Rosario.

'Well, who else could have been the father?' asked Traiano.

He remembered the second pregnancy, when Turiddu was no longer in the house, but he was, and Uncle Caloriu, and all three of them would lie down in the afternoons. He sighed.

'I wanted to talk to you about don Giorgio, to see if you could ask him to be a little more reasonable.'

'Go on,' said Rosario.

He took a swig of Cinzano, and then continued: 'I went to see him. It was awful. He was so unbending. He used to be so kind to me. I wanted to fix a date for the baptism. He said he would do the baptism in the summer. Well, it is now January. The summer is six or seven months away. And he would only do the baptism if I came to Church every Sunday between now and the summer. And there were other conditions. I had to promise that I would not sleep with Ceccina. Well, that is not possible, I fear. Besides, the damage has been done. And I had to, this is where it gets complicated, either marry her when I was eighteen, or decide to have nothing else to do with her at all. I think he has been speaking to her parents. Because I reported all this to them, or some of it, and they were not very sympathetic. I don't think they like me, they just tolerate me. OK, I understand they are not happy that I seduced their daughter; but it wasn't entirely my fault. She played her part, though I know the boy has to take all the blame. But I have offered to marry her. But I am not sure now that they want me to marry her. I'd marry her tomorrow if don Giorgio would let me. But the truth is they may prefer to see the back of me, and stick with the shame of an unmarried daughter and an illegitimate grandson. Well, they are fools and they are hypocrites if that is what they are thinking. They are living in that flat rent free for the next eighteen years, thanks to Uncle Calogero, well, thanks to me, as he only did that because of me. So they take my money. And would I be such a bad son-in-law? Who else is Ceccina going to marry?'

'Do you want to marry her?'

'Of course. She is the mother of my son. How could I not want to marry her? And I do not want my son to be illegitimate.'

'That is not such a big thing these days,' said Rosario.

'It's easy for you to think so, Saro,' said Traiano. 'But Cristoforo's grandmother is a whore and his grandfather is in jail in Bucharest, long may he stay there. Cristoforo needs every advantage he can have in life, and he will have it. He will be legitimate and he will have a good home and he will have lots of money, all the things I did not have; I will make sure he gets them. That's why I want Uncle Calogero to be his godfather. I mentioned that to don Giorgio. Of course I want Uncle Caloriu to be godfather. It is so important to me, and it will be important to Cristoforo as he grows up. Uncle Caloriu himself suggested it. I was so pleased, because I knew it was a great deal to ask and hardly dared to ask it. But he suggested it! Then I told don Giorgio and he went ballistic.'

'Did he?'

'He said under no circumstances can your brother be my son's godfather. He screamed and he shouted, and it went on for ages. He said how he should never have done your father's funeral, as it glorified someone who was a criminal, and how he should never have married Uncle Calogero to Stefania –'

'But he is baptising Renato, isn't he, and he is marrying off my sister Assunta to her husband, isn't he?'

'I don't understand what the logic of his position is,' said Traiano. 'He thinks Calogero is some terrible sinner, well, so am I, so is everyone in this quarter with a very few exceptions. He screamed and he shouted. He said the Archbishop had forbidden people like Uncle Calogero from being godfathers.'

Traiano gestured for another Peroni and a coke for himself.

'Did he say why?' asked Rosario. 'Why my brother cannot be a godfather?'

Traiano was silent while the drinks arrived.

'He said something completely crazy,' said Traiano. 'He said that the Archbishop had decreed that members of criminal organisations were not to be godfathers.'

'Holy Mary,' said Rosario.

'I am glad to see you are as shocked as I am,' said Traiano.

'What he said was true, that members of criminal organisations are banned from being godfathers and banned from being honoured by the Church in religious processions and things like that,' said Rosario. 'But why should he think that applies to my brother?'

'I have not told your brother, but can you imagine how angry he will be when I tell him? And I have to tell him. He expects to be godfather. Am I to tell him that don Giorgio refuses? That's why I am speaking to you. Because this concerns you and your family. It concerns you as a brother, it concerns your mother and your sisters. If Uncle Calogero has his name blackened in this way, how will that reflect on you? And it is a libel. He is a respectable businessman. He is a member of the Confraternity. That's why I need you to go to don Giorgio and tell him to calm down and drop this stupidity that he has got into his head.'

Rosario was thoughtful.

'Saro, I need you to do this for me,' continued Traiano. 'Cristoforo needs this. He has to have Uncle Calogero as his godfather. Who else will look after him and protect him? Where will I be in ten years' time? I might be dead, I might be in jail. But your brother is powerful and will look after my son. When Ceccina told me she was pregnant it was a terrible shock; it was not meant to happen. The boys in the quarter all said the same thing to me – why wasn't I careful? And then they said, oh well, it is too late now, she needs to go to the doctor, the one we all know, Doctor Moro, and you need to go with her, and she has to have an abortion. I absolutely refused, and so did she, thank God. They wanted me to kill my own child, to persuade his mother to kill her own child. Can you imagine? This poor child has no friends, they wanted him dead. He only has me and his mother and he will need Calogero.'

'I do understand that. When did Calogero say he would be the child's godfather?'

'It was when we were in Noto, I think, or it might have been in Syracuse. We talked a lot. Have you been there?'

'Syracuse? Yes. Noto, never. They say it is lovely.'

'It is. We visited the cathedral. You would like it. The stations of the cross are superb. As a religious man, you would really enjoy it. The food was excellent, and we were very lucky as most of the places were shut, but this trattoria was open, just two streets along from the triumphal arch. And the hotel was nice. You should go to Noto. That was the first time I have ever stayed in a hotel. You would really love it.'

'I think I shall. What were the hotel and restaurant called? It is useful to have recommendations.'

Traiano recalled the names.

'The stations of the cross are by a modern artist who paints like Caravaggio. They are really good. You really must see them. The boss knows all about Caravaggio. You would not think it, but he's very well informed. And he was wearing his new overcoat. You know the one... and the suit that Stefania bought him in Milan. One of the suits I should say. I think she bought him several. And the shoes, I could not take my eyes off his shoes. Uncle Calogero always looks so beautiful. So smartly dressed, so handsome.'

'Vanity,' said Rosario. 'Not his but my sister-in-law's. She loves clothes and shoes far too much. She dresses him up.'

'If a man can look good, he should look good,' said Traiano defensively. 'And if he looks good, women come flocking.'

'I have not noticed them flocking to my brother,' said Rosario.

'Well, none of them would dare over here, because Stefania keeps an eye out. But when your brother goes away, it is a different story.'

'What do you mean?' asked Rosario curiously. 'Besides he never goes away. Are you saying that he and Anna... when he went to Syracuse with you?'

'Don't be ridiculous! He does not care about Anna at all, whatever might have happened in the past. He hardly likes her any more as a person. Forget I spoke.'

'Has he got someone else?' persisted Rosario.

'Even if he had, I would not be able to say.'

'So what really happened when you went away. He met some woman?' persisted Rosario.

Traiano became conspiratorial, as he was clearly wanting to.

'As you are his brother… But you know I ought not to talk. He met up with this older woman. She had a younger man with her, who carried her bag, a tough type called Muniddu. Your brother and I were sharing a room, but the boss did not get in until the next morning and he more or less admitted that he had been with her.'

'That's bad,' said Rosario.

'I know you think so. So do I. But it is Stefania's fault. She does not make things easy for him,' said Traiano. 'I know you will defend her, because you like her, and she likes you. But she does not care for me too much. I remind her of things she would rather not know about. But you watch out. One day she will get her claws into you. To get her own back on her husband.'

'Don't be ridiculous,' said Rosario. 'It is not that I disapprove, Traiano, though I do. I just fear the consequences. If she finds out… I mean, he fell in with Stefania when he was very young, and now he is stuck with her for life and she with him. They were thirteen or fourteen when they first started going out. He became entangled and can now never disentangle himself. Stefania is the only person who has power over him, you realise? And there is Anna, she can tell him what to do as well, in a way that no one else can. And look at you, Traiano, you will spend the rest of your life with Ceccina hanging round your neck. You will never be free of her, or her parents. They have got their claws into you. They will never let you go.'

Traiano shrugged.

'Some complications are part of life,' said Traiano. 'Look at you, you have nobody. Besides, I love Ceccina and she loves me.'

'When I look at the relationships around me, I think it is a wise choice. Tell me who this woman was. She may be dangerous. Is she going to be permanent? Will he see her again? Why were you there? Aren't you the bodyguard? You should have kept her away.'

'I am. Yes, she might have been dangerous. She had her own bodyguard. I was surprised that it should be a woman. Not what I was expecting. But you must not tell anyone this, promise? I am only telling you this because you are Uncle Calogero's brother, and of course you would never harm him, or speak about him to someone outside our circle of friends. Her name was Anna Maria Tancredi, and she was there to talk to him about the Messina bridge.'

'The Messina bridge?'

On this topic, however, Traiano was well informed. The longest suspension bridge in the world, the most expensive infrastructure project in Italian history.

'But it is never going to get built, is it?' said Rosario. 'All they do is talk and nothing gets done.'

'Berlusconi is going to do it,' said Traiano. 'You watch. And you know why? Not because it is a good idea, but because he needs to get re-elected. Lots of votes here.'

'And you are too young to vote,' said Rosario. 'For the moment.'

He very badly wanted to make an appointment with Fabio Volta. Later, when he was alone, he would give him a missed call, which would be their signal to meet at the hour of Angelus tomorrow in the Cathedral. In the meantime, as he was getting on so well with Traiano, who had been a fund of valuable information, he knew he had better stick around with him for the rest of the evening. So, after a lengthy and rather dull discussion of the bridge, they decided to go for a pizza.

The pizzeria was another scene of Traiano's work. It was owned by Calogero, and the management welcomed them both with open arms, and there was no question of their paying. The boss, they were assured, had been in earlier, as if this guaranteed the quality of the meal they were going to have. Traiano was in the habit of calling in regularly as well, Rosario could tell, and the management was at some pains to let him know that all was running smoothly, and tonight there was no need for the young

Romanian to bang recalcitrant heads against the marble counter top. That had been last week. A guy who did not want to pay. Traiano had brought his head down on the marble with a terrible thwack. The pizzeria sold pizza, naturally, and delivered it too, but it also dealt in the drugs that came from the establishment once run by the late Carmine del Monaco. Drug users who could not pay were scum, and treated as such. When you lost the ability to pay, you became no one at all. Money was all that counted. Luckily, for every one person who could no longer pay, there were many others who could and did. The amount coming in was huge.

Over pizza, Traiano became more confidential about himself. There were ten, sometimes twelve boys, from a pool of about twenty-five, whom he paid out every night for various services as bouncers and delivery boys. The illegal money amounted to several thousand every night, most of it from the drugs. The prostitutes paid to use the rooms, a fixed rate per hour. In return, he and the other boys were there to keep watch in case there was any trouble. Calogero made his money through the legal activities, the coffee, the drinks, the pizza, and Traiano through the illegal or barely legal ones, the drugs and the rooms for whores. Everything about Calogero was legal, Traiano insisted.

They stepped out onto the street at about eleven. Traiano never went to bed much before dawn, and having visited one of the bars and the pizzeria, there were still more rounds to do. Their first port of call was a dimly lit bar on a side street off the square dominated by the Church of the Holy Souls in Purgatory, a bar that Rosario had never been in before, indeed, had not realised existed. They ordered two cups of coffee to which Rosario added a limoncello.

71

'Everything OK?' Traiano asked the man behind the bar.

'Everything OK,' said the man.

'This place makes a fortune and gives very little trouble,' said Traiano. 'Just you watch.'

Along one wall were three or four teenage boys sipping coke, sitting on bar stools, leaning against a shelf over which hung a mirror. Along the opposite wall were older solitary men, some who looked very subdued, in their turn sipping their drinks. No one spoke. The teenagers played with their phones and looked bored. The older men played with their phones, some of them, or scanned newspapers, or even read books. Occasionally someone came in and everyone would for a moment look up, and then return to their phone or reading matter. Then something happened. One of the older men got up and rather nervously approached the bar, on which he laid a fifty euro note. The barman, granite faced, placed a key on the bar. The teenagers were all attentive for a moment. The man looked at them, gave one an imperceptible nod, and then disappeared behind a curtained door behind the bar. The youngster followed him. Seeing him in the light of the bar, Rosario noticed that he looked very young indeed.

'Finished your coffee?' said Traiano.

They left, and as they did so, Traiano nodded to the man on the door.

'Where do those boys come from?' said Rosario.

'Romania,' said Traiano. 'Luckily I can speak the language. The ones who do not have any luck don't get let in by the security on the door more than once. So the men who go there know that there is quality control. That place is making us a packet, as it is more or less 24 hours a day. Now, do you want to go to another bar?'

'Is there another bar?' asked Rosario.

They were standing on the steps of the Church of the Holy Souls in Purgatory.

'We can go back to the original bar and see if any of the girls have arrived there. As the boss's brother, they would be only too glad to give you anything you wanted. And they are all hot as hell.'

'You are the devil,' said Rosario. 'It will be very hot in hell, you will see.'

'I am destined to die young,' said Traiano, 'So I may soon find out.'

'Why do you say that?'

'Well, one day someone may decide they do not like me at all, and take a pop at me. I have beaten up quite a few people, they may decide on revenge. My father might come from Romania and that would be the end of everything for me. Uncle Calogero would protect me from my father, but he is the only protection I have. Everyone else hates me. Even Ceccina's parents, I sometimes think. It is fine for you. They see you walking around, the people of Purgatory, and they say, 'That's Rosario, the boss's brother, the religious one. He is a lawyer or going to be a lawyer.''

'Is that what they say? The religious one?' said Rosario. 'People say the nicest things, don't they? And as a religious person, I am praying that you do not end up in Hell, or in Purgatory as a Holy Soul, just yet. I pray that you repent. As I am sure don Giorgio does.'

'You'll speak to him?'

'Yes. But you speak to him again as well. Tell him that you want to repent, that you are working on it. And that you will go to confession before the baby is baptised.'

He was not hopeful that this would happen. He felt a sliver of pity for Traiano, who had been so badly used by his brother, so disadvantaged by his birth. Would he survive beyond the age of thirty? Or would there be a knife in the guts for him? Or a long jail sentence? Whatever happened, if and when Calogero came crashing down, Traiano would be collateral damage. Tomorrow, at the hour of Angelus in the cathedral, he would pass on the precious name that he had gleaned: the name of Anna Maria Tancredi, the person Calogero had gone to meet in Noto; or the person who had summoned him for a meeting, to which he had taken his bodyguard. Fabio Volta would be able to do something with that name; they were another step closer to their goal.

Chapter Three

Rosario's elder sister, Assunta, was getting married as soon as Lent was over, on the very day after Easter. This meant a great deal of commotion in the family, particularly in the female part of it. For Rosario's mother, the wedding of her eldest daughter was a matter of great joy, the first proper celebration since the death of her husband, for Calogero had married in the May succeeding that tragic October, which had been too soon in her opinion, though of course the wedding had to be then, as Stefania was by that time seven months pregnant. There would be no hint of scandal about the wedding of her eldest daughter and her chosen young man, a man who was so spectacularly uninteresting that most people who met him had difficulty remembering his name. He was called Federico; neither he nor his future wife were blessed with looks, but both were what one could call steady. Federico worked for the state railways in some sort of managerial capacity about which no one could be bothered to ask; Assunta was a trainee accountant, a heavy girl with glasses. There had been a fear that no one would marry her, so the forthcoming nuptials were considered a great blessing.

One matter that was greatly talked about was that Calogero was giving the couple half a million euros as a wedding present. From this sum he said he would pay for the wedding, and the change would be theirs to do with what they liked. This led to the very first disagreement between the couple: she wanted to spend more on the wedding than he did; he wanted to skimp on the wedding as much as humanly possible and use the money to buy a house, a house, moreover, as far away from Purgatory, and even Catania, as possible. Into this dispute Assunta recruited on her side her mother and her sister, who were both adamant that the wedding must make a good show, for the sake of the family name, and they must not be seen to be mean. Moreover, and this was a sensitive issue, the ghost of the Chemist hung over them still; they had to underline their respectability and wealth, and in so doing help everyone to forget that this was the daughter of a mass murderer getting married. As for poor Federico, it seemed that no one would listen at all to his surely very sensible idea that a wedding was one day but a house was forever; a nice comfortable and spacious house in a good area would be something they could enjoy when the wedding day was but a distant memory. Rosario agreed with this, but no one really cared what he thought. But don Giorgio, who was presiding at the ceremony also agreed, and he weighed in on Federico's side.

'You don't want to look like a bunch of vulgarians,' he told Assunta and her mother, and her sister Elena. 'You don't want to look as if you are showing off your money. Try to keep everything as low key as possible. And buy yourself a nice house with all the money you save.'

There were further rumblings of dissent from the bride and her allies, for Calogero was putting up the half million and the groom's side were not stumping up a penny. It looked a little unbalanced, it seemed to them. As for Elena, the younger sister, she saw that when she married a similar amount would be made available for her, which surely made her more marriageable. As for Rosario, he realised that his brother's generosity was nothing of the sort, given that he had defrauded his siblings of their shares of the paternal inheritance. It was in fact paying them off, if they but saw it. Offering to pay for the wedding was another swindle, too, as Calogero (as at his own wedding) would run up the bills, but never pay them, and the

76

various tradesmen would be far too frightened to insist. It was in his interest that they spent as much as possible on the day itself, as this was money that he would subtract from the half million but never pay out himself on their behalf.

One person to whom economy made no sense at all was Stefania, who had decided that the dress she needed would have to come from Rome, which necessitated a week away to choose it. Moreover, she could not leave the children behind, and they needed clothes too, so they needed to come with her, and therefore her sister Giuseppina had to come as well, to help supervise the children. The expedition, five people, flying to Rome and staying in a decent hotel on the Via Nazionale, would cost a fortune. But a week of peace and quiet at home was priceless, or so reasoned Calogero. While his wife, children and sister-in-law flew north, he himself was subjected to being measured for a new suit by a local tailor on his wife's instructions. She had also arranged that the same tailor should produce something similar for Rosario, and, to the latter's surprise, for Traiano as well. In fact, when he went round for the fitting, in Calogero's flat, he discovered that the idea of Traiano's suit came from Calogero, not his wife.

The measuring up was very easily done and, though tedious, took just a few minutes. Each one of them had to stand on the kitchen table while the tailor measured again and again. There were books of sample cloth to choose from. For Traiano, this would be his first ever adult suit.

After the tailor left, Calogero went to open a bottle of wine, and poured two glasses. Traiano, clearly at home now that the feminine and junior presence in the house was temporarily removed, was swigging coke from a plastic bottle, interspersed with gulps of Cinzano.

The conversation started with a general condemnation of the bride and her sister, and the sheer irrationality of women when it came to weddings. Calogero thought, with some reason, that half a million was a very generous present. But he also thought that the bride hoped, by spending as much as she could on the day itself, that her brother would stump up some more after the wedding day was over. Assunta thought that her mindless extravagance would bring in more cash in the future, because her brother was an endless source of money. And Elena thought the same thing, even though her marriage was not yet on the cards, as there was no young man in prospect. But when there was money to be had, declared Calogero, young men would certainly appear from nowhere and every fortune hunter in Catania and the province would be sniffing around, even though, God knew, the poor girl was no catch. And as for their mother, she seemed to want to get in on the act, talking of all the extra expenses that she was running because of the wedding. Every time he saw her, which was as little as he could possibly manage, she would make some new financial demand. These women were bloodsuckers who thought he was made of money. Of course, they had lived on very little in his father's time, because his father had been parsimonious; and he, Calogero, thought a bit of spending increased one's reputation. After all, his own wedding had been very lavish. But these women needed to understand that their only claim to consideration was that they were his relations. And that they had no money of their own apart from what he gave them. And one day he might well decide to give them nothing at all, which would teach them a lesson.

Another bottle of wine was opened. Calogero, who had once hated smoking, and disapproved of it violently, lit a cigar, and gave one to Rosario as well. Traiano shook his head when offered one. Calogero became expansive. There was no controlling Stefania's spending, he said. The clothes and the shoes. The clothes and the shoes for the children. How was it possible to spend so much on shoes alone?

'You love shoes too,' said Traiano.

Calogero ignored this. Now he began to interrogate Rosario about how much he was being paid by the lawyer Petrocchi, and how he ought not to trust anyone in that office, as they were all crooks looking to pull a fast one. Petrocchi himself, he was sure, had enriched himself at the expense of the Confraternity, but he was keeping an eye on him and one day he would catch him and force him to resign. He was sure he was paying himself far too much for the various legal things he did for the Confraternity, all of which were done by understrappers anyway and for which Petrocchi awarded himself huge fees. As for Rossi, his own lawyer, the man was a crook too, and the worst type of crook, an unsuccessful one. No one ought to trust him; he was neither honest nor rich, therefore despised by all. That law firm was a hornets' nest, and Rosario should be very careful when there. Luckily, he was the brother of Calogero di Rienzi and they knew that, and they would never try to make him look foolish. If ever they did, they would regret it.

At this point, Traiano, who had been lying on the sofa, and who had been up all night, fell asleep. His breathing was soft and regular.

'What about him?' asked Rosario.

'What about him?' echoed Calogero without much interest. 'He's useful. He likes fighting. But now he has got a girlfriend and a child to look after, he is growing up quick. Has he annoyed you?'

'No, not at all, it is just that…. Where is he living?'

'Where he has always lived. The flat I gave to his mother. It has two bedrooms. What can have possessed me to be so generous. Anyway, he sleeps there, though he spends most of his time with Ceccina and the baby at her place, a place that I own and do not charge rent for. Of course they were furious, the idea of their very nice daughter being impregnated by scum like him, but they will get over it. They are getting over it. He hopes to get a bigger flat out of me, and that she will move into it with the baby. It is only one baby, for the moment. But that will change. Or so I hear, or so he tells me. But why should I care? And why should you?'

'He asked me to speak to don Giorgio, about the baptism, about their wedding. Don Giorgio likes him, but he is not being easy.'

'Don Giorgio should be careful and should remember who pays him, and who maintains his Church,' said Calogero with some meaning. 'He is giving Traiano a hard time as some sort of message to me. But I do not care. He cannot hurt me. I shrug it off. Stefania listens to him, my mother does, my sisters do, and even you. But I am beyond all that. And I am a member of the Confraternity and I have other connections. Remind him of that.'

There was silence between them, punctuated only by the regular breathing of Traiano.

'Has he offered to fix you up with any of the whores of the quarter?' asked Calogero, gesturing towards Traiano.

'Not recently,' said Rosario.

'He is a pimp, it is what he does, at least some of the time. The boys of the quarter know that they have to go through him for those sorts of favours. But I told him that if he were ever to try and corrupt my own brother, I would give him one hell of a beating.'

'A good beating fixes everything,' said Rosario.

Calogero took this at face value.

'It is the only thing that works with some people. It worked with me. Our father could be pretty savage.'

There was silence between them.

'Are you seeing anyone?' asked Calogero.

It took Rosario a moment to understand what he meant.

'No,' he said.

'Well, just as well perhaps. It's an expensive business. I don't mean just money. I don't just mean the way Stefania spends my money, or our two sisters want to spend my money. Look what has happened to me and Anna. You were about nine at the time when I was seeing her; I saw her only three or four dozen times. But goodness, in so doing I ruined her life. Everything bad that has ever happened to her is my fault. Lots of bad things have happened to her, even before she met me. So I have to pay for it all. The result is that she has a nice place to live in Syracuse and a cushy way of making money. All at my expense. And is she grateful? Not a bit of it.' He got up and fetched the bottle of his favourite whiskey. 'Sheer ingratitude.'

'Maybe she resents the way you corrupted her son, and killed the father of her child,' said Rosario moderately.

'Turiddu hanging himself was the best thing that ever happened to her, or the child, come to think of it. As for me corrupting Traiano, he has his own ideas about everything, the little skunk. Do you think Traiano is corrupted? Well, you are right, of course. He was corrupted from birth. His mother is a whore and his father a criminal, the scum of the Balkans. He has done well for himself considering such unpromising beginnings. As have I, as have you. We are both the sons of a murderer.'

'You once told me never to speak badly of our father,' said Rosario.

'In vino veritas,' said Calogero, pouring them both two glasses of whiskey. 'Look at you, you are now going to be a lawyer, working for the lawyer

Petrocchi. That is good for a boy whose father blew people to kingdom come. You wear a suit, I wear a suit. We have come up in the world. But let me tell you, we have the potential to destroy ourselves, now that we have got what we want, we have the constant temptation to go too far. And then it will all end with us turning against each other, quarrelling over imagined slights, or over money. Then we would all end up killing each other, or in jail, or in some show trial in Palermo.'

'Do you seriously think so?' asked Rosario.

'It's a worry,' said Calogero.

'Would you kill me?'

Calogero stared at him.

'If I had to. If it were you or me. Yes. I would kill anyone in those circumstances. So, you have been warned. They all know it. They have the example of Turiddu before them.'

Turiddu, who was now lying in his grave in a neglected part of the municipal cemetery.

'Don't you feel any guilt?' asked Rosario curiously. 'Any sorrow? Any fear that one day you will pay for it?'

'Why be frightened when it cannot change anything at all?' asked Calogero. 'And of course I am sorry, sorry for myself. I gave Turiddu everything, and he was not grateful. That was unforgivable.'

'So you killed him.'

'That is the past. It is over. I never think about it. Yes, I killed him. So what? It was no big deal. Traiano did a good job. The police did not even ask questions. They didn't give a damn. No one did. Anna pretends to. But screw Anna. And you do not care either. You hated him with a passion. Admit it. But you have never got your hands dirty, have you, my dear brother? You leave that to me. I take the risk, you get the benefit. You are a hypocrite like Petrocchi. Why don't you join the human race? Why don't you get yourself a girlfriend, even if it is a respectable Catholic one? There will be lots of suitable ones coming to the wedding, and as my brother, you are quite a catch.'

Traiano now opened his eyes, and stirred on the sofa. He yawned. He looked from Calogero to his brother and then back to Rosario. He took in the whiskey bottle.

'I was telling Rosario that he needs to find himself a girlfriend, that this celibacy thing of his is ridiculous. The wedding is the time to meet someone. He will look so smart in his suit too.'

'Though he does not have your looks, Uncle Caloriu,' said Traiano, with the lightest of irony, an unmistakeable reference to his growing weight, something that Calogero, in his vanity, did not pick up.

84

'Is the path you took one you would recommend, Calogero?' asked Rosario. 'Are you so very happy with all the women you've had?'

'I am like you, more or less a celibate. It is true that I had Anna a few times, but then I met Stefania and that was that. And sex with Stefania has been few and far between, I can tell you, what with having children and her going shopping.'

'Stop talking about Anna,' said Traiano suddenly.

'Don't sound so offended. Everyone on this quarter has had Anna. And now most of the elderly population of Syracuse. And that Romanian tough, Michele Lotto. And let's remember who else had Anna a couple of years back when he was just thirteen?'

'I thought you said we would never talk about that,' said Traiano.

'Don't take on,' said Calogero crossly. 'It is what it is. You can screw whoever you like and I can screw whoever I like. Nothing matters.'

'Why did you go to Taormina last week?' asked Traiano accusingly. 'And not take me?'

'What I did in Taormina is my business and not yours,' said Calogero. 'I didn't take you because I didn't need you. I was at a meeting about the Messina bridge about which you know precisely nothing. What use would you have been? If I had been talking about drugs and whores you might have had some use. But I wasn't. Understood?'

'I bet that woman was there,' said Traiano defiantly, now sitting up on the sofa. 'That whore.'

'Yes, she was there. That whore as you call her. She is a very important and respectable person. She has more knowledge in her little finger than you have in your entire body.'

'Did you fuck her?' asked Traiano.

Calogero's silence was thunderous. Rosario froze. He felt that his brother would now hit the boy; but something worse happened. Calogero became, having been very angry, very calm. Rosario felt his insides turn to ice. Only Traiano, realising that he had hit home, seemed unmoved, his face remaining brazen and impudent.

At length, Traiano spoke.

'I need to go home,' he said.

'No, you don't,' said Calogero. 'Go into the kitchen and make some coffee. I am sure my brother would like some.'

Traiano stood up and left the room. A few moments later, Rosario and Calogero could hear the clattering of utensils and the sound of running water from the kitchen.

'What was he talking about?' asked Rosario.

'A woman I am doing business with. An investment matter. It is purely business. Nothing of the heart, I assure you. And yet that little shit is jealous.'

A restlessness had come over Calogero. They sat in silence. There was silence from the kitchen. Both listened to it intently. Calogero got up.

'Caloriu, leave him alone,' said Rosario.

'Mind your own business,' said Calogero, as he left the room.

Rosario sat where he was, poured another drink, and heard the sounds of a huge row from several rooms away. Then there was an ominous silence, a crash and, most worrying of all, a gurgling cry of pain. After a bit, Calogero returned. Then came Traiano, looking shaken. He was shirtless.

'I had an accident with the boiling coffee,' said Traiano.

'Should we go to the hospital?' asked Rosario.

'Don't be stupid, he has had worse,' said Calogero.

'So I have,' said Traiano.

Calogero poured some whiskey.

'That looks nasty,' said Rosario with concern, looking at the huge red mark on the bare flesh of Traiano's stomach. 'Doesn't it hurt? I think we should go to hospital.'

'Shut up,' said Calogero. 'Don't talk nonsense.'

'I am fine, really,' said Traiano, 'And no it does not hurt, much. And I have never been to hospital in my life. They ask too many questions.'

They sat together on the sofa. Calogero put his hands around Traiano's neck and gave him a more than playful squeeze.

'Remember what happened to Turiddu.'

'I am in no danger of forgetting,' said Traiano. 'If you are giving Assunta half a million on marriage, and you will do the same for Elena, how much are you going to give Rosario?'

'A million. A boy is worth two girls.'

'But you can afford to be generous,' said Traiano. 'He is not going to get married. So promise him at least ten million.'

'He may change his mind. Then I would not be able to pay and look very foolish. I will promise him a million. If the Messina bridge project goes well, I will just about be able to afford it. I am confident that it will. My investments will pay off.'

'How much will you give me when I marry Ceccina?'

'That is some way away,' said Calogero carefully. 'I'll treat you as a member of the family. Now, as I am so drunk, I need some peace and quiet, so you two had better go to your respective homes.'

They stood up, in Traiano's case rather shakily. Rosario wondered how badly he had been hurt. He followed Traiano into the kitchen where he found his coffee stained shirt and began to put it on with some difficulty.

'I am going to take you to hospital,' said Rosario.

'Bullshit,' said Traiano. 'But you can take me to Doctor Moro. He is the one who deals with these things. He is a friend. No questions asked.'

Doctor Moro was a retired doctor in his sixties who did favours to a few selected friends, whom he treated in his flat up the Via Etnea quite close to the Borgo station. As Traiano said, he asked no questions, but unquestioningly welcomed them, despite the late hour, and put Traiano on the couch in his study and looked at his very nasty burn which was now turning a horrible colour. He tutted sympathetically, and covered the affected area with ointment, while Traiano flinched.

'Who did you provoke this time?' he asked with some humour. 'How is my friend Calogero? Well, I hope. While you are here I ought to look at that other thing I sorted out for you a few months ago. Is there a nice scar? Not too big a one, I hope. You know,' he said, turning to Rosario, 'This friend of yours is so tough that he always refuses painkillers. Point of honour with him. He took the stiches that time without even noticing it. I have never met you, but I know who you are. I knew your father, you see. There,' he said finishing off the application of the ointment. 'Now let us look at the scar.' He examined Traiano's calf. 'Nice,' he remarked. 'I am pleased with my handiwork. I am going to prescribe some antibiotics in case the burn turns infectious, and I want to see you again in a couple of weeks. How was the birth by the way?'

Traiano sighed: 'It was wonderful. I thought at first I would not be able to bear it, that I would pass out, but then when it happened, I was so happy......'

'That is often the way,' said Doctor Moro. 'How is your mother, by the way?'

'In Syracuse,' he answered. 'She has not seen the baby yet.'

'Ah well,' said the doctor sympathetically. 'Now take the antibiotics and take them all. Three times a day. You don't want a nasty infection. The ointment will help, come back for more if you need it. No doubt I will see you again the next time you come off worse in a fight.'

'You should see the other guy, doctor,' said Traiano.

'Anything else?' asked Doctor Moro. 'Remember, prevention is better than cure.'

'Nothing at all, doctor,' said Traiano.

'Anything for you?' asked the doctor, turning to Rosario.

'Don't think so, thanks,' said Rosario.

Traiano put on his shirt, and then took out his wallet, and passed over two hundred euros. He put the pack of pills in his pocket. A moment later they were in the street and walking down towards the Via Etnea.

'My shirt is ruined,' said Traiano gloomily.

'Who is Doctor Moro?' asked Rosario.

'You ask too many questions.'

'It is just one question.'

'One is too many,' said Traiano, then relented. 'He is just a doctor. He is retired but does what is called private work. You heard him, he was a friend of your father's. If one of us gets in a fight and needs patching up, he does it. It means we can avoid going to hospital and having people ask questions. Calogero knew him when he was very young, when he first got into fights. And the women in the quarter go to him, and he sees to their needs. He has got pills and potions all supplied from somewhere, through connections, all very cheap. He can sew you up, he can cure you of venereal disease, he fixes everyone up with contraceptives. Not that you need to go to him, but he is discreet. Whatever you want, he has got it, and no nonsense about prescriptions, no records kept. I hate him, he knows too much. He asked about Anna, what a cheek. What a bloody cheek. He was the one who would willingly have aborted Salvatore my little brother, and Cristoforo, my own son. The bastard. Did you hear what he said about prevention being better than cure? Last time he gave me a talking to because Ceccina was pregnant. Told me to make sure it did not happen again. Your brother said the same thing. Damn them both. Ceccina and I will do what we like. What we damn well like. All the others take Doctor Moro's advice very seriously. Not me. I would like to kill him.'

'And why don't you?' asked Rosario mildly.

'He has connections. He is just a doctor, but he has connections. But you ask too many questions. You shouldn't. Knowledge is dangerous. The less we all know the better. One thing is for sure, Ceccina goes to a proper doctor, so does Cristoforo, not Moro. I only go to him when I need patching up, when I have to. But the other guys, they all think he is wonderful. You get some nasty infection, he cures you, no embarrassment; one of the girls gets pregnant, and he cures that as well; there is a pill for everything, all done very quickly, no waiting around. He has all the antibiotics anyone could ever need, all of it free, all rerouted from great sources.'

'Well, I am very glad you do not like him,' said Rosario. 'Neither do I. But Calogero….'

'Calogero needs him. I doubt feeling comes into it,' said Traiano. 'I must go home and change my shirt.'

92

They were now standing on the corner of the street that led from the Via Etnea back into Purgatory. Traiano held out his hand to wish him good night.

The wedding took place on Easter Monday, by which time Calogero had recovered from his drunkenness, Stefania and the children returned from Rome and made themselves presentable, and did the same for Calogero; by which time Traiano had recovered from his burn and not developed some nasty infection; and by which time Rosario had driven out to Lentini, half an hour from the city, for a private and he hoped secret meeting with Fabio Volta; and by which time Calogero had spent at least one night subsequent to the night in Taormina, with Anna Maria Tancredi, in a hotel in Catania. Moreover, the Prime Minister had made another speech in which he announced, not for the first time, that the Messina bridge project was going ahead, and there had been some movement in the stock market as a result.

Traiano was showing off the burn marks on his chest (now only barely discernible) in the manner of a soldier returned from war, and at the same time confiding in anyone who was interested that he had impregnated Ceccina for the second time, to the fury of her parents. The remains of the burn marks showed he did not give a damn about personal pain, and the hope that Ceccina was having a second child proved that he did not give a damn about the strictures of her parents. They could go to hell, as could, he implied, anyone else who might disapprove. And while they might take a high moral tone for the moment, they would rapidly come round, because he had more money than they did. Meanwhile Ceccina was moving in with him, as soon as he secured the new, bigger, flat. Ceccina was receiving quiet congratulations from other girls present and shyly showing them the engagement ring that Traiano had bought her.

'I suppose I am in the end going to have to marry them,' said don Giorgio wearily.

'How did my brother react when you told him?' asked Rosario when Traiano told him the news.

'He shrugged. He claims not to be pleased, that he disapproves, that he thinks I am too young. But I know him. I think he is pleased, secretly. He likes children. He thinks men should get married and have children. He is old-fashioned in that regard. That's why he wants you to find someone. One of lovely Assunta's friends.'

'Shut up. He may be old-fashioned, as you say. How is his mistress?'

This was a matter of interest to them both, though for different reasons. Traiano had actually seen her, and described her appearance: old (by which he meant in her mid-forties) and very beautiful and rich. Smartly dressed with russet hair. A good figure. Rather surprisingly, he viewed her as a terrible mistake on the boss's part. She would use him and she would throw him aside. Her task was to get him to invest in one of the companies involved in the Messina bridge project, but she would use him for her advantage not his. Calogero was a big tough man, who could use his fists if he wanted to. Anna Maria Tancredi came from a different world, the world of clever people and high finance, about which the boss knew little.

It struck Rosario that this was true: Calogero knew little about fraud, but he could learn. The fraud under way was massive, he knew that, for Volta had told him, and the fraud would make Calogero even richer than he was at present. But it struck him that perhaps the lady herself was making a mistake, given that Calogero had no real feeling for women or anyone else for that matter, whereas she might be driven and weakened by sentiment. It was possible that she was not as heartless as him, and therefore, in any personal duel, somewhat vulnerable to making misjudgements. If she thought she could manage him, she would find herself mistaken, he thought.

'Saro, you don't understand your brother at all,' said Traiano. 'And yet you grew up with him. He lives to dominate other people by inflicting pain on them. But he is old-fashioned and would never beat up a woman. As a result, all the women in his life have given him the run around. Look at Anna. My God, look at Anna. He is like a little boy in her presence. Look at Stefania. She can do what she likes. And now along comes this Tancredi woman. He will be putty in her hands. Because he can dominate men, but he cannot dominate women. He tends to keep away from women. He knows they are dangerous. And he told me that he only slept with Tancredi because he thought this would make it less likely that one day she would have him killed.'

'I suppose a psychologist would have great fun with my brother,' said Rosario. 'But there is very little to understand beyond what is summed up by the phrase that it is a great consolation to have companions in misery. My father beat him, very badly, I think, when he was young. So he beat me, then he beat Turiddu, now he beats you. And I think he beats all the boys in Purgatory.'

'So what? I don't mind.'

'You may well shrug now. He rewards you to compensate for the beatings.'

'Saro,' said Traiano, with great patience. 'You are not like the rest of us. We grew up fighting. I have my first fight, my first proper fight, when I was about six. I got my first knife when I was about eleven, and I got a gun when I was fourteen. That is what we do round here. We grow up fighting, and we fight because it is what we are good at, and it is what we love doing. You fight to stay ahead. And that is a great feeling. Uncle Calogero is the best fighter around. He could beat anyone and he did. He beat up Turiddu's father when was fourteen. He could beat any man from the age of fourteen. So, he became the leader. He can still fight and win. But you know, I am strong, and I could beat him if I wanted to. But I let him win. That's what he likes. But don't tell him. He wouldn't like it. With Anna Maria Tancredi I am not sure he will win. Because she does not fight in the same way.'

'Do you know what every Sicilian woman says when she orgasms?' asked Rosario.

'Do you?' asked Traiano.

'I read it in a book,' said Rosario.

'Ceccina just says 'O Jesus, Jesus, Jesus',' said Traiano. 'Which I take as a compliment. I make her call upon the Lord in desperation. I imagine that Tancredi shouts out something about the Messina bridge, if indeed she orgasms at all.'

'They all call upon the Holy Name,' said Rosario. 'It is what Sicilian women do.'

'I will listen out for it in future,' said Traiano. 'Remember I am just a poor Romanian. And you should get to hear it first hand, Saro, instead of just reading about it in books.'

'The point is this: what is it you say when you are dying, if indeed you can speak?'

'I was listening in those catechism classes! You call upon the Holy Name. How interesting. They say that orgasm resembles death, the feeling of dying, though how anyone could know.... We are familiar with orgasm, but death will be a once in a lifetime experience. That is how Turiddu died, you know, officially at least. At least it is one of the rumours that went around. He hanged himself by accident when he was masturbating with a ligature round his neck, something that people do to make their orgasm feel more intense.'

'Jesus!' said Rosario. 'Sex is death. At least it comes very close to it. That is why no doubt Calogero thought of death after he had slept with signora Tancredi.'

'She would kill people who got in her way,' said Traiano. 'She has a thug called Muniddu who accompanies her everywhere. Or he was with her the first time she met him, and I was with him. But I have not seen her since, and perhaps when they meet they trust each other enough to do without bodyguards. But they can't kill each other, can they?'

'Why not?'

'The peace of Palermo. Palermo lays down the rules, Palermo judges and Palermo condemns. If someone were to take someone out just because of a personal quarrel, Palermo would be annoyed. Look what happened to Carmine del Monaco. If you break the peace, you suffer for it. And thanks to that peace, we can make money, lots of it.'

'That is good in theory, but in practice there are people like Carmine del Monaco getting killed every day. And people like you and my brother. Look what happened to Ino.'

'What happened to Ino? Remind me.'

'Someone stabbed him outside the hospital.'

'Ino was a nonentity. Someone we knew ages ago. I barely remember him. I think he left the quarter when I was seven or eight. Palermo would not care about him. No one cared about him, not even the police. But as you say, it is indeed a dangerous world,' said Traiano. 'The strong rule it, and there are risks. But it is better to be one of the strong. You are so lucky to have your brother looking out for you.'

'Is that what he does?'

Don Giorgio joined them.

'They have told me the news,' he said wearily to Traiano. 'To think that you were once one of my better altar servers.'

'Father, I was at Mass on Sunday; and the Sunday before.'

'I noticed you,' said the priest.

'Please can we get Cristoforo baptised before the new baby is born?'

'That will not be before summer. I suppose we can say June, something like that.'

'And we want to get married.'

'Impossible without parental consent at your age. Can you bring her parents round to it? I have the awful feeling that I am being boxed in to something I don't want to do, again.'

'One wedding begets another one, as I was saying to Rosario,' said Traiano. He turned to Rosario as the priest ambled off. 'I know I can't be a good Catholic ever again, not with the present nature of my work. But I would like to get married to make my children legitimate, before I die. But being a good Catholic like you is a bit boring. Living like me and dying young, is a lot more interesting. Sex is death; well, that sounds a lot more interesting too. I imagine it gives your brother a real thrill in sleeping with a woman who might one day dispose of him. Like the spider, the black widow.'

'She will end up in jail. Whatever is being planned with the Messina bridge, a bridge that will never happen, is too transparent a fraud. You watch. She is clever but not that clever.'

'Why do you say that?' asked Traiano sharply.

'Because she has fallen in with my brother, that is why. Not a clever move. You will see.'

The very same brother now approached. He was completely sober, unlike the last time, and he was wearing the special suit that Stefania had had made for him, as indeed were Rosario and Traiano. His brother sensed that he was in a very expansive mood. He put an arm around each of them.

'Have you seen his burn marks on his chest?' he asked Rosario. 'I gather he was showing them off to everyone, unbuttoning his shirt, though it takes a real act of faith to be able to discern them now. But it was a nasty burn, eh? But he is tough. And if he is scarred for life, he may grow some hair on his chest eventually and cover it up. We will see. I gather you met our good Doctor Moro. He is here somewhere, as an old family friend. That was one invitation Assunta did not object to. Well, she does not know him. As for this little friend of ours, she did question why he should be here. Well, he is here, if only to annoy Assunta and to remind her who is paying for things and who is really in charge. And you have heard that he is going to be a father again? And still not quite sixteen years old. What a man.'

'I am glad you are not annoyed with me, boss,' said Traiano.

'Of course I am not annoyed with you. If I were, you would be crawling out of here bleeding with broken bones. But you have to marry her. I know the parents are being uncooperative. I shall go round to see them in person and make them cooperate. It should not be hard. They are living rent free, are they not? That should make them see reason. Now,' he turned to Rosario, 'I have persuaded our fat new brother-in-law, whose wedding this is, if you have not forgotten, to invest every spare penny he has in a company whose value is going to go through the roof very soon. And he has quite a few of those, if you remember. I don't want you to be left out, so you can do the same, and I will give you the money discreetly. You, Traiano, have a bank account with a fair amount in it, I should hope. The company is called Straits Limited. It is an umbrella company for lots of construction and property firms, all of whom are going to make a fortune when the contracts are awarded for the Messina bridge.'

'And you have been told by a certain person that this company will land these contracts?' asked Traiano.

101

'Yes,' said Calogero. 'All of us must bet the farm on this. And then get out before it is too late. OK?'

'I can imagine all sorts of disasters,' said Rosario.

'I trust her,' said Calogero. 'I trust my instinct.'

He was feeling, just then, incredibly pleased with himself, and this owed much to Anna Maria Tancredi. She was going to make him rich. He was already rich, but she was going to project him into the league of the superrich, and with it open many doors for him. But it was not just the money. The thought of having a mistress, any mistress, was cheering, but such a mistress, so rich, so powerful, and so hungry for him in bed. Looking round the wedding, at his bespectacled sister and her portly new husband, he felt he was rising fast above his origins. Of course, it had annoyed him that Traiano had mentioned Anna Maria in front of his brother, but only because he was addicted to secrets. But on the other hand, the more people who knew about her, and one day they would all know, the more his prestige rose, he reasoned.

The lawyer Petrocchi was Rosario's boss, and Rosario was one of the most junior members of the firm, but when he asked to see the lawyer Petrocchi to discuss an important and urgent matter of mutual interest, the very day the office reopened after the Easter holidays, Rosario was invited to present himself at the lunch table at the small restaurant where Petrocchi ate every day. It was some years since he had had the honour, but he knew the rules. Petrocchi ordered the same thing every day, and it was best to order what he had for the sake of convenience. And he knew too that the waiters were spies, and that what was discussed here might easily and swiftly get back to Calogero.

As he sat in front of his plate of lasagne (was this what they had eaten beforehand, he could not remember), he told Petrocchi that some of the people working in the restaurant were from Purgatory, and they were in the habit of passing information back to Calogero. Petrocchi raised an eyebrow. He was not surprised. Indeed, that was the sort of thing one would expect of Calogero di Rienzi. Not to have the place bugged, but to have ears listening out for his own name. So they decided not to have the main course, veal cutlets with spinach, after all, but to go and walk in the Villa Bellini.

'I know what you want to talk about. Straits Limited. Your brother has been speaking to me, or rather not to me as me, if you see what I mean, but as me as the head of the Confraternity. He wants us to put everything into this company. Sink all our ready money into it. He has a tip off that the government is going to award some very important contracts to Straits Limited. In other words, Straits Limited is going to have major access to the trough that is the spending of the Italian state. The wasteful spending. The thing is, my dear boy, your brother, has good instincts. He is a rich man and he became so by being clever with money. But I would like to know, and you perhaps can tell me, where his inside information comes from.'

'I can tell you. He is relying on information given to him by a woman called Anna Maria Tancredi.'

103

'That is a name I know,' said Petrocchi. 'Let's say you were playing roulette, and someone told you that a certain number was bound to come up. So you bet the house on that number. And then it does not come up, even though they swore to you that they had fixed the table that it would. You would be left looking very foolish, wouldn't you?'

'Do you know signora Tancredi, sir?'

'By reputation. She is a highly reputable banker with links to lots of politicians. Highly reputable. She is the very worst sort of crook because she does not look like a crook. I believe she is very charming. How interesting that she should have alighted on your brother as her partner in crime. Though she may have others.'

'Is it a crime?'

'Of course. It is conspiracy for a start, conspiracy to defraud. It is insider trading. Don't touch it with a bargepole, my son. If the financial police can prove that you knew that this was going on when you invested, you would not be in a good place after the crash. And crash there will be. This whole bridge project is a mirage. This time next year it will be cancelled, and then Straits Limited will sink without trace. The other thing is it will not take intelligent people too long to guess that Straits Limited is a cover for Tancredi and her friends. Anyone investing will either be a complete fool or else a stooge for you know who.'

'You mean…?'

'Don't even mention them. They are the bane of our life. They have ruined this island. Look at us, in the world's most beautiful city, on the world's most beautiful island, set in the middle of the Mediterranean, and we are an object of international pity. Let's not embrace our abusers and executioners.'

They returned to the office. It was thus something of a surprise and a disappointment to discover that very afternoon that the lawyer Petrocchi had changed his mind. After work, at six in the evening, Rosario walked home, and went to the small fourth floor flat in Purgatory where he lived alone. It was a single room, with a tiny kitchen and a bathroom, which overlooked a narrow street, and had no view of the dome of the Church of the Holy Souls in Purgatory, and very little natural light. It was the property of his brother, naturally, who had given it to him on his return from Rome. As soon as he got home, which took ten minutes from the office, he did what he usually did, he undressed and got into the shower. As a result, the sound of the water masked the sound of the key turning in the lock, and it was with great surprise that he walked into his bedroom to find someone there.

'Hi,' said Traiano. 'Your brother asked me to drop by.'

'What for?'

'To check that you have looked into your bank account, seen the money he has given you, and invested that money in Straits Limited, which you can quite easily do online, and which you need to do this evening.'

'No,' said Rosario, clutching the towel round his waist.

'That is what Petrocchi said this afternoon, over the phone to your brother. But then he said yes, when your brother called in person. I was there too. Petrocchi has invested a shedload of cash in the company. He will have to explain that to the Confraternity as best he can when they look at the accounts. But by that time the share price will have risen, and the Confraternity have made a vast profit. That is why you have to buy your shares now, before they shoot up. But the real reason you have to do this is because your brother wants you to. He sent me because he knows we are friends. He might have sent one of the other boys.'

'No,' said Rosario again.

'You will,' said Traiano. He sat on the bed and took out his gun. 'Let us avoid any unpleasantness, shall we? You will do it, because you realise that doing this little thing is better than getting stabbed in the buttock or shot in the leg. And if I shot you in the leg or stabbed you in the rear, you would then do it anyway. So you might as well do it without having to suffer first. But the real reason you will do it is the same reason I am doing this: because he wants it. And what Calogero wants, we want too, and so Calogero always gets what he wants.'

'What did you do to Petrocchi?'

'Nothing much. I held a gun to his head, and he then co-operated. People usually do. Guns are persuasive. People always take the easy way out. There are very few martyrs out there, and I would not advise you to become one of them. At least not yet.'

'If not now, then when?'

'Too difficult a question. One thing at a time. Now go to your computer and buy those shares.'

'No,' said Rosario once more.

Traiano came and stood in front of Rosario. He nudged the towel with his gun. Rosario felt the metal of the gun's barrel against his genitals. He was glad it was the gun and not the knife, which he had always thought the more terrifying weapon. He had felt cold with fear, but now he felt a sudden surge of confidence. Perhaps Traiano sensed this too. He brought the gun up to a position under Rosario's chin.

'You have got to do what he says,' he said, a note of entreaty entering his voice, a note that told Rosario that he had won this contest of wills.

'I don't, and neither do you,' said Rosario.

'Oh but I do. He will be very angry if you defy him. The only question is whether he will take that out on me or on you.'

'Anna stands up to him: why can't you? Why can't I?'

Traiano sat on the bed, dispirited, and put the gun down. He held his head in his hands, and said: 'Holy Mary!' He seemed defeated and depressed.

Rosario sat down next to him.

'You and I can fight him,' he said.

'Really?' said Traiano.

'Yes, he is not all-powerful.'

Traiano shrugged his usual shrug. Then very swiftly, he bent down, held the gun against Rosario's bare calf, and pulled the trigger.

'So, you shot my brother?' said Calogero some twenty minutes later.

He was standing at the door of his flat. Behind him came the noise made by the children and their mother, Stefania.

'He is on his way to Doctor Moro?'

'Yes, boss. I suggested he go and see Moro. He knows the place.'

'I wonder what my mother will say?' mused Calogero. (He rarely wondered what his mother thought or felt about anything, but this was a novel idea and it amused him.) 'I wonder what Stefania will say. I wonder what Petrocchi will say when he limps into the office tomorrow.'

'I am wondering what you are going to say, boss,' said Traiano.

'I say well done, my son,' said Calogero, pulling Traiano towards him and kissing him on the forehead. 'Well done for teaching that hypocritical bastard a lesson. Now, come in, and we will break the news to Stefania. And you can join us and the children for supper. The girls both adore you and often ask about you.'

In they went.

'You will never guess,' he told his wife. 'Someone has shot Rosario. No, not seriously. Flesh wound in the leg. Traiano just saw him. I wonder what can have happened? You would think that a nice clean boy like my brother would not get shot in his own flat by some gun-carrying criminal. How on earth…?'

'Holy Mary!' said Stefania. She turned to Traiano. 'We are having prosciutto crudo. I know you like that. Draw up a chair. I like your hair like that. You look very handsome. Have we fixed a date for your wedding yet?'

Rosario knew they expected him to go to Doctor Moro, the man who did not ask questions, so he did the opposite. He went to the hospital instead.

In the emergency department, Rosario was glad to discover, gunshot wounds went straight to the head of the queue, and because it was early evening, he didn't have to wait.

The doctor who examined him was sympathetic but brisk.

'We see a lot of these,' he said. 'They know where to aim: it goes in one side and comes out the other and hits no arteries or bones. If they had wanted to hurt you, they could have done a lot more damage. Are you in much pain? I thought not. You do not require surgery, you just have to rest for a day or two and let it heal. We will clean the wound, give you some pain killers and some precautionary antibiotics so that you do not develop an infection. I don't know who has done this to you, but you have been largely spared. Next time you may not be so lucky.'

He lay on his bed in the cubicle, while a nurse fussed over his bare leg. He obediently took the pills they gave him. He listened to what they said about keeping the wound clean and dry and how long it would take to heal.

Then the police came: a single policeman.

'Hi,' he said. 'I am sorry to hear of your misfortune. Did you see the man who did it?'

'Of course. It was someone called Traiano, Trajan Antonescu, who lives in my quarter.'

'OK,' said the officer. 'Let me take down your details.'

He was asked for his name, his date of birth and lots of other information, and then to describe the 'incident'.

'This Traiano, a Romanian with a name like that?' said the officer, who, Rosario noted, had a pronounced lisp. 'Bad people the Romanians. Best avoided. Why was this Traiano in your flat? Were you buying drugs off him?'

'No!' said Rosario outraged.

'Were you soliciting him for prostitution?'

'No!'

'Are you quite sure? I know it is embarrassing, but most of these wounds of this nature do involve prostitution or drugs or both. I see you live in the Purgatory quarter. Not a good place. Full of drugs and prostitutes of both sexes. How old is this Traiano?'

'He is fifteen or sixteen at most, but -'

'Soliciting a minor for prostitution is a serious crime,' said the policeman sententiously. 'Why did you let him into your flat, and why were you naked?'

'I didn't let him in!'

111

'We have been round there and there is no sign of a break in. Your clothes are all over the place, and you came in wearing your dressing gown. So: you were in your flat, naked with a sixteen-year-old, no fifteen-year-old, Romanian, who shot you. Of course, I am not making a judgement, sir, but you see how this will look in court.'

'I would very much like it to go to court, actually,' said Rosario. 'Now please take down the details and make sure you file this incident properly.'

'Are you saying I wouldn't?' said the policeman in an offended tone. 'I just want to save you embarrassment. If this Romanian teenager is known to you, could you tell me his surname again? And his date of birth? And his address?'

Rosario gave all three.

'So you know him quite well,' observed the policeman. 'Why did he shoot you?'

The policemen listened to the explanation, and shrugged. Then he put away his papers and his pen. He stood up.

'We will have him arrested,' he said.

'Can I go home now?' asked Rosario. 'Is that all you need?'

'That is all we need,' said the lisping policeman. 'But you cannot go home. Your flat has been sealed off as it is a crime scene.'

He groaned. He would have to go and stay with his mother.

'What is your name?' he asked the departing policeman.

'Fabrizio Perraino, at your service,' said the departing officer.

He was back in his old room at home, and had been there a week, when his brother Calogero came to see him.

'How are you?' he asked tenderly. 'They told me that you have been back at work. But still not at home?'

'The police have sealed it off.'

'But not very efficiently. I was able to send someone in there to use your computer on your behalf, to make that purchase. Since last week, since the night you were so unfortunately shot, you have been the owner of some shares in Straits Limited. You bought twenty thousand euro worth of them, and that has almost doubled in a week. Don't worry, I will tell you when to sell, and when I do perhaps then you will do as I say. I won't ask you to roll up your trouser leg. I can picture what the wound looks like. You will have a small round scar for the rest of your life. A nice little reminder to you always to co-operate with me. By the way, Traiano wants to see you.

He wants to kiss and make up. He is so sweet. He likes you a lot, you know. He was very sorry that he had to do it. For that you must blame me. But you knew I was heartless, didn't you? By the way what has our mother said about all this talk about you being shot by a male prostitute?'

'Very funny,' said Rosario. Then he added: 'Caloriu, don't go.'

That day, he had met Fabio Volta, at the usual place and time. What he now did was difficult, but necessary. Fabio had said that he had to do it, otherwise he would no longer be trusted by Calogero. But Rosario knew that Calogero had one weakness, his vanity. It was that he had to speak to now.

'What?' said Calogero from the door.

'I am sorry. I should have listened to you. I should always listen to you.'

His face was burning red as he said this.

'It is not easy being a younger brother,' said Rosario.

'It is not easy being an older one,' said Calogero. He came and sat down on the bed next to his brother and embraced him.

'Do you want me to put a bullet in your head?' he asked.

'No.'

'It could happen, but I hope it won't. If anything happens to me, you have to be here to look after our mother and our sisters, but to look after Renato and Isabella and Natalia, and to keep an eye on Stefania.'

'Is something going to happen to you?'

'I hope not. But just in case. If it does, if I am killed, then you have to marry Stefania. She and I have discussed it. That is the best for the children and for her. She's always liked you. You are my post-death insurance policy. I need you. Don't make me kill you.' He got up to go. 'I will tell the police to let you get back into your own place. Naturally they will now leave you alone. What did you think of Fabrizio Perraino?'

'The one with the lisp?'

'Correct. Carmine del Monaco broke his jaw in three places. Nasty. Well, Carmine paid for that. In many ways, one can understand why Carmine did it. But he broke the peace of Palermo and paid the price for it. By all accounts Perraino is a little shit. Perhaps one day I shall break his jaw or some other part of him. But he is useful to us. He is Anna Maria Tancredi's nephew.'

He went home later that evening, glad to escape his mother and her grim disapproval. There had been no sympathy in that quarter, only the supposition that he had brought it on himself. As he walked up the stairs to his flat, Traiano was waiting for him, sitting on the stairs.

'What?' he said.

'I have come to say that I am sorry,' said Traiano.

He let him into the flat.

'I didn't think you would dare do it,' said Rosario. 'So, I miscalculated. I shouldn't have pushed you.'

'You were not to know,' said Traiano. 'I owe you one. If ever you need someone dealt with, I will do it for you, no questions asked.'

'That's nice to know,' said Rosario. 'I need a drink.'

'Have you got any coke?' asked Traiano.

Chapter Four

Rosario was disappointed. He was disappointed with Fabio Volta, whose advice he had reluctantly followed, which was to make peace with his brother, and not to press charges with the shooting incident. Rosario, with his legal training, thought that there was a good chance of getting Traiano arrested, tried and convicted for causing actual bodily harm, or malicious wounding, or whatever it was called (like everyone else who worked for Petrocchi, his expertise was in property and commercial law, not crime). And if they nailed Traiano, he could perhaps be persuaded to shop his master, Calogero. But Fabio Volta had been much less sanguine about any such outcome. For a start, he was convinced that Traiano would never ever betray his master, and would much rather face a couple of years inside one of Sicily's notoriously lax youth offender institutions, which would have been the equivalent of a holiday for him, to the certainty of being killed by Calogero for betrayal. And Calogero would certainly kill him, as Traiano would know. For if Calogero was happy to put a bullet through his brother's leg for non-cooperation, what would he do to his chief collaborator if he went over to the police?

Besides which, there was the whole problem of the police. As soon as Rosario had been wounded and gone to hospital rather than Doctor Moro, Calogero had sent a few messages (he never made calls) to ensure that Captain Fabrizio Perraino attended the hospital to take the victim's statement, and to warn the victim not to make a fuss. Sure enough, though Perraino had done the initial paperwork, this had then been conveniently lost which delayed the entire process for a few days, enabling the victim to have the opportunity to think about whether he really wanted to go forward. He would have done, but Volta overruled him, for one simple reason: the Messina bridge affair was maturing, and this affair, Volta was convinced, would bring them to the very top of the organisation. For what made the organisation strong, he explained to Rosario, was not the thugs at the bottom who put bullets through the calves of the innocent, but the bankers, the money men and women and the politicians. As he reminded Rosario, Al Capone was never sent down for his many crimes of violence, but for the much more mundane misdemeanour of tax avoidance. Three things made the organisation successful: the use of violence, the ability to move large sums of money around undetected, and the cooperation of politicians; of these three, the latter two were the easier to tackle.

Anna Maria Tancredi was one of the people who knew of this triple alliance better than most. She represented the money, and she knew the politicians, and she was currently in bed with the man of violence. He was telling her about the way Traiano had shot his brother through the calf. She found the story rather amusing, but at the same time a little dark. If this was how he treated his brother when he annoyed him, how might he treat her one day? For just as he rather feared her power, she feared his; and that added an edge to their relationship.

When she asked him how many men he had killed, he would only answer that it had been as many as required. Of course, he had killed Carmine del Monaco, she knew that, the man who had so cruelly beaten up her formerly handsome nephew Fabrizio and terrorised her sister, Fabrizio's mother. Fabrizio's mother had thought it her influence with Palermo had assured the punishment of del Monaco, but it had been her, Anna Maria, who had brought it about, really. How she had loved her beautiful nephew, as a

118

teenager, and as a young man; how disappointing he was now with his misshapen jaw and his lisp that no surgeon could do anything to cure. What a disappointed man Fabrizio was too, even if he had been promoted to be a captain – but how useful, to her, to the people in Palermo, and to Calogero himself, in dealing with his brother, the tiresome Rosario. But Rosario was now in line, as were the others, even the self-righteous Petrocchi. He described how Traiano had held a gun to his head. She had seen Traiano at Noto, a youthful, handsome, well built young thug. She'd liked him. When she commented on his good looks, Calogero had looked annoyed, as if he were jealous.

She had never married, and now, approaching the age of forty-five, she saw no point in it. She would never have children, but she would have, already did have, a fine substitute: lots of influence and lots of money. What she had now was success, the magic dust, the blessing of the gods, the sense that when she entered a room, people noticed her, people, if not feared her, waited to hear what she would say. That was very pleasing for anyone; it was very pleasing for a woman in Sicily.

Early on in her banking career she had mastered a few techniques that could be useful for those who might have an excess of cash but no legal place to put it. Her speciality was the use of charities. You gave ten thousand, for example, to the shrine of the Madonna of Wherever, and the shrine in its turn spent nine thousand in a completely legal business that you owned. You set up a charitable foundation designed to help missionaries in the third world, and sent a million euro out to Kenya which came back in a variety of ways into your own pocket. Of course, it had been she who had seen the potential of the Ancient and Most Noble

Confraternity of the Holy Souls in Purgatory. You stuffed it with money, that came in as charitable donations, and then the money was disbursed as you saw fit, as supposed charitable donations. Gone were the days of men carrying briefcases full of high denomination notes. Now everything was done by wire. One sat at a computer terminal and vast sums and sometimes smaller ones moved around the planet. Payments were made to drug lords in Colombia through supposed donations to funds earmarked for non-existent hospitals and schools. Whoremasters in Brazil received payment through funds that were supposedly being donated to the missionaries in the Amazon. For the last ten years she had run her own bank, inherited from her father, who had taught her her trade. It was called the Bank of Donnafugata, named after the town she was born in. Of course the bank had nothing to do with the town itself, but she liked the name. The bank maintained an office in Palermo. It dealt with a very restricted list of clients, most of whom, but not all, were completely blameless. She employed several people but essentially the bank, the real operation, was herself and her computer.

Of course banks were regulated, and so was hers, but, and this was important, the regulators were not interested, as the bank specialised in charitable accounts, which was something of a niche market. Some of these accounts were in fact genuine, in fact the majority were. There were quite a few religious orders, including the Jesuits, who used her services; and so did several Sicilian dioceses. This provided a veneer of respectability, and she was always full of deference to the clergy. She delighted in genuflecting before bishops, abbots, provincials and archbishops, and even the Cardinal himself. The depth of her abasement merely served to underline who was really using whom, who really had the power. She had

120

a large collection of beautifully modest dark dresses fit for religious occasions. In recent years she had even bought a few lace mantillas, which she thought gave exactly the right impression: devout, serious, dedicated to doing God's work in the world. To the Church she was a wonderful person they could trust; and to the organisation headquartered in Palermo, she was a wonderful person they could trust too. Her femininity was ideal from their point of view, the perfect cover. No one would ever suspect a woman of being so closely involved with them, surely?

Her femininity was also a disadvantage in that it meant that she would never be admitted to the very highest counsels of the organisation for which she worked. Where they met and what they did, she had a pretty firm idea. They were supposed to meet, traditionally, in the Grand Hotel in Palermo, and they still did from time to time. But most meetings of the top men took place in other hotels in other places: Taormina, Cefalù occasionally, but generally closer to the epicentre of life, places like Mondello and Bagheria. Nothing was ever trusted to paper, nothing was ever communicated electronically; messages came in person, sudden visits from strangers. It was curious how they always knew where you would be.

She had a beautiful flat in the nineteenth century part of Palermo, near the Politeama, a series of lovely high-ceilinged rooms in a Liberty apartment block, inherited from her father; she had a house near Donnafugata, in the province of Ragusa, which she had bought herself, where she spent some time, indeed, as much time as she could. This property, done up with understated good taste and unobtrusive luxury, was her pride and joy. It was her reward to herself for all her hard work. It had a vineyard, an orange grove, olive trees, a garden and a swimming pool. One day she

121

would live there permanently, and grow oranges and lemons, and cultivate the garden; but that day was far off still.

She had always had a weakness for agreeable young men. One summer, the first summer she had owned the house in Donnafugata, she had studied from behind her dark glasses the shape of her nephew Fabrizio under his bathing trunks, as he got out of the pool, his long muscular legs, his broad chest, his wonderful smile. That had been a memorable summer. That was long before Fabrizio had had his jaw broken, and with that disaster become petulant and spoiled and complaining. Or rather, he had always been those things: it was just when his good looks vanished that you noticed his character more; when he started lisping that you noticed he was not, per se, an attractive person. But though ruined in looks, he was still useful, and his spoiled character made him just the sort of person one could use. There had of course been others after Fabrizio, all years younger than herself, none blood relatives, all young men who had in the end been dismissed with kind words and generous presents. All had been pliant, obedient and eager to please. None had lasted more than two or three years at most, before her boredom set in. They wanted too much from her, they wanted attention she could not give; they failed to understand that sometimes she had to cancel meetings at short notice, that her work had to come before pleasure; neither did they entirely grasp that when she wanted pleasure, it was pleasure she wanted, and she did not wish to have to spend her time unruffling male feathers, or making men, any men, feel good about themselves. She wasn't really interested in their mental state, their interior wellbeing. That bored her. She just wanted to have her needs fulfilled; that was all.

This was, of course, selfish. She knew that. But she felt that she was entitled to enjoy herself, as compensation for all her hard work, for all the things that she did for other people. It was thanks to her, and thanks to the lawyers and accountants (most of whom had no idea) she employed, that many people had become rich. They used her, and she was entitled to make use of others, especially when those others she used benefitted hugely from her attentions. Many were employees who moved onto other companies with a wealth of experience and high recommendations.

But Calogero di Rienzi was a little different. He was not from the same social background, for a start. He had no education that she could discern, though he was well-informed when it came to art and architecture. He did read books, mainly books about history, and his focus was almost always the Risorgimento or the world of late antiquity. After his first decade, he had never regularly attended school, so this interest in history, and the way he confined himself almost exclusively to these two periods was remarkable. He hated Garibaldi, he loathed Cavour, he disdained Victor Emmanuel II. He had a sympathy for Pius IX and for the Bourbons of the Two Sicilies. He admired Nelson alone of all the English, but he also admired Napoleon. He referred to Anita Garibaldi exclusively as 'that bitch' and refused to drink anything from a bottle marked with the name of her infamous husband. He disliked Mussolini as yet another oppressor of Sicily, and alone of all the men of the twentieth century he admired Salvatore Giuliano, the famous bandit and outlaw who had campaigned for the independence of Sicily after the Second World war. His feelings for Giuliano were almost slavishly devoted. He carried a picture of him in his wallet. The only other pictures in his wallet were a holy picture of Saint Augustine, and a holy picture of the Spanish Madonna of Velasquez. She had remarked that he looked a bit like Salvatore Giuliano, and this had pleased him immensely. He had pointed out that Giuliano had died at the age of twenty-seven, an age he himself was fast approaching. But he did not seem to think that this early death was too much of a tragedy, for Giuliano had become immortal. There was a film about him, even an opera about him, numerous books. He was simply the greatest man who had ever lived, the Achilles of his day, one who had exchanged longevity for glory.

She had asked him whether he did not want to live a long life, so as to enjoy his already considerable wealth which was bound to grow, especially with the Messina bridge project. But he had shrugged. Who knew what the future would bring? He had children, it was true, unlike Giuliano, but his brother who had never been in trouble and never would be, would look after them if anything happened to him. When he read about ancient Rome, and the world of late antiquity (much to her surprise he had found time to read both the *Confessions* of Saint Augustine and the *City of God*), he had noted that for the Romans ambition had been everything, even though the chances of ambition ever being rewarded were extremely slim. Every Roman of the third or fourth century that you had ever heard of, it seemed to him, had sacrificed all for very little. It was human nature, this desire to get to the top. She herself had had a comfortable upbringing in Palermo and in the province of Ragusa. He did not want to exaggerate, but Purgatory was not the ideal place to grow up. You had to use your fists from an early age. If you didn't, people took advantage of you. The better you were at fighting, the more fearless you were, the more you rose. He had risen to the top partly because of what his father had achieved before him, but mainly because he had been fearless and pitiless. Hence the putting the bullet through Rosario's calf. One could not tolerate dissent.

Poor Rosario, he only had himself to blame, as he had admitted. He had to learn, the hard way if need be.

He wasn't a violent man as such; at least he was not an angry man who gave way to acts of violence. Violent acts had to be planned and considered and committed with proper deliberation. Losing your temper was a very bad idea – look at Carmine del Monaco. That man had been too stupid to live. He failed to control his temper and had become a liability.

She liked the idea that he was a violent criminal, and she liked even more the idea that he was controlled in his violent impulses. He was, she could see, clever, bold and calculating. She wondered what part she herself played in his calculations. At the same time, she wondered what part he could play in hers. He was married, which was just as well; for he was not the sort of man any sensible woman should marry; besides she was twenty years his senior. Anna Maria knew she was beautiful and had known it since her early teens; Calogero was attractive rather than beautiful, though he may have been beautiful in his teens. He now showed, in the face at least, a sort of handsomeness gone to seed, even though he was only in his mid-twenties. His eyes had lost the sparkle they once might have had; they surveyed every room he entered, she noticed, with marked suspicion. He was immensely strong, she could tell, and his smooth brown flesh enclosed a powerful frame of musculature.

He knew that she found him attractive for all the wrong sort of reasons, that he was a tough man and she was not used to tough men; he was her idea of an excursion into dangerous territory. For his part, he found her easily the most interesting woman he had ever met. That in itself was not remarkable. He had loved his mother as a small child, but now felt very little for her. His mother had adored him, and done everything his father could ever have wanted, but this sort of personal devotion bred contempt rather than love. His sisters were objects of complete indifference to him. Anna, who had introduced him to sex, Anna the Romanian prostitute, who had lain back on her bed in that squalid ground floor room, her skirt hitched up, her top pulled down, showing off her hugely inviting breasts and her shameless vagina, Anna who had given him a memory picture that could never be expunged, Anna the mother of Traiano - Anna he now regarded as one of the great mistakes of his life. The prostitute had not made him pay then, but she made him pay now. It was not simply a matter of money, it was the way she constantly tried to make him feel guilty. She did not entirely succeed, but she did annoy him. She was a burden, and being a woman, he could not simply get rid of her. One had to carry her through life. The same was true for Stefania his wife, a clever woman, an asset to him with her looks, her smart appearance, the way she had effortlessly embraced the middle-class life. She had given him a son too, which was of the greatest possible importance. They had been together since the age of fourteen and married since the tender age of seventeen; as a teenager he had not expected to have profound feelings for her, and such profound feelings had never come. In fact, the only deep feeling that had ever taken possession of him was his love for his son Renato, still an infant. That perhaps would grow. But Stefania, for her he would feel little more than he felt for her now, a wary sort of respect. She was the mother of his children. That was surely position enough for her, and it suited him too.

Moments of passion with Stefania had been rare, if indeed there had been any at all. He could not understand the boys in the quarter, particularly the ones he employed, who were constantly in search of girls. He could not understand how Traiano, not content with sleeping with Ceccina and making her pregnant twice, continued to be so uxorious. By contrast he rather understood his brother Rosario who had spent his life up to now avoiding women. Self-control was all. If one wanted to rise, one had to plan, and if one was going to plan, one had to have a firm grip on one's own mind.

He had done his best to show that he had been flattered and delighted by her invitation to join her in her hotel room at Noto, but his real motivation was not the desire to be with her as such, but the desire to get one stage further into the organisation. She represented one step up, though as a woman, she was not in the innermost circle. But he could use her as a stepping stone. Luckily he did not need to act too much as the devoted lover, as she seemed to like the idea of a rather passive and withdrawn man in her bed. He had let her take the initiative that night in Noto; it would never have occurred to him to proposition her; but she had propositioned him, and that was an advantage as far as he could see.

Stefania never asked him about his work, which was wise of her, as one day she might well have to avow that she knew nothing about his work, and it would be all the more convincing if it happened to be true. As a result he was able to go away frequently without any questions being asked. And indeed the nights spent in hotel rooms were, as far as he could see, work. In giving her what she wanted, he was ensuring that she gave him what he wanted, which was a huge slice of the Messina bridge project.

The season after Easter had been busy. Easter Monday had seen his sister Assunta marry her fat husband. A month later, Renato had been baptised, and Rosario, now recovered from his wound, had been his godfather, as a way of compensating him for the indignity of being shot through the leg. There had been a big party after that. Then the next Sunday don Giorgio had given in and baptised the son of Traiano and Ceccina, Cristoforo, and allowed Calogero himself to be the godfather, which had pleased Traiano no end, and rewarded him for the trouble he had taken in shooting Rosario in the first place. Rather to Calogero's surprise, Rosario and Traiano were now reconciled. Then it was fixed, in July, that Traiano would marry Ceccina.

This had taken some fixing, as Calogero knew. Ceccina's parents had to consent for the marriage to be legal and that had meant a considerable bribe. He was the owner of their flat, and he had to give them the title deeds. This did not hurt so very much, as he had already promised them an eighteen-year rent free tenure, and the property was not so very valuable. Moreover, Traiano, who had saved up a lot of his own money, promised that he would compensate the boss for his loss, as well as pay the boss for the bigger flat the boss would give him and Ceccina. This seemed generous, but there was a catch. On the drunken night when he had poured boiling coffee over the boy's chest and Rosario had accompanied him to Doctor Moro, he had made some sort of promise that he would give Traiano a handsome wedding present. He had given his sister half a million euros. And now, it was hinted, he had promised to do the same for Traiano. The two flats would not come to half a million all told; he was pretty certain that if he gave the boy fifty thousand that would more than suffice –

after all, Traiano was known to have saved a great deal, and the idea that he should give him half a million and then be paid back out of what he had given seemed ridiculous. But even the fifty thousand was problematic. While in the past he had always had plenty in reserve, right now he had nothing at all, as he had sunk everything into Straits Limited. In a month of two he might well be awash with cash. But for the moment he was cleaned out. He had even had to explain this to Stefania. Of course, he could borrow, but he had already borrowed a great deal and had a horror of borrowing even more, and there again, couldn't all these people who wanted his money just wait for a bit? If he could tell Stefania that there were cash flow problems, then surely he could say the same to Traiano?

At the back of his mind was the fear that the Straits Limited scam might leave him badly burned. A further investment had been made after Easter, as the markets opened, and the price had climbed steadily since them. The balloon was inflating. But would it burst before they got their money out? He worried about this, though Anna Maria counselled calm and patience. Money was to be made by knowing when was the right time to sell; but that moment was still far off.

He rather wished that Traiano would put his wedding off till the autumn when this matter might be resolved. But this was impossible, partly because Ceccina was pregnant and would be in no fit state to walk down the aisle of the Church of the Holy Souls in Purgatory by autumn; and partly because don Giorgio had agreed to the wedding after much persuasion, and to put it off now might risk him changing his mind.

As the thermometer climbed so did the price of Straits Limited. Every newspaper, every television chat show was full of the talk of the opportunities that the bridge represented. It would link Messina and Reggio and make them one city (just how this was supposed to help anyone, was never explained). It would join Sicily to Italy even more than at present (which to Calogero's mind would be a thoroughly bad thing). It would mean thousands of jobs in construction, on the bridge itself, on the new railways, on the new roads. It would bring trade and prosperity in its wake. It would cost a fortune but the initial outlay would pay for itself many times over. It would be the envy of the world. It would make the British Channel Tunnel look like a petty little thing in comparison.

Traiano was to marry on the first Saturday in July. The weekend before that Calogero had been invited to Donnafugata. This was an invitation he was keen to accept, not that he relished a weekend alone with Anna Maria, but because he was very desirous of seeing her house there. He had heard her speak of the orange grove, the garden and the swimming pool. He had always wanted to see the town and province of Ragusa. There was a castle at Donnafugata which was surely worth a visit. He was aware that being invited for the weekend to her preferred place, rather than a hotel, was a great honour. He knew, with the price of Straits Limited reaching stratospheric heights, that he must not do anything to upset her now. The trouble was, the weekend before the wedding was more or less earmarked for entertaining Traiano, and he had promised his faithful retainer that he and Rosario would take him out to dinner on the Saturday night in Taormina and perhaps stay the night at a hotel there, as a sort of farewell to bachelordom. To cancel this, coming on top of the disappointment about the wedding present would be unwise, he felt.

The best he could manage, in order not to disappoint both parties was to ring up Anna Maria at her office, and ask if she would not mind too much if he brought his driver with him. He knew that this was not so outrageous a request, as whenever they had met in the past, her minder, Muniddu, had never been far away. Anna Maria was, as it turned out, happy with that. Her house had a room above the garage on the far side of the orange grove, where Muniddu stayed, and Traiano could stay there with him. He accepted the offer. Then he went to sell the offer to Traiano.

Traiano did his best to hide his disappointment. He had been looking forward to the stag party in Taormina, but now he was going off to the countryside to spend time with Muniddu, whom he had only seen once, while the boss screwed Anna Maria, and he was left twiddling his thumbs. It was not much of an exchange. Moreover, the boss still had not broached the matter of the money that he had promised to give him for the wedding, and the wedding was bringing in its train much more expense than he had realised, thanks, in part, to Ceccina. He needed a few thousand at least, and he did not want to ask for it; he wanted the boss to give it freely. He was paid a regular and generous salary by the boss, and he had savings, but at present, with nothing forthcoming, he did not know just how much money he would have when all was over, if indeed he would have enough. He needed the boss to tell him how much he was going to give him, so he could calculate accordingly.

And so it was on the morning of the last Saturday of June that they left Catania together, with Traiano driving, to go to Donnafugata. Traiano did not have a driving licence and it was a very expensive car, but he thought it best to let the boy drive as he would enjoy it and it was a way of showing that he trusted him.

As they sped south along the motorway, Calogero asked:

'Are you looking forward to the wedding?'

'You bet.'

'Is Anna coming?'

'Of course.'

'Is she bringing Salvatore?'

'Of course.'

'Is she bringing Michele Lotto?'

'I haven't invited him. I hope not.'

'And is everything paid for?'

'Not yet. We will get all the bills after the wedding, I suppose,' said Traiano.

At this point he expected Calogero to say something along the lines of 'Don't worry, I will make sure you have plenty of money to pay whatever you need,' but there was silence, which was disconcerting. Calogero had adopted an uncharacteristic and studious silence.

'In fact, it is going to be a bit of a struggle paying everything off, I think,' said Traiano. 'Both Ceccina and I thought we would have rather more in hand than we in fact do. That has led us to spend rather more than we would have done. Her parents too have been extravagant on our behalf. They appear to think that I am made of money, and they don't have a penny themselves.'

'When they send in the bills, ignore them. They won't be insistent. They know who you are. You are not the sort of man who can be chased for debts.'

He paused, then went on.

'Right now, things are a bit tight,' Calogero finally brought himself to say, knowing what Traiano wanted. 'I have put everything into this bridge project. I have even had to tell Stefania to spend less.'

'I see,' said Traiano, tight-lipped, and clearly disappointed.

Calogero sighed. This was not going well. He felt annoyed that Traiano did not realise how the bridge project trumped everything else, and if that worked their fortunes were made. (If it didn't, well, they would start again, though he dreaded to think about that.)

As for Traiano, he felt annoyed that the boss did not realise that his wedding trumped everything else.

'How are the wedding preparations going? With don Giorgio and so on?' he asked, trying to sound more friendly and less annoyed.

'Oh fine. Ceccina and her mother are the ones who are overseeing everything. The night before I have to go to confession. Don Giorgio said so. Did the same happen with you, Uncle Caloriu?'

'I remember it did. He said I had to go to confession. It is some sort of church rule. So I said I would and I said I would go to the Cathedral. But of course I did not, as I think he probably realised, but what could he do about it? They urge you to do it, but they cannot verify that you have done it, as confession is anonymous.'

'I should have thought of that,' said Traiano. 'I made an appointment to see him on Friday with Ceccina. Ceccina is very keen on me going. And so is her mother. They want to make a reformed man out of me.'

'That's quite an ambition,' said Calogero.

The irony was lost.

'I have been speaking to Rosario about it. He has been helping me with what I should say. There are certain things that are a bit embarrassing.'

'Like what?'

'Like having sex before marriage.'

'He knows you have a child already and you have another on the way,' said Calogero. 'That is the least of your worries and embarrassments. Unless you mean your other carryings on.'

By which Calogero meant the way Traiano had presumably slept with several of the prostitutes who worked in the bars of the quarter. These were girls with whom Traiano might well have had passing and transient fun before he met Ceccina. But they did not in his estimation 'count'. What did count was the thing that he and the boss had once agreed never to mention.

'I thought we agreed we would never mention that,' he said with burning cheeks.

'I wasn't mentioning it,' said Calogero, realising what he meant. 'Look, it happened, and it does not matter, OK?'

But they both knew it did matter, and that they could not forget it, and even if they could, Anna would not allow them to do so.

'Well, maybe you should,' said Calogero at length, oppressed by the silence. 'Go and confess to don Giorgio that when you were a child of thirteen you did things in bed with your own mother and that it was not your fault but my fault. That it is all my fault. Go and confess to don Giorgio not your sins but my sins. And don't forget the murder of Turiddu. You did it, but I made you do it. Because you are not a man, but a boy, a manipulated child. And tell him you have decided to have no more to do with drug dealing or prostitution in future.'

'Fuck you,' said Traiano, blinded by tears.

'No, fuck you,' said Calogero evenly and calmly. 'I remember that afternoon so well. Perhaps your memory has warped. I was lying on the bed with Anna and it was so hot. We had taken most of our clothes off. Then you appeared and joined us. You fell asleep or pretended to be asleep. Anna and I started to play with each other, then I fell asleep and you woke up, or pretended to, and you started playing with yourself and then you finished off inside Anna. Then we all fell asleep, and Turiddu saw us. Yes, we agreed not to talk about it, but we have. It happened. So what? Now stop snivelling and concentrate on the road.'

'Can you blame her for hating me?' asked Traiano at length.

'No. She hates me too. So what?'

'She is not your mother.'

'Thank God for that. Though my mother is not easy. Have you discussed all this with Rosario?'

'No, of course not.'

'With Ceccina?'

'God forbid.'

'Well then, let it be. Now let's try to be less dramatic, shall we? I have a lot on my mind. Not least the prospect of Anna Maria Tancredi, and the price of Straits Limited. But I want to see her house. When I am rich, and that may be soon, I shall buy one just like it.'

'May it be soon,' said Traiano. 'But I have a bad feeling about this Straits Limited.'

'You do?'

They were now in the depths of the countryside, the motorway long behind them. The roads were narrow and not the smoothest. On either side of the road were dry stone walls and barriers consisting of prickly pear. It was an alien landscape to someone who had spent their entire life inside the city.

'Yes, I have a bad feeling,' said Traiano. 'The idea is that everyone invests in this company, and its value goes up and up, artificially inflated; then it collapses and goes bankrupt and you keep the money?'

'Something like that.'

'But the money you put in is their money?'

'Most of it. Some has been my own. We take that out before the company goes pop.'

'I see. So the idea is to defraud investors. But what if the idea is to defraud you?'

'That has occurred to me,' said Calogero.

'Of course if they cheated you, you would come after them, with everything you have got. But what if they planned to put a bullet in your head first? And if they were planning on doing that, what better place to do it than out here, in the middle of nowhere? Of course, they would have to kill me too.'

'I said I was bringing you,' said Calogero. 'Would she have agreed to that, if she were planning what you say? Besides the plot still has got some way to go. You don't trust her, do you?'

'And I do not trust that Muniddu, either,' said Traiano.

'Well, if they were going to kill me, that would be because the *pax Panormi* would no longer guarantee my safety. And if the peace of Palermo is withdrawn from me, I am a dead man wherever I go. But keep an eye out. Keep an eye on Muniddu. Did you bring your gun? And your knife?'

'Of course, boss. Did you bring your knife?'

'Of course,' he answered.

The house, when they arrived, was everything he had hoped it would be. It was mid-afternoon, and the heat was stunning; the gate opened at the press of a button, and the long driveway was lined with pine trees. The house was an eighteenth-century construction, a series of rooms spread out over a long south facing terrace, covered with an awning, overlooking first the pool, then the orange groves. She greeted them at the front door, and then sent Traiano round with the car to the garages, above which were the staff quarters, where Muniddu would be waiting for him.

'The thing is,' said Anna Maria, as she watched him get out of the pool, 'is that we have a slight problem. Not that it is a problem that we cannot solve, you understand.'

He stood in front of her, rubbing his head with a towel. He was wearing his new swimming trunks, bought particularly for this occasion. They were black, a colour which he thought suited him. She had told him he could swim naked, but with the typical modesty of all Sicilians of his class, he thought that would be unsuitable behaviour. She herself was naked, and as he placed his towel around his neck, he took in the magnificent bosom which he had only just enjoyed, the distractingly shapely legs. But he allowed himself to be distracted only a for a moment. He had feared there would be problems along the way. That was only to be expected. The whole scheme had seemed too easy.

'You had better explain,' he said.

139

'There's a man going round. He works for one of the politicians. He is what they call a researcher. That is to say a professional busybody. He has been asking questions. He has been speaking to various financial journalists. As you know we have several financial journalists, backed by their editors, who are leading the choir that sings from our hymn sheet about how Straits Limited is the best investment opportunity for a generation. We are very lucky in that the leaders of the choir are the government itself, constantly telling people that Sicily is going to turn into a paradise of money making with this new bridge and that you need to get in now, early, before the boat sails. But we have this one dissonant voice and he is trying to get someone in the media to take up the counter-narrative.'

'To say that the bridge will never be built and the whole thing is a scam?'

'Yes. Of course the bridge never will be built, we all know that, our whole project is based on this, but we could do without anyone trying to ruin our party.'

'Who is this man?'

'His name is Fabio Volta. We have been warned about him by our people who work in the media. Volta is retained by some self-righteous deputy, and by people in the Catania town hall, whose main campaigning position is the fight against corruption.'

'And has anyone tried to corrupt these politicians?'

'That I do not know. They may just retain Volta as a useful cover; but they may be genuine, at least for the moment. So far Volta has not got anyone to take up his story.'

'I know that man; he used to be a policeman. Nine years ago, back in October 2001, he was the one who came round to our house and told us my father was dead. Later he had me in for questioning. Later still he was removed from Catania, round about the time del Monaco was dealt with, in 2006. They got rid of him as a trouble maker then. He should have stayed away. It is not wise to put your head above the parapet. To do so twice is positively foolish. Besides, I do not like the way he seems to have developed an interest in me and my affairs. Of course, that may be a coincidence. But I fear coincidences don't really happen.'

'So....'

'I think I should kill him, don't you?'

She smiled.

'It would be an excellent warning to other potential troublemakers,' she said. 'If this man carries on it might endanger the whole project. It had better be done soon.'

'It shall be done soon,' said Calogero. 'I remember the man well. He was an annoying little bastard. Now I think of him, I seem to remember that he was always deserving of death. It is high time I settled that score. I will think about it. Nothing happens at weekends, but by Monday I will have a plan.'

Traiano and Muniddu were getting better acquainted. Above the garage was a single large room, envisaged as the chauffeur's quarters, where Muniddu spent his time when Anna Maria Tancredi was at Donnafugata. There was a wide balcony at the front, and a staircase going up to the roof, from which one could survey the entire property, the orange grove, the garden, the vines, the surrounding countryside and the distant hills. There was a chair under a canvas sun shelter on which reposed a shotgun. This was where Muniddu sat guard over his employer and her property. Through the trees one could see the house, and also a glimpse of the swimming pool, if one stood in the right place.

Muniddu, so used to solitary guard duty, and like Traiano, a child of the city and a hater of the countryside, was positively garrulous now he had company. Traiano had been much disposed not to like him; he did not like Anna Maria, and he distrusted the scam connected with the Messina bridge. This seemed to him a dubious way of making money; far more honest were the bars, the girls and the drugs, all backed up by the power of the fist; this idea of defrauding people through fake investments, which he did not quite understand, so hard was it to visualise, struck him as intrinsically dishonest and fundamentally unreliable. He did not like the lady, and felt that she should keep out of what was essentially a male business. And he did not like Muniddu, who worked for a woman, which, he thought, was undignified. And his own boss too was now working for a woman, or working with a woman, which?

Yet Muniddu was older than him and came from Palermo, the epicentre of the world where their business was concerned. There might be something to learn from him, and thrown together as they were, he was determined to be friendly, even confidential.

They talked about their children and their wives, or in Traiano's case, the wife-to-be. Muniddu was in his late twenties, had been married five years, and had two young children. His father-in-law and his brother-in-law were in the same business, in Palermo, where his wife and children lived. He was often away from home, but he never played away from home. Traiano had been with Ceccina for well over a year, they had one child and another on the way, and they were marrying in a week's time, but he had been faithful to her, and he was sure he would be after the wedding was over. He thought that Muniddu's puritanism in this regard implied a criticism of Calogero, who, while they sat on the balcony was busily committing adultery a few hundred meters away with Tancredi. He imagined too that the brother-in-law and the father-in-law might be the sort of men to discourage Muniddu from adultery. His own prospective parents-in-law were people he was not frightened of in the least. But he loved his future wife, and he loved the time they spent together, though he felt that no wife should really expect her husband to be her lapdog. Why would she even want that? Didn't wives have other things to worry about, other things to enjoy, apart from their husbands' company?

Then the discussion moved on to work. How many major jobs had he done? Traiano admitted that he had killed more than one man; but it seemed that Muniddu had done seven or eight, and that he was an expert with the gun, rather than the knife. Traiano said he liked both. The knife was more intimate, though, he admitted. It was clear as the conversation progressed that they both enjoyed the prospect of killing other men. There was something so satisfying about it. It was part of the administration of justice, for the people they killed or would kill were people who asked to be killed, deserved to be killed or knew that they were risking death. There were no innocent victims.

Muniddu was an expert at getting rid of bodies, of not just killing people but making them disappear. This was an art: someone disappeared, then there was a rumour that they had turned up in Naples, or Rome, or Milan. These reappearances of the disappeared were cleverly staged to create doubt as to whether the person was dead or not. Sometimes someone used the person's bank card all over Italy, giving the impression that they were on the run, when all the time they were in fact safely dead. This muddied the waters of any investigation, and there were several open enquiries into missing people where everyone knew, even the police themselves, that the person was not missing but dead. But the complete destruction of a body was a difficult matter. Some were weighed down and dropped from boats far out at sea, so that the fish took care of their mortal remains. This was a pretty good way of doing things, as there never yet had been a case of some body part being washed up on a beach; or if there were, the beach was too distant to count. Some of these people were consigned to the deep while still alive, but they were always allowed to say a prayer first. That was only right.

As for throwing people down the crater of Mount Etna, that was myth, though like so many myths, one wished it were true, it was such a good story. The lava fields of Etna were enormous, and one could hide a body under the pieces of lava in some remote spot, and hope for another eruption to come and bury it even more definitively. Some of the lava fields consisted of black sand and it was said that every now and again some hunter with a dog came across a mummified corpse in the sand, dressed in the fashions of a hundred years ago. But it was risky taking a body out to Etna, as the place was exposed and the distances were long. Better the drop into the kindly forgiving Mediterranean Sea.

In prisons, not that he knew this from personal experience, it was sometimes necessary to kill someone to stop them talking. A few spectacular murders there had been, with cyanide delivered in coffee or cake, but the preferred method was to suicide the person, by creating the impression that they had hanged themselves. Traiano nodded at this, for this was something he knew about.

Darkness was falling, and Muniddu urged Traiano to go to the fridge and help himself to drinks, while he, Muniddu, fixed them something to eat. There was one fridge for food and another for drinks, and it was to the latter he was sent. What he saw in the fridge delighted him for a second: it was full of coke and Cinzano. He habitually drank coke (the diet variety) and sweet Cinzano was the only alcoholic drink he ever touched. And here were his two favourite drinks in quantity. His heart froze. They had prepared for his coming.

He returned from the fridge with the same relaxed walk with which he had gone there. With his bottle of coke, he joined Muniddu, his mind racing. The gun was in his bag, and the bag was on his bed. The knife was in his pocket: a small retractable and deadly blade. He was able to resist, if indeed he was marked for death right now. But he reassured himself that this could not be. They would not kill him here. That would be too difficult to cover up. But who knew they were there? Perhaps the secrecy of the weekend away was part of the plot. His blood began to pound. But why would they want to kill the boss? And they would only want to kill him if they wanted to kill the boss. It seemed clear that the Cinzano and the coke were there to make him feel at home, and some deep-laid plan was afoot, which might mean they were thinking of killing the boss at some future point. Perhaps Muniddu's mission was to win him over, to lull him into a sense of ease; perhaps this would take some time, and then, later, much later, months from now, they would strike.

Muniddu asked him about Romania, a country of which he denied all knowledge. It was true his parents were both Romanian, but he had no memory of any place apart from Catania. His father was still there, in jail. Muniddu was sympathetic. Traiano shrugged. He had no sympathy, as his father was unknown to him. There was always the worry that he would turn up in Sicily and make himself known, which would not be pleasant. After all, his father had no money, as far as he knew, and would only be coming to scrounge. He himself had done well, though it was all being spent on the wedding, to his dismay. His mother had done well, considering she had started with nothing, and the boss had been good to her. She was now living in Syracuse.

At the mention of Syracuse, Muniddu asked him whether he had heard of Michele Lotto, a Romanian, recently arrived.

'I have met him,' said Traiano shortly, with caution.

'He had some bad luck in Romania, I was told,' said Muniddu. 'But they say he is very professional, and that the people at the top will use him whenever they need to carry out a really big job. Apparently he is untraceable, just like your boss's father was untraceable. Such a man comes but once every generation.'

They went out and sat on the balcony where there was a table. The shade of evening had come after a terribly hot day. He heard a whistle from the garden, and there was Calogero standing in the trees, looking up at him. He left the food with a show of reluctance and went down to him. He was relieved to see him; with a gesture, he invited Calogero to join him in the garage.

'What?' asked Calogero, immediately sensing something was wrong.

In a low voice he explained the fridge.

'Why did they do that? And who told them?'

'Be on your guard,' said Calogero.

'You too, boss.'

'They want us to do a job for them,' said Calogero. 'That is what she has told me. Someone has been trying to undermine the whole project. He needs sorting out.'

'Let me do it,' said Traiano.

'We both will,' said Calogero. 'I wanted to tell you now, so you would know. It will be next week. It will give us something to take our mind off your wedding preparations. How are things?'

He looked upwards towards the balcony on which Muniddu sat, no doubt straining his ears.

Traiano shrugged, and they parted.

It was with great relief that they both left the next day to return to Catania in the evening. Traiano had found spending the weekend with Muniddu oppressive; and Calogero had found it claustrophobic spending so much time alone with Anna Maria, though he hoped he had given no clue of this to her. He knew that he was not cut out for conversation, eating, drinking and lovemaking in a beautiful setting; in fact Stefania was the ideal mate for him, because she understood his needs, amongst which was the need to be left alone, to reflect, to be silent, to have his own space. Stefania never pestered him, never made him feel that things were expected of him. He felt a new respect for his wife after his weekend of adultery.

As for Traiano, he had been frustrated by the bucolic setting, and bored by being stuck with Muniddu, whom he had come heartily to dislike as well as to distrust.

His question, when they were in the car and speeding away at last, was very simple.

148

'What do we know about Palermo, boss?'

'Only what Anna Maria Tancredi tells us,' said Calogero thoughtfully. 'Though we may learn some more soon. When we get the order to get rid of Fabio Volta. She has spoken of it, but the authorisation has to come from Palermo. They will be in touch.'

'I hope Palermo realises that I am getting married this week,' said Traiano. 'Do you think they have someone on our team, Uncle Caloriu?'

'Because they know you like sweet Cinzano? Is that such a secret? Don't you drink it wherever you go? It means that they have eyes in our quarter, that is all. I suspected as much. Indeed, I would have been surprised if they had not. They are professionals. They like to know what is what. But they are not planning to kill us, at least not yet. They need us. And when they do kill us, they will use Michele Lotto.'

'Unless we kill him first,' said Traiano.

'Precisely,' said Calogero.

Chapter Five

On Monday at four in the afternoon, having just woken up, washed and dressed, Traiano came downstairs from his flat to discover a man in early middle age standing at the bottom of the staircase.

'Hi, kid,' he said. 'They told me you were a later riser. I suppose most of your work is at night. I almost thought of going in and waking you. Go and get your boss, and bring him back here, can you?'

The man smiled. He had not said who he was or who he represented. But there was no need. Traiano nodded, and within five minutes he had returned with Calogero. In silence the three of them went upstairs to Traiano's flat. This was the place he was due to leave later this week, for the new marital home. It had a dirty and neglected appearance. The smart man from Palermo wrinkled his nose.

'I have had meetings in worse places,' he observed, sitting on the bed, throwing off his coat. He looked at Traiano, and then looked at Calogero.

'He stays,' said Calogero.

'Good,' said the man. 'Why don't you both sit down and make yourselves comfortable, as there is much to discuss. I am, in case you are wondering, Antonio Santucci. And yes, I come from that place you hate and fear, Palermo. But though you should fear us, you should not hate us, as we are ones who make sure you get the drugs you need to sell and the girls you need to work your bars, and we keep the riff raff away from your quarter, and very nice you have made it too. Thanks to the peace of Palermo, you are making lots of money, or so my father and my uncle, for ours is a family business as you know, tell me. Not that they tell me everything, you know, but that much they tell me. You may remember my father, you met him in Messina five years ago. And they tell me too that you are brave and fearless, and how you got rid of del Monaco. And it is not just them who speak about you, Calogero; there is all the talk that, if I can put it this way, that seeps in on the ether; about how brilliant you are. And now what strikes me is that you have fallen in with Anna Maria Tancredi – of course we allowed that, we arranged that – and that shows an aptitude for, well, business of a higher sort. My father knew your father, as I think he told you, and liked and respected him, for his dedication, his discretion. Renato di Rienzi was a fine man; it is a great shame that his career ended in failure. But his son will do better, I am sure, we are all sure. I have long wanted to see you close up. I have of course seen you from afar. I was the one who put the piece of paper in your pocket in Messina. I was the one who gave you the message through one of the little boys of the quarter to summon you to Noto.

'I am not surprised that Anna Maria has taken to you. I have known Tancredi for some years, as you would expect. I even remember when she was the lover of that idiot her nephew, Fabrizio Perraino, an idiot but a useful one for us. Quite often women have a weakness, and in her case, it was for Fabrizio. But he is in the past now. Now she has got you. As you will have imagined there have been others. One day she will throw you aside, but nicely. But I know you will not mind, because you see her, wisely, I think, as a business proposition, someone who is going to make you millions, and who indeed is going to make us all millions. Tancredi

151

and her bank are useful to us. We are using her. She is not one of us. She can't handle a gun, to put it bluntly, let alone a knife. Remember, that is what we are: people with guns and knives, who know how to use them, and who do not debase the currency, because we use them sparingly. But of course, Tancredi takes us into those places where we might not otherwise reach, into the higher levels of the Church and the state. So we will continue to use her.

'And you,' he said, turning to Traiano. 'There has been lots of talk about you. Congratulations on your coming wedding, and on the arrival of the second child, and on all your hard work. In Palermo, yes, even in Palermo, they have spoken of you. The handsome Romanian boy is what they call you. A sweet smile, and a hand holding a dagger. Nice combination. We will have lots of work for you. This man Michele Lotto, whom you have met…. Yes, we know about that. One of our elderly friends, a retired magistrate, has been keeping an eye out in Syracuse. He goes to see your mother, and she is very kind to him, and she tells him things. We are not entirely happy with Lotto….'

'But he is your man,' said Calogero. 'You brought him over here. You are supposed to be making use of him.'

'That was the plan. Our friends in Bucharest sent him over here because they had to get him out of Romania, and because they said he would be a help to us. But in fact he is a thorn in our side. But the sort of thorn that has not yet become intolerable. But we are keeping him under review. He talks a very great deal. That is not good. I suppose having spent all those years in jail he now feels the need to talk a great deal. That is never wise. He is coming to the wedding; did you know that?'

'No,' said Traiano. 'I did not invite him.'

'Precisely. An uninvited guest. Lotto has no finesse. When he comes, please keep an eye on him. Listen to what he says. That would be a service to us. And if it turns out that we cannot use Lotto after all, that he is just an encumbrance, or worse an embarrassment, well, in that case....' He smiled broadly. 'In that case we might very well turn to you as best placed to deal with the problem. Talking of which, we need to speak about Fabio Volta. There have been discussions. When the name of Fabio Volta was first mentioned to you, these discussions had not reached a conclusion. There were three possibilities with Volta, the man who seems determined to persuade everyone that the Messina bridge project is a fraud. The first was to silence him with a bullet in the head, or a knife in the guts, to send a message to those who were, shall we say, not getting the message about the Messina bridge being the greatest opportunity for a century. We thought in the end that that would be counterproductive. It might just alert people to the fact that there was something fishy about the Messina bridge project. Then there was the idea that we should just make him disappear. This is still on the table. But it was thought that the best thing to do was to try and get him to co-operate. Now, you know the man....'

'I last saw him nine years ago. And even then I just saw him once,' said Calogero.

'Yes, you may not know him at all, but you have met him, and there is this way in. But it is something else. We have every reason to believe that his obsession with us stems from his investigation into your father. It would make perfect sense for you to approach him and ask him how that investigation went, why he left the police (he is now working as a political researcher) and then quite calmly ask him whether investing in the Messina bridge project is a good idea or not, as you know that he knows something about it. Let this be a challenge to your acting ability and your intelligence. See if there is not something that can be done with him, if there is not some chink in his smooth surface, if there is not some way we can get leverage with him and neutralise him. If there is not, then we use hard power. Then we will send Traiano here to shoot him in the leg or something; and if that does not work, we will disappear him. But it may not come to that. After all, if this Fabio Volta does disappear there is no guarantee someone else will not come along making trouble. So, please arrange an accidental meeting with Volta, and let us see what happens. I know that he will be delighted to talk to you. After all, you are the man he has been sniffing around.'

'He has?' asked Calogero, alarmed.

'We have had him in our sights,' said Antonio, without giving anything further away. 'For years. That worthless piece of rubbish, Fabrizio Perraino, has been passing us information about anyone who asks too many questions. Volta has left the police, but he has contacts. See what he wants. See if he can be distracted. Would you recognise him?'

'Yes.'

'That helps. Every day he goes for coffee first thing in the morning at the bar closest to the Elephant. You know the one I mean? It's close to the office of the politician he works for. He has his coffee and his croissant standing at the bar, every day, at eight fifteen sharp. He never changes his routine. The sign of a man who has no idea he is in danger. Perhaps you could be there too?'

'I will.'

Antonio stood up to leave.

'I will be in touch, naturally,' he said. 'The old man your mother is kind to is her Tuesday afternoon gentleman,' he said turning to Traiano. 'A message to him will always get me. But Anna Maria knows how to reach me, of course. Good luck with the wedding. Watch Lotto. Until we meet again.'

He shook hands and left.

Fabio Volta saw him as soon as he came into the bar: the handsome but fleshy man with the well-cut hair in the very expensive suit, poring over the newspaper, with a cup of coffee in front of him. He knew him at once, even though he had not been so close to him for nine years. He was of course older and heavier, but whereas all those years ago he had given off an air of thuggish menace, which had by no means disappeared, he now announced to the world a picture of importance and prosperity. This was still the man who as a boy had broken another boy's nose against the marble steps outside the Church of the Holy Souls in Purgatory, who as teenager had threatened and beaten his way to power; but the stink of the slums no longer hung around him. He was plainly rich; the suit was fine and a glance told him that his shoes were the very best money could buy. Fabio Volta had been trained as a policeman and in his heart was a policeman still. He was used to looking for evidence about character. Those shoes... He himself had just come into the centre of the city from spending the night with his latest girlfriend, a woman who possessed an entire small room stuffed with shoes, and who constantly offered him advice about what to wear on his feet. His mother had been pressuring him to get married for years, and he feared he was destined to disappoint her yet again, and was heading up a dead end though scenic road. The Shoe Girl was wedded to shoes; or at least he did not want to marry her, given that her heart clearly belonged to her footwear. Perhaps Calogero's wife was a similar shoe obsessive. Odd to think that a man like Calogero di Rienzi was perhaps not particularly happily married. He was sleeping with Tancredi too. He wondered how that was going. Tancredi was voracious, or so he imagined. She was also, in his estimation at least, very attractive. Looking at Calogero as he read his newspaper, open of course on the financial pages, he felt almost sorry for him. But of course Tancredi might flatter his vanity: a child of the slums managing to get into bed with a member of the upper middle classes, a powerful banker, a well know financier. Vanity, he knew, was the man's weak spot.

He knew that this meeting had to be a set up. He never varied his routine, at least not yet, as he did not think he was worth assassinating, or rather he assumed that they would see any assassination as hugely counter-productive. Indeed, ever since the spring and summer of 1992, now eighteen years ago, they had laid off the spectacular assassination as a weapon of choice. Assassinations represented a loss of temper, a loss of control, a single moment of satisfaction at seeing an enemy gone, followed by months, even years, of unintended consequences. Assassination was the weapon of the weak. The strong used something else: persuasion. The strong did not need to gun you down or to blow you up; they did not need to be so crude. You did as they said, you obeyed.

Of course, the Chemist, whose son now sat at a table with his paper just a few feet away, not taking his eyes off it, which was most unusual surely, the Chemist had been an assassin, but his victims had not been policemen or politicians or magistrates, and his most spectacular jobs had been designed to create fear and uncertainty, to destabilise the people in power, to get them to realise that co-operation was the only real way forward. And of course there had been the surgical removal of people who would not co-operate, chiefly other criminals. But the Chemist had always operated on the further side of the Straits of Messina. On this side of the straits it was the peace of Palermo that reigned.

Calogero was sitting at one of the tables, affecting not to have seen him, and having bought his coffee and croissant, Volta moved over to him and said: 'We know each other.'

Calogero looked up, feigning surprise: 'The face is familiar,' he admitted.

He gestured very slightly, indicating that Volta should sit down.

'I was the policeman who worked on the case of your father's death. I am Fabio Volta. We met, when, nearly ten years ago.'

'No, only nine years this October,' said Calogero with a rueful smile. 'My father died in October 2001, though it seems a lifetime ago. My eldest daughter Isabella is eight this summer. She came into the world the night we were told of my father's death.'

'That is a detail I had not forgotten,' said Volta.

'I have three children now,' said Calogero. 'My son was born at the beginning of this year. We named him Renato after my late father.'

'Congratulations,' said Volta. 'I see you are reading the financial pages.'

'The bridge project,' said Calogero carelessly.

'You think it will ever be built?'

Calogero put down the paper. He knew he was being asked to tell a lie, a lie that they would both recognise. There was a moment of understanding between them.

'What do you want?' asked Calogero.

'What do you want?' replied Volta.

The tension between them dissolved.

'I want to warn you off becoming too interested in the bridge project. As far as I can see, the project was decided on in Rome, far to the north of here. It concerns neither of us. It is an opportunity for investors, and like all investments it is a gamble. Right now it is full speed ahead, but we know it is possible, indeed, likely, indeed I would say almost certain, that in less than a year it will hit a brick wall. But by then we will all have got out; it is true that a lot of people will be badly burned. But caveat emptor, let the buyer beware. This a gamble. No profit without risk.'

'It is not a gamble, it is a confidence trick,' said Volta. 'It is the South Sea bubble all over again. It is a way of hoovering up a huge amount of cash, dirty money, and supposedly throwing it away on a company that will go spectacularly bankrupt. The smaller investors, the ones who do not know, are going to be screwed. And let me tell you something else. One person will come out of this well: Anna Maria Tancredi. She is brilliant. She knows the markets, she has experience, she knows what she is doing. Fraud comes to her in the way that painting came to Caravaggio. She could do it in her sleep. She is the most deceptive woman in Sicily. That I realise is saying something. She is deceiving you. At the end of this you are going to be bankrupt along with a lot of other people. The people who will do well are Tancredi and her masters in Palermo. She would never deceive them. She is frightened of them. They have links with America and the rest of the world. You can never get away from them, so you never offend them. But you, my dear sir, you are an amateur. You are a big fish in the small pond of Purgatory; a medium fish in the medium pond of Catania, but you are nothing elsewhere. You have forgotten your limitations. You think you are using her, but she is using you.'

Calogero felt an enormous wave of anger cross over him and almost convulse his body. He silently fingered his coffee cup. He looked towards the marble topped bar and imagined how he could have brought Volta's face down on it time and time again with force, leaving him a mass of bruises.

'I know Tancredi better than most,' he said at last.

'Oh, so you have slept with her. So did that jerk Fabrizio Perraino. Her own nephew. What a disgrace. She likes naughty things. She screwed her eighteen-year-old nephew under the eyes of her own sister, his mother. He used to boast about it. But she went off him when Carmine del Monaco wrecked his handsome little face. Perraino is a worthless person.'

'So, she only sleeps with worthless men?'

'Don Calogero,' said Volta, 'I remember meeting you when you were sixteen. You were a tough boy from the slums. We were all struck by your self-confidence. You certainly believed in yourself. Your brother, poor boy, not so much. But that often happens in families. Now you think you are Salvatore Giuliano come back to life. You remember the story of him and the duchess?'

'Yes, there are so many legends,' said Calogero. 'No doubt every woman fell in love with him. Can you blame them?'

160

'And you think Tancredi is in love with you?' asked Volta.

'No. She is not romantic. I am not romantic. I am practical, so is she. She just likes screwing a boy from the slums, as you put it. Some of these women do.' He paused. 'What we have is mutually beneficial. Unless you have some specific warning for me?'

'Yes, I do. When the whole scam is revealed for the fraud it is, then someone will be thrown to the dogs. And that someone may well be you.'

'But the Prime Minister himself has said that the Messina bridge is happening....'

'And it is that that makes the fraud possible. Tancredi's proxies would never be able to sell all these dodgy shares if it were not for our dear Prime Minister. Do you believe him? Maybe some people do. Maybe he is sincere in wanting to get the bridge built. But Italy is heading for bankruptcy, and by this time next year we will be in a real crisis and the first thing to be cancelled is the bridge, which was only a pose to start with. The government will blame the bankers of Brussels. But people here, who will they blame? They should blame Tancredi. But who has heard of her? But have you noticed that the woman is whiter than white? She has no whiff of criminality about her. She will emerge smelling of roses. She always has. Everyone trusts her; she is so respectable. But you... when they look at you, they see a slum landlord, a whoremaster, a druglord, a gang leader and a crook.'

'You insult me,' said Calogero.

He felt the force of his stare.

'Don Calogero, I am merely telling you the truth. I know all about the peace of Palermo. It's your licence to make money. A licence that Carmine del Monaco held for many years. Well, you are cleverer than him. But you are not a member of this organisation. You are someone they make use of, but you are not one of them. I know you want to be one of them, but you are not. Perhaps you think you will be after this. But I wonder...'

'Tancredi is not a member either,' he pointed out.

'She can't be, so that is her excuse. They would never ever have a woman or someone who was not a Sicilian. They are very conservative. They are the one thing round here that never changes. But they like her a great deal and she is necessary to them. She is a banker, for goodness' sake. All crime these days involves financial crime. She can move money round the world, she can make it disappear. She can make sure no one can trace it. Money has no smell. But your money?'

'Bars and pizzerias take cash,' he said.

'I mean big money. Millions not thousands. The huge rake offs from government contracts. You benefit from the peace of Palermo; she benefits, and the people in Palermo benefit, from the pax Romana, the peace of Rome. The peace of Montecitorio and Palazzo Madama. That is where the friends who count are to be found: in the chamber of deputies

162

and in the senate. In the very office of the Prime Minister and the other government departments. They are the sort of people who can make sure things happen and more importantly do not happen. They can appoint judges who dismiss cases on technicalities. They can allot funds to interesting projects; they can discourage questions. They are the ones that make it happen. Not you. You are the muscle. They are the brains who get round the law. Without them the whole lousy edifice collapses.'

'Why are you telling me this?'

'Because one day they will put a bullet in your head or a knife in your guts. And that one day may be soon.'

'Someone else was saying that to me, just this weekend,' said Calogero. 'Perhaps for a family like mine, it takes three generations not two to arrive at a position of real power. But there are more terrifying things than death, you know.'

'I cannot think of one,' said Volta.

'Tell me, Volta, what did you discover about my father? Because you know, to us he was a stranger.'

Volta was surprised. This was one question that Rosario had never asked him. But for Rosario the Chemist was a figure of horror. For Calogero, the Chemist was the founder of a dynasty and an inspiration.

'The investigation was largely an exercise in archaeology. Your father only used cash, never used a mobile phone, never used a bank card. He had several false identities, and always checked into quiet hotels using a false identity card. He must have had about two or three of them; some think more; wherever there was a bomb there was someone staying nearby who we were unable to trace. After a bit, it became farcical. It was as if there were multiple identities, hundreds of them, and as if he were responsible for every crime in the history of Italy in these years. Thinking he was all these people, it became tempting to think he was none of these people. But he must have had places where he worked, where he stayed. But we never found them with certainty. It is hard to trace people in hotels because they have so many people moving through. Then there was the question of his contacts. We eventually knew about Vitale, but Vitale was a dead end. We never found out who Vitale's contacts were, though Vitale did spend a lot of his time driving around the island: Enna, Caltagirone, Caltanisetta. Perhaps when he was travelling, he met people, perhaps he was a sort of postman; but there was nothing written down, nothing traceable. And Vitale had no relations, no family, no friends. It was supposed that your father got his instructions from Vitale, and Vitale, we thought, received instructions at places like the filling station outside Enna. But who your father met when he was in Italy, we do not know and could never find out. Naturally we knew he was doing business, but did he have no friends, no people he spoke to?'

'When I was young, I sometimes thought he had another wife and family,' said Calogero.

'He didn't. That sort of fraud is pretty hard to carry off. He had no one, just his work.'

Calogero was thoughtful. The Chemist's life had been empty. There had of course been the life in Purgatory, the life in Catania. But when he came home, what then? He remembered accompanying his father on his visit to tenants and properties, but that had been work. The Chemist perhaps had loved his wife, but how could one tell? He had ignored his younger son, and ignored his daughters. And as for Calogero, until he reached the age of fourteen, he had beaten him mercilessly, not that that had done him any harm. He must have known the risks he ran as a bombmaker. Had he banked on surviving, of leading a happy retirement, of having some sort of life? But one could not defer life. One had to live it now. Was this the life that he would lead? Like his father's life, would his end before he ever got to enjoy the result of his hard efforts?

He looked rather sadly at Volta, and realised that he had a mission with him, one that he did not really wish to fulfil, or rather which he felt was not quite his metier in fulfilling. He would rather hold a gun to the man's head, or break his legs. But this art of gentle persuasion was not his thing at all.

'You should meet my brother,' he said. 'I am sure you would like him. You questioned him when he was a mere child. You should catch up with him.'

Volta handed Calogero a card.

'I will instruct him to speak to you,' said Calogero, who then got up, picked up his newspaper and walked away. As he left the bar, he passed Traiano, who had been there the whole time, and gave him a slight nod of recognition.

'These people have got nothing on us, nothing at all,' said Calogero. He and Traiano were standing on the steps of the Church of the Holy Souls in Purgatory. It was Tuesday evening. The night air was hot; they had finished the wedding rehearsal two hours previously. The people who really cared about weddings, that is to say the bride and her mother and her friends, had all gone home some time previously. The two men had gone out to eat, and now stood enjoying the slightly cooler evening air. They were waiting too for Rosario.

'What they want us to do is to make a mistake; that is their strategy; to cause us to panic so we throw away our advantages. This Volta, who I do not trust, and who no one should trust, clearly wants me to be afraid of the people in Palermo and afraid of Anna Maria Tancredi. He wants me to upset the whole project, to panic, to pull out just as it is approaching its end; to throw in the towel just as we are winning. He wants me to think that Anna Maria is deceiving me, and that she would put a bullet in my head. Or get Muniddu to put a bullet in my head. But why should she? She needs me. And he thinks that I will be so panicked I will put a bullet in her head. Why should I? She is a money-making machine for us. We are all benefitting. Anna Maria is our cash cow. Palermo cannot make money

166

without her; she can't make money without Palermo; and as for me, and doubtless others, they need us to do some of the legwork, to create enthusiasm for the project.'

'Would you kill her if you had to?' asked Traiano.

'Of course,' he said without hesitation. 'Rosario once asked me if I would kill him if I had to. Of course I would. I killed Turiddu, didn't I? Well, you did the legwork, but I was the one who decided he had to go. I know you do not trust Anna Maria or Muniddu. Did you sleep on Saturday with your gun in your hand, and your knife under the pillow?'

'I barely slept,' said Traiano. 'You are right, I don't trust him, and I don't trust her. Did you sleep with your knife under the pillow, Uncle Caloriu?'

He laughed. 'Don't be ridiculous. You think I trust her because I am in love with her, or something like that. That is ridiculous. I am with her and giving her what she wants because it pays to keep your business partners happy. Look at Fabrizio Perraino. He used to screw her and he is set up for life. She is not some black widow spider, just a woman who likes sex and is grateful when she is given it. That is all. For me it is not personal, it is business. It is always best to keep the personal out of business; it warps your judgement. One needs a clear head. One needs a steady hand. We need to approach the problem of Lotto very carefully. They do not trust him. It may be that we will do them an immense favour by getting rid of Lotto. That will not be hard to do, provided Anna cooperates. And cooperating is always a bit of a challenge for her, but she owes us both a great deal. You remember the layout of Anna's place: a bedroom with an adjoining bathroom. One of us hides in the bathroom. After he has done whatever he does with Anna, he comes through to the bathroom either to have a shower or to piss. One of us is hiding behind the door and knifes him in the back. There will be a lot of blood, but bathrooms are easy to clean, and hers has tiles up the walls. They may well discover his DNA there, and yours or mine, but that is natural enough. As long as we do not give them any evidence that he was killed there. Then we dump his body in the sea, which is right next to her place. That will have to be at night; he will float around and some unfortunate will eventually discover his naked corpse. His clothes will have to be got rid of; but when the police find him and identify him, what will they think? A recently arrived Romanian, with a criminal record, with a false name… well, any number of people might have wanted him dead.'

'If he is not called Michele Lotto, what is he really called?' asked Traiano.

'Find out at the wedding. It might be interesting to know. And at the wedding let us also try to find out what it is that Lotto is up to, and why Palermo has gone off him. Anna may be able to tell us something.'

'I will try my best, boss, but don't forget I am getting married that night.'

'I had not forgotten. Ah,' he said, seeing Rosario coming into the square. This was what they had both been waiting for.

Rosario approached them. He had just been having dinner quite openly with Fabio Volta, a man he had been seeing secretly for some time. The complexity of relations was beginning to overwhelm him.

'Well?' asked Calogero.

Rosario looked at him. 'It is hard to know where to begin. I want to ask Traiano how the wedding rehearsal went. I was sorry not to be there.'

Calogero looked momentarily annoyed, and Traiano surprised. It did not do to keep the boss waiting.

'I will come up and see you in ten minutes,' said Rosario.

They watched Calogero leave.

'Why do you provoke your brother?' asked Traiano.

'Do I?'

'Yes, you do. He adores you, and you just provoke him. Then perhaps you wonder why he gets angry.'

'I am not as good as you at handling him,' said Rosario. 'I suppose you are the expert. How were the things in Church?'

'That's what you really care about,' said Traiano. 'Church, the things of God. The things of don Giorgio. He and I had a talk, since you ask. Your brother did not ask, by the way. Perhaps he is not interested. Perhaps he does not want to know, perhaps he feels that whatever we discussed was not important. But it was. Very important. But not in quite the way you would expect. He wanted me to confess my sins, and receive Holy Communion on my wedding day. I told him I could not. To repent is beyond me, and for two reasons. The first is practical. My work. I have no other work to go to. If I were to say that I was giving up enforcing the rules of the drug trade and the rules of prostitution, what would I do then? Dig? I am not strong enough. Well, I am, I am just too lazy. And as for the other things, I am just not sorry. If I were sorry, I would have to break with your brother, and that is something I cannot do. And it is not just the money, it is something else. You belong to him because he is your brother. You tried to escape, but you failed. He can mistreat you all he likes and you will still belong to him. But I belong to him because I chose to belong to him. That is a harder bond to break. In fact it is unbreakable. I really do not care what happens. He may get killed, and I will get killed with him. So be it. He may one day kill me. Well, if that is the price I have to pay, so be it.'

'Death may be closer than we all imagine,' said Rosario, sadly. 'You are sixteen, getting married, one child already and another coming, and all you talk about and all you feel is the approach of death.'

'Not all the time, but some of the time. So does he, I am sure. He is haunted by it. Look what happened to your father. Look what happened to Vitale. Look what happened to Carmine del Monaco. Look what happened to Turiddu. Look what happened to Ino. It is all around us. Is it so very frightening?'

'I had better go up to see him,' said Rosario. 'I am looking forward to the wedding.'

His brother was waiting for him in his flat. Stefania was nowhere to be seen, and the children presumably asleep. Calogero was wearing a pair of silk pyjamas that Rosario had not seen before. They were the palest shade of cream. The night was still hot, but the pyjamas gave off an aroma of almost oriental coolness.

Calogero poured two glasses of whiskey from a bottle that bore a name that Rosario found incomprehensible. Rosario took his and sipped it. The flavour was strange.

'It is very expensive,' said Calogero. 'Drink it slowly.'

They sat down. The distance between them was immense.

'I have given you everything,' said Calogero. 'And you have given me nothing in return.'

'What do you want me to give you?' asked Rosario quietly.

'Brotherly love,' said Calogero.

'And if I have none to give?' he asked.

'Then there is something wrong with you,' said Calogero. 'Tell me about Volta.'

'He knows that this bridge project is a fraud. But you know that already and I know that too. All sensible people know that. The market has not caught on, but it will. This we know. Your success depends on your getting out of the bridge project before it all collapses.'

'My success? Yours too.'

'Indeed. As I am sure you want me to acknowledge.'

'I do want you to acknowledge it. It just happens to be true. Tell me what you found out from Volta. I do not like the man. May I remind you that you are all that stands between Volta and a good beating or much much worse. We cannot afford the project to be derailed at this point. Your task is to keep the project on track, and to keep Volta alive. The first only counts for me. For you, I imagine they both count.'

'Volta is playing a game. He works for a politician, as you know. He wants to stir up suspicion between you and Tancredi. That is his strategy.'

'I know that.'

'He wants to know who is behind Tancredi.'

'In Palermo?'

'No, in Rome. He doesn't care about what happens here, in Purgatory. He cares about Rome, what happens there. The political powers that give Tancredi her licence. The pax Romana.'

'And he wants to know that because then his political masters can use it to destroy their opponents.'

'I suppose so.'

'You see, in the end, all they care about is power. I have no idea who is behind Tancredi, though the Santucci family have something to do with it. I suppose the list of her bank's clients might give you a clue, though Volta will have thought of that. And the bank's clients will mainly be charities or anonymous companies, the real owners of which are obscure. But you need to keep him talking and keep him alive. Otherwise we will come after him. And when we do, we will use you to get to him. So, it is in your interest to keep him talking to us and not to other people. Understood?'

Rosario nodded.

'Are you looking forward to the wedding?'

'Yes, I am.'

'Good. What are you wearing?'

'The suit I wore at Assunta's wedding.'

'It will be hot.'

'I can take the jacket off.'

'True. Have you got some shoes?'

'I have got shoes, yes.'

'I mean nice ones, new ones?'

'No.'

'Disappointing. You should try and make a good impression. You are my brother. People will be looking at you.'

'No one will be looking at me,' said Rosario.

'Are you going with anyone in particular?'

'No.'

'You may meet someone there. It happens.'

'I am sure I will meet plenty of people there.'

'That is not what I meant,' said Calogero. 'You know what I mean. I want you to meet someone.'

'You want it and I don't. Has our mother been nagging you?'

'Does she nag you?'

'No. She never gets a chance. I never see her.'

'Why not? It's not natural.'

'Because of you, because of our father. She prefers your type to my type.'

Calogero sighed. 'You need to find a girl. It doesn't look good at your age. You are my brother and you need to look normal. Some nice girl. That is what you need.'

'I am happy as I am,' said Rosario.

'Oh, go away, go away,' said Calogero.

Rosario put down his whiskey glass and stood up to leave.

'Come here,' commanded Calogero.

His brother's embrace was warm on the hot night. The silk was smooth, his cheek was rough, the smell of whiskey and male perfume overpowering.

'You keep on provoking me,' said Calogero. 'You think I will never kill you, but I have told you, I will, I will, I will. Now go.'

He went.

Don Giorgio had spent years trying to get couples to spend less on their weddings, but weddings in the Purgatory quarter just seemed to be getting more and more extravagant. The beautiful Church of the Holy Souls in Purgatory was awash with expensive flower arrangements, which were brought in a few hours before the Mass began, and which would be taken out at the end of it, in order to bedeck the hotel where the reception was taking place. As was always the case, while there would be hundreds at the reception, and don Giorgio always went to receptions as he was driven by the curiosity to see who would be there, there were never so many at the Mass itself. The marriage vows taken in the presence of God, taken in front of the image of the Spanish Madonna by Velasquez, that exquisite painting, were all very well, but what really counted was the extravagant party that would follow, the size of the buffet, the number of bottles and the noise made by the band. Calogero's wedding eight years ago had been hugely expensive; his sister's on Easter Monday had been ruinously extravagant, and now this child's, this pair of children's wedding, this wedding of these two teenagers, was going to be the worst yet. How he wished that it would be that ideal yet never realised thing, a quiet wedding. But such things simply did not happen, at least not here in Purgatory.

He had nothing against the girl Ceccina and nothing against her parents; as far as he could tell they were decent people. The parents had been outraged by Traiano sleeping with their daughter and impregnating her, not once, but twice. Anyone would have been. Theirs was the right reaction, but of course there was very little they could do to stop the wedding, though they would have liked to have done so, as indeed he would have liked to have done so. But the damage was done, the girl deflowered and pregnant, not

176

once but twice, and the boy Traiano had the backing, the unquestioned backing, of Calogero di Rienzi. With that there was no arguing.

There were no parents to deal with on the groom's side, that was for sure; Anna the Romanian prostitute had fled to Syracuse. He had always liked Anna, and had known her since she had first come to the quarter, when Traiano had been a tiny child of about three years old. Of course, she had been a prostitute, which was not good; there had always been prostitutes in the quarter, and there still were, the only difference was that the new ones operated in a slightly more discreet and classy way. But Anna had been a down to earth prostitute of the old school, sitting on her doorstep and waiting for passers-by to take her into the shabby little room behind. There was no romance in such a life, she had told him, but there was a living. And of course, there was a husband back in Romania, a terrible man, who had subjected her to unimaginably awful violence. It had been her fate to attract the wrong sort of man, she said. Traiano's father, he remembered, was currently in jail, but there was always the possibility that he would come to Catania on his liberation, to pick up the threads of his relationships, to see his wife and his son. He had felt intensely sorry for the little boy, admired how Anna had insisted he went to school, and how she had brought him to Church, so he would be exposed to good influences. He had not been a very good altar boy, but he and Rosario, five years his senior, had always got on well; and then one day, suddenly, don Giorgio had noticed that Traiano had gone to the bad, become yet another minion of Calogero di Rienzi. These things happened, and by the time you realised that you should step in and intervene, it was already too late. But it could have been different. Traiano was not a naturally bad boy, and he liked him. If he had become bad, that was because Calogero had corrupted him.

The Mass was like most nuptial masses: there was a visiting soprano who sang Ave Maria, always the same soprano, always the same song. The couple themselves looked rather overawed by their surroundings. He alone could see their faces; the girl Ceccina was serious, her pregnancy not too visible; and as for Traiano, he obviously looked older that sixteen and at the same time a lot younger, despite his broad shoulders and his height. He looked almost intimidated by what was happening to him, by what he had done, by having come so far already and knowing that he could not now turn back. He was like a man who climbs a cliff and finds the going easy, but who suddenly looks down and realises that the drop is high, and the top is still distant, but he has no choice but to go on. It was as if he could not help admitting to himself that his lifelong bond to Ceccina was one thing, but the other lifelong bond he had was equally constricting, his lifelong bond with Calogero.

At the wedding reception it was very interesting to note that there were a couple of dozen young men in matching suits with matching flowers in their buttonholes, all young, but most older than Traiano, all of whom, he could see, worked for Calogero. They were big, tough, rough and noisy. Their suits fitted them poorly, and their faces were the faces of the slums of Catania; he knew most of them, and he knew their parents and grandparents as well; and he recognised them all: some were on duty in the pizzeria Calogero owned, working as delivery boys; others working in the bars; one, more refined than the rest, was the one who would often make him a cup of coffee when he called into the bar in the square. Another, a big strong chap with a bruiser's face, was the one who used to stoke up the woodfired pizza oven, and oversee the deliveries of firewood. All of them, though don Giorgio did not know this, but he could see it and understand it subliminally, were practised young toughs who had no problem administering a beating to any troublemaker: anyone who did not pay for their pizza or their coffee of their ice-cream, or for the use of the upstairs rooms, or anyone who made trouble with the girls or indeed the boys who worked in those upstairs rooms. These twenty were the core of Calogero's little gang. They settled at a large table, and began drinking; each had brought a girl with him; not one of the girls, but one of the better class of girls from the quarter or the city. Not intimidated, don Giorgio, went round the table and shook hands with them all. Each boy (the eldest were twenty-five and had been at school with Calogero) stood up and shook hands respectfully with the priest, a little shamefacedly. As he looked into their barely mature but roughened faces, he recognised them from their First Holy Communions and their Confirmations. The girls too, some of them had stood in the Church of the Holy Souls in Purgatory in little white bridal dresses, symbols of girlish purity, looking so pretty. And now, here they were, plastered with makeup, their skimpy dresses hardly covering their flesh, sitting next to boys, in some cases actually sitting on their laps and allowing the boys to stroke them. Alas, thought don Giorgio.

One boy, the one who had been at school with Calogero, the one called Alfio, a boy he remembered so well, if only because he had such strange teeth, introduced him to another youth who was not, he was told, from the quarter. This was Gino, he said.

'Hi, Gino,' said the priest. 'Where are you from?'

'Agrigento, don Giorgio,' said Gino respectfully.

179

'And how did you two meet?' asked the priest, conversationally.

'We were in Bicocca,' said Alfio. 'Stealing cars, you may remember, don Giorgio. My mother told you all about it. Gino was there for another reason.'

The priest looked at Gino questioningly.

'I stabbed a friend,' said Gino apologetically. 'It was a misunderstanding. I mean, the judge did not realise it was in self-defence. I got a year, but half off for good behaviour. And I met so many nice and good people like Alfio inside. The chaplain was so good to me, he really opened my eyes. Do you know him, don Mimmo he's called.'

'It's a tough job being prison chaplain,' said don Giorgio. 'Yes, I know him. A good man, one of the best. Very hard worker.'

'The Mass, don Giorgio, was beautiful,' Alfio now felt impelled to say.

'You were there?'

'No. But my mother said so.'

'Your mother is a good woman,' said don Giorgio. 'She was very upset when they put you in Bicocca. Especially as your father was doing time just then in Piazza Lanza.'

'I know,' said Alfio, looking sad. 'My father is still in Piazza Lanza. It is not nice there. They want to punish him, but in fact they punish my poor mother. But I have learned my lesson in Bicocca. I have no intention of joining my father in Piazza Lanza, or ending up in Ucciardone like Gino's father.'

All the boys round the table looked sad and serious for a few moments. The girls seemed merely puzzled. No one was going to imprison them, thought don Giorgio, and even if they did, Italian women's prisons were notoriously soft. But what crimes were these girls likely to commit? Crime was a male thing. It was interesting to note that while these boys all seemed to know of a relative in jail, and two at least had been in Bicocca, the young offenders' institution, a horrible concrete bunker out by the ring road, many had not been imprisoned, but probably ought to have been. Presumably they were too clever to be caught, or the law too slow to catch them. Or if the law caught people, it caught the wrong people. And if you put people like Alfio and Gino in Bicocca, what good did it do them? What reform ever came out of a reformatory? And Piazza Lanza? What penitence ever came out of a penitentiary?

He could see Calogero approaching, and so he drew himself away from the young men's table, leaving them to their idol. He watched how Calogero approached them. The various girls he smiled at and greeted, but otherwise ignored. He was not interested in them. They did not work for him, and never could. The boys, his employees, these were the ones who counted; these were the useless riff raff of the slums, the otherwise unemployed and poor, whom he had given purpose and employment to, and above all money. He had made them important. Each one was given the magic touch, an arm around the shoulder, a clasp of the hand, a ruffling of the hair, sometimes a kiss on the cheek. Each one stood while he addressed them. Each one did not smile, but was awed by his presence and rejoiced in it. Each one felt that they were in the presence of a god.

Then Calogero left them, and there was silence, succeeded by fervent conversation. They discussed his suit (linen, bought in Rome, made in India, a light cream in colour); his shoes (highly polished brown brogues, from England, the most expensive money could buy, made by hand); the stuff he put on his hair; the fact he had no beard, and the fact that they had all followed his example; his silk boxer shorts, that none of them had seen but had heard about; the man who cut his hair in a small barbershop near the opera house, and who had cut it for the last ten years. In short, his perfections, his presence, his beauty. A few years ago he had put on weight, but now he had lost some of it, and he looked better than ever.

The groom was going round the tables, and met his master doing the same thing.

'Are you enjoying your wedding?' asked Calogero.

'Yes,' said Traiano. 'And the best is still to come. I am looking forward to getting into that hotel room. And so is Ceccina.'

'Good. I need to speak to Anna, and to Michele Lotto. I have been putting it off for now. The boys are enjoying themselves. They will be pleased to see you. Until later.'

Anna and Michele Lotto were sitting on their own in a quieter part of the room. Anna had an obviously new dress, he noticed, and Lotto, though wearing a suit and a tie, still looked like what he was, a hired killer and thug. Behind him he heard the uproar from the boys' table with which they greeted their leader Traiano. Anna looked over towards the boys. She knew them all, more or less, with the exception of the one called Gino, the boy from Agrigento. She knew them from the quarter, she knew them as friends of her son, and she knew them, she reflected bitterly, because they had more or less all at one time or another, been through her door to test their teenage sexuality out on her. She remembered their grunting, their sweating and their grinding of teeth. And now here was Calogero, another one who had done the very same thing. She managed a smile.

Calogero beamed at her. There was some desultory conversation about Syracuse and how things were there. Calogero remarked on the beauty of the place, the wonder of the nymph Arethusa's spring, right next to the sea, and so close to where Anna now lived. Then he turned to Michele Lotto.

'So, how is business?' he asked.

Anna stood up. It was time to leave these men to discuss their affairs. Besides, she was wearing a new dress, and she really ought to show it off to the room. As well as that, her son was the groom, and she ought to show herself to the guests, and renew a few old acquaintances. She saw don Giorgio. How she loved that priest. Well, she loved all priests, but him especially. She moved in his direction.

'How is business?' echoed Lotto. 'I think you know the answer. The people here are not putting much business my way. I am getting a bit bored. The thing is that you Sicilians, not all of you, and not you, but most of you, do not like or trust Romanians. You do not like foreigners, unless they are Americans. You love America.'

'Yes, we love America,' said Calogero conversationally. 'I may go one day. But you were saying…'

'I am glad that you treat Traiano like a son, and that you regard him as one of your own.'

'That's what he is.'

'We Romanians are Romans, and he has the name of a Roman emperor. You have accepted him, you have adopted him. But in certain circles, someone born in Romania can never be accepted.'

'Certain circles in Palermo, you mean?'

'Exactly. We have been very helpful to them. Very helpful, but they look down on us as pimps, whores, drug dealers and guns for hire. They consider themselves a cut above us.'

'That is not something that I would ever think,' said Calogero. 'Besides, let's not be snobbish about drugs and whores and pimps. They are very necessary for human beings, and as a result very profitable for us. I know though that our friends in Palermo are now getting more interested in fraud rather than the usual traditional activities.'

Lotto looked over to the other side of the room.

'How many of those boys of yours could stick a knife into someone or use a gun?'

'All of them. That's what I pay them for.'

'But....?'

'They threaten people, they rough them up, they cut them up, they break bones. That is all that is necessary, usually. But they all know that they are expected to use maximum force if need be. And they are ready for that. Of course, Traiano is the best, but the others are not far behind. If they were no good, I would not employ them. I get lots of applications. Some I take on then let go when I think they are no good; I get many more applications than I can handle. The whole of Bicocca wants to come and work for me once they are out, but I am wary of the ones who can't control themselves. I need quality, not quantity.'

'Very wise,' said Lotto. 'You train them?'

'They know what to do. Naturally I prefer to take boys from this quarter, they are more reliable. Boys in this quarter, if they are any good, grow up as fighters. They are naturals. They imbibe it with the air of Purgatory. They know what to do, they do not need to be trained.'

185

'Like Iasi, like Bucharest; if you come from certain parts of the city, you know what to do. You grow up quickly.'

Calogero nodded.

'In Bucharest, they are looking to expand their operation,' said Lotto slowly and deliberately.

From the boys' table came a huge roar or laughter and whoops of ribald enjoyment. Calogero looked at Lotto and put a finger to his lips.

'You are staying here?'

'This hotel, yes.'

'Nice place, good choice; the swimming pool is nice, the indoor one.'

Lotto nodded.

Calogero got up to leave; as he did so he passed Anna. 'Tell him ten in the morning,' he told her. 'He will understand. Do it so no one else hears.'

At the boys' table the groom had opened his trousers to expose himself, which was the cause of great ribaldry; it was only the boys present, for the girls had drifted away. Someone was explaining the joke to Rosario. Back in the nineteenth century, in order to be sure that his wife was a virgin, a man of honour on his wedding night would prepare himself by painting his penis green; if the bride seemed surprised by this, he would shoot her. Several of the boys had bet that Traiano would not do this, but he had, and he had just proved it. Those who had lost the bet were now passing him fifty-euro notes, which he was pleased to pocket.

'But will the paint come off?' asked Rosario, with a laugh. The whole matter was absurd to him, given that the bride had one child already and was pregnant with another.

Calogero joined them at the table. Rosario noted that some secret intelligence seemed to pass between him and Traiano.

'I was just speaking to your mother and Lotto,' said Calogero.

Traiano nodded.

'Boss, have you seen what he's done?' shouted one of the more drunken lads. 'It's green. What will she think?'

'No, don't show me,' said Calogero, handing over a fifty euro note.

Chapter Six

Michele Lotto the Romanian was up to his neck in the waters of the indoor pool. It was clear, then, that he was not wearing a wire. Next to him, equally submerged, was Calogero. The man's appearance revolted him: the barrel chest, the thick dark hair on his arms and shoulders. He felt a slight passing sympathy for Anna and what she must have to put up with.

'How is Anna?' he asked conversationally.

'I cannot complain, don Calogero. When you spend time in jail, you dream of finding someone to look after your needs when you get out, but Anna surpasses anything I could have dreamed of.'

'I know, I know,' said Calogero. 'She is very memorable. She…'

He contemplated her attractions, and was silent.

Clearly Lotto was doing the same thing.

'We are very happy,' he said.

'Perhaps you could marry her,' said Calogero evenly. 'I mean, if you are happy and she is too. It is a new thought, Anna being happy.'

'She is already married. I know her husband. And I am married too. But I have what I want. I know she sees these old fellows in the afternoons. But I see her every Tuesday, Thursday and Saturday at 7pm. It is all very well regulated.'

'What is your real name?' asked Calogero.

'You are a cautious man,' observed Lotto, referring to the meeting in the swimming pool, and making clear that his real name was not important, for he too was cautious.

'I have to be,' said Calogero. Around them were some early morning swimmers, making lots of noise. There was no chance of anyone overhearing anything. 'I ask for your real name because, well, perhaps you might like to settle down here, join with us, make Anna permanent. All that could be arranged. I happen to know,' he continued, 'that they have their eye on me, and that they have their eye on you. They are watching us all, and trying to hear as much as possible. They may send men with wires, or they may put bugs on our clothes. It is possible. They told me that one of Anna's old men is one of their people.'

'Which one?'

'No idea. But you should be able to find out. Not that it matters. But they have him watching you, and perhaps they are eavesdropping. They are suspicious of you. They told me that.'

'Do you think one of your boys is working for them?'

'No. they are nearly all from the quarter. They are loyal. They do not like people from Palermo. One is from Agrigento, but I don't fear him, as he is too stupid. But people talk, people overhear things. It is not what they might overhear or see that worries me, but the fact that they think it necessary to watch in the first place. But if they are terminally suspicious, that is something that we all have to be. But what I want to know is why they are suspicious of you.'

'I give them credit for it,' said Lotto. 'I came here from Bucharest, as you know. I was inside there for some time, and in that prison I made a lot of useful contacts. When I was released, I followed up the contacts. I came here, but not before going to America first. I was in New York. I spent time in Brooklyn, in Staten Island, and I went over to New Jersey. I think you said that you had never been?'

'Never.'

'Well, if ever you got bored of Catania, it would be the ideal place for you. The land of opportunity. And if ever Catania got too hot for you, America would be the place; the United States, or somewhere to the south. But that is not what I want to talk to you about. Having spoken to lots of people, having listened to them, I come, if you like, as an ambassador.'

'For whom? For Bucharest?'

'Yes, for Bucharest, but, and this is important, with the approval of the Americans.'

'Then what you are about to say is of the very greatest importance, I am sure,' said Calogero.

'The people I represent are not happy. They see this bridge project as the height of folly. They do not trust Anna Maria Tancredi. This sort of fraud is not our traditional work; it may bring in millions but it will not provide a steady income in the way that our usual work does. Tancredi is clever, and she will use us to enrich herself, indeed, she has already done so. And the thing is, Tancredi is a woman, and this is a man's business, it has always been a man's business and should remain so. Women should keep out. I mean, would you ever discuss business with your wife?'

'Of course not,' said Calogero. 'But, the people in Palermo think we need to modernise. That is the impression I have. And that through modernity comes profit.'

'Profit comes from selling goods and service that people want to buy, that people will always buy come what may: drugs, gambling, prostitutes, and the people who ensure the smooth running of these things, the muscle power. Palermo has taken its eye of the ball. They have moved, shall we say, into banking, but forgotten that the real source of power is the fist. At least Antonio Santucci has done so; but he has not taken everyone with him.'

'What on earth are you thinking of?' asked Calogero, horrified at the thought of what was coming.

'It is not as bad as you think. America says yes, and Bucharest, and others, can provide the physical power. The people in Palermo on our side will just sit back and wait and watch.'

'I am one of the others?'

'Of course. In fact you are an important piece of the jigsaw. Palermo has bet heavily on Tancredi. If she is removed from the scene, their entire strategy is vaporised. They lose a shedload of money, their own, and worse, other people's. Their credibility is shot. We would have sixty men over from Romania, top men, and then we would pick them off one by one, and inherit their network. The smaller men, who resent the bigwigs, would not make any problems for us; in fact, given that many of them would lose all their money, they would be quite pleased to get rid of them. And the Americans would like to see a smooth transition of power. Look, you are a big talent, and Purgatory is too small for you. You could run the whole of Catania, and be acknowledged by the other local bosses as the commander in chief.'

'And who would take over in Palermo? A load of Romanians?'

'Yes,' said Lotto. 'But not obviously so. We have our people in Palermo, don't forget. And we need you too. It has to be a Sicilian operation, it has to look like a Sicilian operation. Nobody likes a foreign takeover. We need to get rid of the dead wood and have fresh talent at the top. You are fresh talent. This is a very big chance for you. Very big. In ten years' time, you could be at the top.'

'I can see now why Palermo was anxious about you,' said Calogero. 'I know exactly what needs to be done. But when it comes to destroying the bridge project, timing is everything.' He smiled. 'I need to think, and I need to consult.'

Rosario awoke with a start. The bells of the Church of the Holy Souls in Purgatory were sounding the hour. He tried to count; he thought they said ten; he looked at his mobile phone on his bedside table; it said twelve. He groaned softly to himself. His mouth was dry, his head was fuzzy. He had not left the wedding until two in the morning. He was wearing most of his clothes from last night, minus the shoes. (The shoes, the shoes, why was everyone so obsessed with shoes?) It was Sunday. He would go to the evening Mass, the one in the Cathedral. Right now he desperately needed some water, and some coffee, and some time to recover.

He hauled himself out of bed and very quietly made his way to the kitchen, where he filled the coffee maker, and put it on the stove. Then he poured out two glasses of water, and went into the flat's small living room. As he came into the room the girl on the sofa stirred, and opened her eyes. She accepted the glass of water with gratitude.

'I have some paracetamol somewhere if you need any,' he said solicitously.

'It's OK,' she said.

'You slept well?'

'Yes, thanks.'

'You could have had the bed, and I could have had the sofa,' he said.

She smiled: 'You are too tall for this sofa. It would have crippled you. This water is good.'

He went away and came back with the coffee.

'You said last night that in this quarter you are all dead men,' she remarked as she sipped the life-giving liquid.

'I must have been drunk,' he said.

'You were, but only a little bit. I think you were serious. The quarter is full of dead men. That is what you said. It is not a nice thought. Is it true?'

'I think so. Who did you come with?'

'Gino, the one from Agrigento. The one who met up with Alfio in Bicocca. Alfio is my cousin. He introduced us. You know Alfio?'

'I was at school with him. He is a few years older than me. He was in my brother's year. The one with the teeth, right?'

She giggled.

'The one with the teeth. Poor Alfio. He is not good-looking and he has still not managed to get a girl. And after last night, after the wedding, they are all talking of getting married.'

'Are you? Talking of getting married?' he asked.

'To Gino? He's nice enough. Would I do any better, I wonder? He will do for now. Where did he get to, do you think?'

'They all went off somewhere, they all scattered. They are all asleep somewhere in this quarter, Purgatory, the land of dead men.'

'Well, Gino is there when I need him, most of the time. A girl has got to take what is on offer. She can only dream. And you, Saro, are not available. We have established that. Every girl has waited for you to ask, and waited without result. And then one girl asked last night, and you said no. Well, at least I tried. This coffee is good.'

'You fall in love, you get married, you have children to carry on the human race. Our race ought not to carry on. If you marry Gino you will be a widow at the age of thirty with two small children and a lot of unhappy memories. I am sorry, but that is how I see it.'

'Poor Gino, poor Alfio; my uncle is in Piazza Lanza, you know. So that is their choice, an early death or prison. But it was never really a choice. They grow up round here fascinated with fighting, with guns and with knives. They all carry knives. Do you think they would kill someone?'

195

'Yes. That is what knives are for.'

'But the boys with knives and guns are also the boys with money. Look at the ones who don't have knives and guns; they are without a single lira. I am sure some are nice boys, but…. Did you see Ceccina's cousin there, the one called Arnaldo? He is a nice boy, but no job, no money, no prospects. But he is still young, isn't he, not more than twelve or thirteen. So sweet, but what future does he have? But the ones like Gino only want a girlfriend because it looks good. They are not that interested in girls as such. I don't mean…'

'I know what you mean. Listen, go to university, get a job, go to Milan, go to Turin, go to Germany, just get away from here.'

'Those are all cold places,' she said, not unreasonably. 'And far from home. Far from family. And Gino is not so bad. Maybe he will be lucky. Maybe he will change.'

'People never change,' said Rosario decisively. 'Don't delude yourself.'

'You are right, you are right,' she said. 'It is like we are all living on the edge of a volcano, and one day it will start to erupt and we will all be killed or lose everything, everything we know will be swept away.'

'We do live on the edge of a volcano,' observed Rosario.

Her face was eloquent of the sudden despair she felt. He realised that he did not have the gift of reassuring people or making them happy, least of all girls. But in the circumstances they were in, was reassurance the best way forward? She looked as if she might cry.

'I am sorry, I am sorry,' he said.

He moved to embrace her. There was total utter silence in the small room. He was aware of his own breathing, and of hers. The inevitable kiss came; then another. He felt the intoxication the kiss brought with it.

'You need to brush your teeth,' she said quietly.

Behind him, the door clicked. There was only one person who had a key of his own and entered unannounced. It was his brother. He sprang away from the girl, his cheeks burning, conscious that his clothes were in disarray.

'I hope you did not miss Mass, either of you,' said Calogero mildly. 'Hello, gorgeous,' he said to the girl. 'Congratulations. Not often I find my brother in flagrante delicto.'

She giggled, and got up, to go to the bathroom.

'Please excuse me, don Caloriu,' she said.

He looked questioningly at his brother.

'Catarina,' he said. 'Alfio's cousin. She came last night with Gino.'

'Then we had better keep it quiet,' said Calogero. 'I am sure she will. He might stab or shoot her. Or stab or shoot you. Now listen. There is a change of plan. We are not going to harm Volta. We are going to use him. I want to meet up with him: you, me and he. Can you arrange that? And soon? Good. Now you can get back to doing whatever it was you were doing.'

And he was gone.

Calogero and Traiano were having pizza on the night after the wedding.

'How long does food colouring mark the skin for?' asked Traiano.

'What?'

'You know, the green stuff that comes in a little bottle that they use for cakes.'

'Ah, that,' said Calogero. 'For ever. It is like a tattoo. I think it says on the bottle that you should be very careful when handling it, because it stains indelibly. That is the word. Indelible.'

'Really?'

'Yes. It stains skin and hair as well. But why are you asking?'

'Ceccina is furious.'

'Oh that? Well, she will get used to it. She may even come to like it. You know how women are. They like things that are unique. It may catch on. You may be the envy of all your friends. I am sure they will be madly jealous.'

Calogero looked concerned, but could not maintain his seriousness. He burst out laughing. Eventually, Traiano had to join in.

'I am going to take your advice about Tancredi,' he said suddenly. 'We never speak on the phone but we meet up from time to time as you know and each time, we fix on the next appointment. The next time I am expected in Donnafugata is Saturday 17th July. After that, who knows, and who knows where it will be. It might be here in Catania in a hotel, or in Taormina. The key thing is the timing. One needs to sell the entire holding in the bridge project first thing on the Monday morning. The fact that she has been killed will come out on the Monday, after the beginning of trade. That is vital. Because as soon as she is dead, the share price will collapse. So we have to take our profit and run, so to speak. I and others have decided to pull the carpet from under the bridge project. Once she is out of the picture there will be panic and it will be seen for the scam it is. But our money will be safe. Maybe Petrocchi's too as I can't see the point of ruining the Confraternity. But no one must know this at all. And we have to co-ordinate the timing with Lotto.'

He explained what Lotto had proposed.

'So, you have decided, boss, that you do not trust her, and you do trust Lotto?'

'I trust no one. I can make more use at present of Lotto than I can of her. This is a rare opportunity, to clear out the old guard in Palermo and have an entirely new management, and promotion for me and of course for you. You in particular. The current regime in Palermo do not like non-Sicilians, by which they mean people like you. You are one of us, and I regard their attitude as stupid. If anything happens to me, the legal stuff will be inherited by the children, and the illegal stuff by you. You will be in charge, and the fact you were born in Romania is not important. Once Tancredi goes, Palermo will be in crisis. For a start they will not know who did it. They will assume it is anyone of numerous enraged investors. One by one Lotto and his men will decapitate the Palermo men, and they will all suspect each other. He is going to unleash havoc, and we will benefit.'

'Boss, if you sell your holdings in Straits Limited the moment before the price crashes, won't that look suspicious? And Palermo knows that you are Tancredi's lover, don't they?'

'She has got several lovers, or has had. And on the Monday after her death, everyone will be selling, and the Palermo gang will have other things to worry about.'

Traiano nodded.

'Her house in Donnafugata is a nice quiet place, I am sure you will agree. Terribly quiet. High wall, security gates. If it happens there, so much the better. It will be easy. There will be Muniddu to take care of, but that we shall turn to our advantage. Her routine at weekends is always the same, is it not? She goes to Mass at eleven, then comes back for lunch. She never misses Mass. And what happened when she went to Mass last time? I stayed in the house reading a book. And someone came and swam in the pool.'

'Muniddu. He only uses the pool when she is not there.'

'You didn't swim?'

'I didn't know there was a pool and I had not brought my swimming things, otherwise I would have.'

'Good. She goes to Mass, and while she is praying, Muniddu swims, you join him, I join him, and we drown him. He is strong, but there are two of us. We will have a dress rehearsal on my next visit. We will lull his suspicions. Horseplay, so when it gets serious, he will realise too late. Then we put the body in the pool room nearby. Then she comes back, and he always keeps in the background when she is around, so she will notice nothing strange. And when she comes back from Mass, the first thing she does – '

'Is swim,' said Traiano.

'She likes fooling around by the poolside and even in the water, so she will not realise the danger before it is too late. Then we put both the bodies in the water, and we scarper. And we go somewhere and construct an alibi. The bodies in the water means that time of death will be hard to determine. The crucial thing is that no one sees us there or near there.'

'But you will have left your DNA all over the place, boss. In her bedroom, in the house, on the sheets, on her body, in her body…. That's how they catch people these days. It is so unfair. Unless of course we burn the house down, as you did with Vitale. With del Monaco the whole place was trampled over a thousand times.'

'I suppose we could both arrive and kill them straight away before going into the house. But the thing is we have to arrive, spend the weekend as if nothing is wrong, and then strike, in time for Monday morning.'

'I would prefer to go there and get it over with,' said Traiano. 'The idea of spending twenty-four hours drinking coke with Muniddu and listening to him talk, and then having to drown him like a rat…. It is a little depressing.'

'It does not pay to be sentimental,' said Calogero. 'I have been screwing the woman since January, but that was business and this is business. And she would have me thrown off a cliff if it helped her.'

'You feel nothing for her?'

'Why should I?' he asked. 'Look, I agree that leaving my DNA everywhere is a problem. Maybe we will have to soak the whole place in petrol and set light to it. But that would create its own problems. Maybe we are looking at this from the wrong perspective. Perhaps we should be thinking of someone else doing the job for us: but the truth is that we are best placed to strike, and that is what Lotto wants; that is our contribution to the Lotto conspiracy. If we do this, it guarantees us a place in the sun when the new world emerges. But one thing is for sure. We need to recruit more boys. We need to organise more of an army. The ones we have got are good. I told Lotto that. Which are the best? Which can be promoted?'

'We get applications all the time,' said Traiano.

'We need tough little bastards,' said Calogero.

'Bicocca is full of them, and so is Piazza Lanza. And all they talk about in those places is us.'

'Good,' said Calogero. 'Next week let us go to see Anna in Syracuse. And the week after it will be Donnafugata for the dress rehearsal. The opening weeks of your married life are going to be busy. And there is something else as well I have decided on. You and some of the boys are going to go on a little day trip up the mountainside. To be exact, to Nicolosi. It is nice up there. You'll like it.'

Lunch had been arranged in a restaurant near the fish market which had air conditioning. In the blistering July heat, Fabio Volta crossed the Cathedral Square from his place of work in the City Hall, feeling the heat from the lava cobbles beneath his feet, working its way through his shoes. He slipped into the restaurant with gratitude at the wave of cold air that greeted him as he opened the door. There at the back were Calogero and his brother; the former smiled, the latter looked uncomfortable. He joined them and the three of them shook hands. Calogero got down to work at once.

'I have decided, and naturally this must remain between us, to divest myself of the considerable holding I have in Straits Limited. It strikes me that the whole thing is fundamentally flawed. The bridge is never going to be built. The Prime Minister can say what he likes; and of course he may not be Prime Minister much longer. The other thing is that the whiff of illegality' – at this phrase, Volta raised his eyebrows, and Rosario rolled his eyes – 'hangs over the whole thing. It is very important for me, and for my brother, who is a lawyer, that everything should be above board. We do not want the financial police sniffing around. Now, the question is this: how can I sell things off without getting burned?'

Volta said: 'The price keeps on going up. If you sold today, people would say that you were taking a profit and think nothing of it. And that would be that. There would be no story.'

'But for you there is a story?'

'Of course there is. The story is the crash, when it comes, and the way thousands will lose their money and where that money will go. It will disappear into the pockets of criminals.'

'That's not a story. That is everyday life. The rich get richer, the poor get poorer. The story is this: the timing of the crash. They expect a crash, they have built it into their calculations. But if the crash comes early and takes them by surprise, then that will really be your story, Volta. Because you see, then the crash will not take down the ordinary small investor about whom no one cares much (apart, obviously, from myself, whose sympathy is always with the little man). If the crash comes when they do not expect it, before they plan it, then the people who suffer are Anna Maria Tancredi, and her backers. Her backers in Palermo and her backers in Rome. They will be severely dented by this. It is not just the loss of money, it is the loss of prestige. Anna Maria Tancredi always goes around with a bodyguard. If the crash comes before they expect it and they lose everything, then she will need more than a single bodyguard to protect her. Rome will cut her loose; Palermo will cut her loose; Rome and Palermo will fall into mutual recriminations. What is the bit in Shakespeare?'

'Lady Macbeth?' asked Rosario.

'No, Julius Caesar. Cry havoc and let slip the dogs of war.'

'Are you saying,' said Volta, 'that the people in Palermo will come after the politicians in Rome?'

'That is exactly what I am saying,' said Calogero.

'You really are a bastard,' said Rosario. 'You have known this woman since January. You have been sleeping with her on and off since then, and now you are planning to throw her to the dogs. Have you no feelings? At the very least you will be exposing her to grave danger from these murderous thugs in Palermo.'

Calogero looked at Volta.

'My brother is an idiot, please ignore him. Anna Maria Tancredi knew all the risks she was running right from the start. She chose to work with the people in Palermo and she chose to link up with the scum of the earth in Rome. And I have no obligations towards any woman I sleep with apart from the mother of my children. How is Catarina?'

'Who?' asked Rosario.

'The girl you slept with on Saturday night after the wedding?'

'I did not sleep with her,' said Rosario, raising his voice. 'She slept on the sofa in my flat.'

'That is not what it looked like to me,' said Calogero, 'When I called round in the morning. Does her cousin Alfio know? Does Gino? I think they would both like to know.'

'Did you find them in bed together?' asked Volta.

'More or less,' said Calogero.

'He did not,' protested Rosario.

'Have you seen her since?' asked Calogero.

'No!' said Rosario.

'You do not know how to behave to a woman. So do not lecture me on Anna Maria.'

'I wasn't.'

'Ah, here comes the waiter,' said Calogero.

'To get back to the matter in hand,' said Volta after they had ordered. 'The question of timing is important.'

'Absolutely. It has to be a Monday morning that I sell, first thing, as soon as the markets open, before everyone has got over the weekend. And just as a single snowball starts off an avalanche.'

'There may be other things that happen on that Monday to help the avalanche along?'

'Yes. And if it is in August when they are all at the beach, all the powers that be, that will hamper their ability to make a co-ordinated response.'

'There is never much news in August,' said Volta. 'It is the dead season. The newspapers and the people who broadcast will pick the matter up and their talk will bring the price crashing down. As you say, one snowball. A snowball in August. Just when you do not expect it, when you are lying on the beach. Nice.' He paused. 'Of course we know who the Palermo people are. We have known them for years. But who are the people in Rome? How can we expose them?'

'You don't have to. They will be exposed not by their enemies, but by their friends.'

In Nicolosi, high up on the lower slopes of Mount Etna, things were cooler. There were trees there, and a breeze. It was a nice place to escape to, to get away from the heat of the city. Traiano decided that when he was richer than he was at present, he would buy a house in Nicolosi, for the summer, for Ceccina and the children. Little Cristoforo would like it, as he grew older. And perhaps they could get a dog. He always wanted to have a dog, but you couldn't keep one in the city, in a flat, especially in Purgatory, which at this time of year was hot and airless as hell itself.

He was looking at a dog right now. A very small dog, a Chihuahua in fact. They were, he had read, fashionable. Rich women liked them. But it was unusual for a man to have one.

'Tell me about your dog,' he said to the man.

The man frowned.

'It is my daughter's,' he said. 'She is on holiday. I am just looking after it while she is away. But look, the man on the door told you, you are not supposed to be here. This is a private club. You are not members. You are not guests. He asked you to leave, and I am telling you that he was right. In fact, you have to be eighteen to join this club, and you, sir, do not look eighteen, though your friends may be.'

Traiano ignored this.

'It would be a pity if your daughter came back from holiday and found that something had happened to this poor little animal,' he said. He beckoned the dog, who came to him, and sat on his lap. 'It would be a pity if your daughter came back from holiday and found that something had happened to you, sir.'

'Who the hell are you?' said the man with horror in his voice.

The dog was sniffing Traiano's knife with great interest.

'I have never eviscerated a live dog,' said Traiano. 'Even with a small cute dog like this, it would not be a nice sight. But I can do so, and you can watch, and then you can imagine what I will do to you when I stick this knife into your guts and butcher you. There will be blood everywhere, all over this nice office. But perhaps it will not come to that.'

Alfio and Gino came and stood either side of the man at the desk. He tried to speak. Eventually he managed to say: 'Fabrizio Perraino is one of our members.'

'The one with the lisp? We know him. Why not call him now, and invite him over? We will cut him up in front of you and throw his remains into the volcano. But I don't think he can help you in any way, even if he wanted to. You see, we like this place. We don't want to damage it, we want to use it. We want to come here and train ourselves, perhaps with the help of your instructors, and we do not want silly questions about who we are, how old we are, membership fees, paperwork, identity cards or any of that nonsense. We just turn up when we want to, use the facilities and that is that. Do you understand?'

The man nodded dumbly.

'And we are fair people. We will make sure you do not suffer financially.' He released the dog. 'Go to daddy,' he commanded. 'And as for Perraino, please do not worry about him. We can take care of him if he makes any trouble. Perraino is not a problem. At least not for us. Now, perhaps you can give me and my two friends a tour of the premises. And you are going to be seeing a lot of us and the rest of our friends as well.'

He smiled.

'So,' said Volta, 'To sum up. You are proposing to collapse the whole rotten house of cards, and as a result break the peace of Palermo, and the pax Romana as well?'

'You might well put it that way, Volta, if you so wish,' replied Calogero. 'I would see it like this. I take my money out of Straits Limited. The company collapses in price earlier than expected, and recriminations follow. So, I pull out one brick from the bottom of the house, and the whole structure totters? Yes, maybe. But it was a pretty unstable structure to begin with. Like one of those cheaply built houses that falls down in the first earthquake.'

'Aren't a lot of people going to get killed as a result?' asked Rosario.

'Well done, Saro, you are catching on,' observed his brother. 'Or look at it in a more Catholic way. Aren't a lot of people going to have to face the consequences of their actions? Anna Maria has been a thief and a trickster, and working for thieves and tricksters for far too long. She is a banker, running a private bank, but that is a pose. She is the associate of criminals who just happens to be very good at masking her activities. She uses the Church to do so. She is a hypocrite. What is going to happen is that her hypocrisy is going to be revealed.'

'You are going to get her killed,' said Rosario.

'If she gets killed, she will have got herself killed. She was crook long before she met me.'

'What about that Romanian, what has he got to do with this?' asked Rosario.

'Traiano? Nothing.'

'Not Traiano. The man who came with Anna to the wedding. The one called Michele Lotto.'

'He has nothing to do with this. Why do you think he might? He is just a friend of Anna's. Who have you been talking to? Who have you been listening to?'

'Traiano mentioned him. I know that Traiano does not like him.'

'Well, Traiano does not like anyone who sleeps with his mother,' said Calogero mildly.

'Does that include you?'

Calogero sighed.

'You are very cheeky, Saro. Volta, do you have a younger brother? No? Lucky you. Do you have some very good Catholic relative, a fanatic who goes to Church every Sunday and who criticises your behaviour at every turn? Well, I do, it seems. And this is his revenge because on Sunday morning, when he should have been in Church, he was with some cheap tart, and I walked in and found them together on the sofa, and he was bright red in the face and his trousers were round his ankles.'

'They were not,' protested Rosario.

'So what if they were,' said Volta mildly.

'So what?' asked Calogero. 'Indeed so what. But it is the hypocrisy that gets me. I am never allowed to forget my sins, and his sins are never spoken of. This is what I have to put up with. You must excuse me a minute.'

Calogero left them.

'I am sorry, I am sorry,' said Volta. 'He is very difficult, very bullying. I do feel for you.'

'Never mind that, I am used to it, and none of it is true. He is just about to make trouble for me. What we need to consider is why he is doing this now? Why does he want to pull the rug from out under Tancredi and Palermo now? And it has got something to do with Lotto. Did you see how he reacted to the mention of his name? That is not his real name, of course. But who is Lotto and what is he doing here? My guess is nothing good. And are we really going to allow him to expose Anna Maria to sudden death? Is he going to leave her naked? Do we warn her? Or are we part of a conspiracy to murder here?'

'If we warn her the whole thing is off,' said Volta.

'I don't like it,' said Rosario. 'We are sinking to his level.'

They fell silent as Calogero returned.

'I was just making some phone calls,' he said.

'Signor di Rienzi,' said Volta deliberately. 'If you go ahead and pull out your money and the whole thing collapses, and some of her former friends murder Anna Maria Tancredi, won't you feel guilty?'

'No,' said Calogero.

'Can you find out for me who her backers are in Rome? I know you are not interested in politics, but I am. The people I work for are.'

'The people you work for are politicians,' said Calogero. 'Obviously they want to do down their rivals. I can understand that. Your lot wants to find out something bad about the other lot. And I know what you are going to ask me to do. And I can do it. I believe it is illegal, but you want me to steal her mobile phone.'

'Or to replicate it. It is illegal, yes, and such evidence cannot be used in court. But if we could get the contents of her phone it might give us vital clues. There will be a number in that phone that will be her link to the office of the Prime Minister. After all, that is where the bridge project was born, in what passes for the mind of you know who. I doubt she talks to him, but she talks to someone who has sight of his desk, his plans, his papers, his diaries.'

Calogero looked at Rosario.

'Would Traiano know how to replicate a phone if he had five minutes alone with it?' He turned to Volta. 'I don't even know how to make a phone call. I use carrier pigeons. And I keep all my useful numbers in my

214

head. But we can use Traiano. That is a job he would enjoy. I am going to Donnafugata next weekend. You can have the phone on Monday. I will send Traiano, no, I will send my brother, to your office first thing on Monday morning. Then we need to agree on a date for this pulling out of the rug. I need you to study the market and tell me when.'

'The first Monday in August would be optimal,' said Volta. 'That would be the second August.'

'Let's work to that date,' said Calogero.

They stood up and shook hands. They left the restaurant; Volta hurried across the Cathedral square to his office, and Calogero watched him go; Rosario headed up the Via Etnea to return to his office at the lawyer Petrocchi's. Calogero waited in the square for a few moments until they were gone, and drifted over to the statue of the elephant with the obelisk on its back.

'Hi, handsome,' he said to a little boy of eleven who was leaning against the statue.

'Hi, don Caloriu,' said the child, the one called Tonino Grassi.

Calogero kissed him and ruffled his hair.

'I have got a job for you,' he said. 'So listen carefully. Alfio and Gino – you know Gino, the boy from Agrigento? – they have both gone to Nicolosi with Traiano. I want you to look out for them, and send them

215

straight over to me, as soon as they get back. I shall be at home. Tell them to come to me at about quarter to six. And tell Traiano to come too. Then when you have done that, at about 6pm, stand outside the lawyer Petrocchi's office and when you see my brother Rosario coming out, tell him that he is wanted at home urgently. Don't tell him why. Just make him anxious. Have you understood that?'

'Yes, don Caloriu.'

Calogero carelessly took out a fifty euro note and gave it the boy.

'Well done my little pigeon. Give me another kiss.'

'Don Caloriu, can I ask you something? Is it true that Traiano's dick is green?'

'How do you know that?'

'Everyone is talking about it.'

'It is true. It glows in the dark. It means his wife can find it easily in bed. He dipped it in food colouring. Make sure you do not do the same.'

'I won't,' said the boy, running off.

Rosario came hurrying home, sweating through the heat of early evening. The boy who had met him outside the office had been completely incoherent with worry and fear, and this feeling was catching. His breath came in terrible heaves as he crossed the square and passed the façade of the Church of the Holy Souls in Purgatory. He then went down the shady alley to his own door, where he found the street door open. Walking up with dread, wondering what he would find, when he came to the third floor, and his own front door, Alfio and Gino were waiting for him, leaning against the wall.

He was surprised, and a little fearful. He caught his breath, and realised that there was some sort of difficultly ahead, and he thought he knew who had caused it.

'Hi,' he said politely and firmly. 'What do you want?'

They were silent.

'Come in,' he said, taking out his key, and letting them into the flat, which, luckily, had been tidied since the weekend. He knew that these two would only have come round because his brother allowed them to come round, and they would be acting with the full permission of Calogero. If Calogero had given them permission for them to beat him up, then that was bound to happen. But he doubted that. The main thing, the only thing, was to keep calm.

The three of them sat down. Alfio, the one had had known for years, a big strong man with very bad teeth, the one who had been locked up in Bicocca, God knows what for, was the first to speak.

'You know Catarina is my cousin, Saro,' he said.

'I knew that, Alfio,' he said.

'And I have been going with her for six months,' said Gino, the one from Agrigento via Bicocca, who he knew less well, and whose physical strength seemed to fill the entire room.

'We know she was here on Saturday night,' continued Alfio. 'Can you explain that?'

'After the wedding was over, you disappeared,' said Rosario. 'We were talking. She didn't want to go home and wake everyone up as they were not expecting her, so she asked if she could stay with me. She slept on the sofa, I slept in my bed. Then in the morning, she and I had coffee and then she left.'

Alfio and Gino looked at each other. After the wedding broke up, at around midnight, all the boys had gone to one of the bars owned by Calogero, and drunk whiskey until dawn, and flirted with the prostitutes, and in one or two cases, more than flirted. In their pleasures they had all temporarily mislaid their girlfriends. Since then Gino had not spoken to Catarina except over the phone; and they had not spoken, merely screamed and shouted.

218

Gino began to mumble something.

Alfio held up a hand to stop him.

'Don Caloriu said that he came round here and found you on Sunday morning,' said Alfio.

'That is correct,' said Rosario.

'And he said you were on the sofa together and you were very embarrassed.'

Rosario considered. 'My brother Caloriu has a great sense of humour. I promise you both that there was nothing like that happening. Nothing happened between me and Catarina. And just think for a moment: why would Catarina look at me, when she has you, Gino?'

'It is true that you are not good looking, but you are the boss's brother,' said Gino.

'But am I the one he trusts with his confidential business?' asked Rosario.

They looked at each other. Rosario realised that he had said something of importance.

'That is true,' said Alfio. 'He trusts us a lot.'

'You have just come from his house, haven't you? I suppose that little boy summoned you, the one who called me back here.'

They nodded. He wished he could find out what they had spoken about, apart from himself. He waited.

'Tell us about this guy, this Fabrizio Perraino,' said Alfio.

'I met him in hospital. He is an absolute bastard.'

'Should we discuss this?' cautioned Gino.

'Saro is the boss's brother, he trusts us, he trusts him. Besides it may be important. Tell us everything you know about Perraino.'

'He is the worst type of policeman. He is very greedy. He fell out with Carmine del Monaco, whom you have all heard about.' They nodded. 'He used to be very good-looking, and del Monaco broke his jaw in two places. Since then Perraino has lost his looks and he speaks with a lisp, which makes him ridiculous, especially as his misfortunes have not taught him any humility. Caloriu knows him, I am sure, though they may never have met. This Fabrizio used to be the lover of his own aunt, but she dropped him when he started to lisp.'

He could tell that this last detail shocked them.

'But why do you want to know about him?'

'There is a shooting club in Nicolosi, where the owner mentioned his name as some big cheese we should be frightened of,' said Alfio.

'He had one of those small dogs,' said Gino. 'A Chihuahua. Traiano threatened to stab him. How that scared him!'

'He threatened the dog, not the man,' explained Alfio. 'The dog was sweet, I thought. But this Perraino is no good, you say? That is nice to know.'

Rosario stood up and got three bottles of beer and opened them. The two visitors gratefully accepted.

'Carmine del Monaco hated Perraino,' said Rosario. 'But look what happened to him as a result. Perraino has friends. If he didn't, he wouldn't just have a lisp for his trouble, he would be long dead.'

'That is the trouble with people like Perraino,' said Alfio. 'They think they have friends and they become arrogant. He insulted you?'

'You could say that.'

'He did that with his aunt?' asked Gino. 'My God, that is so disgusting. He deserves to die just for that.'

Then the subject turned to other matters. To Catarina, who was being so unreasonable, because of what Gino had said to her on the phone, and because he had left her on the night of the wedding; to the wedding itself; to what don Caloriu was wearing at the wedding, the suit of pale linen, the shirt from India, and the wonderful shoes; and how Traiano had stained himself green with food colouring.

'Holy Mary, green,' said Alfio accepting another beer.

'Holy Mary, did you see it?' said Gino. 'Everything was green. Even his curly hair had gone blackish-green. Did you notice? I wonder what Ceccina thinks of it all?'

'She tries not to look, I should think. She lies back and closes her eyes. Particularly on the wedding night.'

There was laughter.

'Eh, Saro,' said Alfio boldly, 'Is it true that you have never done it?'

'Yes, that is true,' said Rosario.

The two visitors looked at each other.

'I told you,' said Alfio to Gino. 'But he would not believe me. Well, perhaps not doing it is a good idea. When we were little they told us that in catechism. Wait until you were married. You told the children that, Saro, when you taught them catechism. At least you practice what you preach. I believed it once, but then you grow up and everyone else is around you, and you cannot resist. Oh Jesus, the girls in this quarter...'

'You mean the whores,' said Gino. 'Best in Catania. Real quality. We can introduce you, and as you are the boss's brother…. No?'

'Are they all from eastern Europe?'

'Most. Romania… But do you think it is true, what they say about the boss? That he is seeing someone? A few times now he has been away, on one occasion back in January he drove off with Traiano, and again in June, and a few times in between as well,' said Alfio.

'If he is, he cannot want Stefania to find out,' said Rosario sensibly.

'Could she blame him?' said Gino. 'A beautiful man like that needs more than one woman. Hell, we all need more than one woman, and if we could get more than one, we would. Apart from you, Saro, apart from you. You are not good-looking, it is hard to think that you are brothers, but you are good, you are good….'

'Of course he has a new woman. He must do. Why else is he wearing these silk boxer shorts?' said Alfio.

'Have you seen them?' asked Rosario.

'I have!' said Alfio. 'And so has Gino. We were there this afternoon and we were having coffee in the kitchen and there was a pile of ironing there. I am going to get some. I can't afford shoes like his just yet, but the boxers are not so very expensive. You can get them on the Via Etnea.'

'Hmm, beautiful,' said Rosario, going for more beers.

They did not leave until all the beers were gone.

Chapter Seven

On their way to Donnafugata for the dress rehearsal, they decided to call in at Syracuse; Traiano telephoned Anna to let her know that she was to expect a filial visit at around lunchtime; they were expected at Donnafugata at mid-afternoon. The July sun shone harshly on the waterfront, and on the fountain of Arethusa, so they took refuge on the other side of the island, which faced north, and where there was a breeze, near where they had left the car. They walked along the sea, Lotto and Calogero going first, deep in conversation, Traiano and Anna following, the child Salvatore sitting on Traiano's shoulders.

'Is my father going to be released soon?' asked Traiano. 'Will he come here? How will you explain Salvatore if he does?'

'There would be a lot more than Salvatore to explain,' she said. 'Salvatore is the least of my worries, poor little boy. The explanations I owe your father, are in his eyes at least, very long and complicated. In fact it is too hard even to begin to formulate them. But will he come back? Back, I mean to me, not to Sicily. Yes, I think he will. Your grandmother knows we are here, and she will tell him, in all innocence. I mean she knows. She knows I only came here to get away from him, but she believes in reconciliations and happy endings. And when she tells him, he will come. He has unfinished business with me and with you. Me, he tried to kill. You were three years old, so you do not remember it, though you were there. Though I think it must have had an effect on you, when your father tries to kill your mother in front of you.'

225

'I know, I know, but why?'

'I don't know,' she said. 'He was very violent, and his rage fell on me. I was there in the wrong place at the wrong time. I did not want him to mistreat you. I stood up to him. I paid the price. Anyway, I got away, to this.'

They were, she reflected, in one of the most beautiful places on earth. But one never truly got away. There was no freedom, only temporary reprieves. There was always a debt to pay, always a reckoning.

'And if he comes? When he comes?'

'Lotto will warn me, and when the time comes, protect me. Your father is not completely irrational, and he knows that if he takes on Lotto he cannot win. So I am safe.'

'You like Lotto?'

'No. But I need him.'

'Am I safe?'

'No one is. But you can defend yourself, can't you? Besides, your father will see in you something of himself, and will leave you alone. At least he will not try to kill you. He will probably try to squeeze you for cash. Me too. After all, you are richer than you have ever been, and so am I.'

'I am poorer than I have ever been. I have a wife, a child and another on the way, and now I am married I pay for everything.'

'You have been married two weeks today, haven't you? You are richer than you have ever been. And he is making a fortune as well, out of all the drugs and girls and pizzas. Make sure that as he gets richer you get richer as well. How much have you got put away?'

'Do we have to talk about money? Nothing at all. The wedding was expensive. Besides, I am the only one in the whole of Ceccina's family who seems to earn anything. They all need looking after. But do not worry. Calogero is expecting a huge amount very soon, and he has some big jobs lined up for me. And the money from the bars and the pizza place is still coming in.'

'Well, be careful,' said Anna.

'I am careful,' said Traiano with asperity. 'I am grown up, for goodness' sake. I am not the sort to get caught and I can look after myself.' They sat down on the sea wall, and he took Salvatore in his lap, observing not for the first time that the child did not look like his natural father, the man he had killed, but more like himself, his half-brother. 'By the way, one of the old men who comes to you in the afternoons works for Palermo. He is long retired, but he is passing things on. They told us themselves. They are watching Lotto. They don't trust him. It is quite possible that they have bugged your house. Palermo have that sort of equipment. Though what they would hear, I don't know, apart from a load of old men coming. And

Lotto coming too, I suppose. Electronic surveillance of a brothel must make very monotonous listening.'

Anna laughed.

'All those faked orgasms,' she said. 'Each one the same as the last. Jesus, Jesus, Jesus!'

He remembered that Rosario of all people had said something on the same matter. That all Sicilian woman called upon the Holy Name as they climaxed. But his mother faked it. He wondered for a moment about Ceccina, his wife.

At a distance of fifty metres, Calogero was also explaining the matter of the electronic surveillance to Lotto, warning him. Lotto shrugged. If someone in Palermo was listening, all they were hearing were the creakings of the bedsprings and Anna's noisy orgasms. That didn't bother him. Far more important was the fixing of the date. He agreed with Calogero that timing was everything. The shares would be dumped on Monday 2nd August. The lady and her bodyguard would meet their maker on Sunday morning. On Saturday evening, Fabrizio Perraino would have a meeting in Purgatory late at night from which he would never return. It was necessary to prevent him avenging his aunt. He was also an important cog in the Palermo machine. All these things coming together would create the perfect catastrophe for Palermo.

At four o'clock the security gates of the house outside Donnafugata opened before them in response to the press of the button. Traiano drove him in, and dropped him by the front door, then took the car round to the garage on the other side of the orange grove. The front door was open. Calogero stepped into the dark coolness of the hallway. After the glare of the sun, it took some time to accustom his eyes to the change of light.

'Hello,' she said, standing at the top of the stairs.

She was naked.

Carrying his bag, he walked slowly up the stairs to meet her.

On the other side of the orange grove, Muniddu was pouring a coke for Traiano.

'Actually, I am glad to see you,' he said. 'Usually, I find these weekends in the country very boring. At least it is not as hot as in Palermo. The heat there is incredible. My poor wife, my poor children. The heat makes them fractious. So at least here I get away from that. How is your wife? Congratulations by the way. When is the new child coming? December? It won't be so hot then. Have you air conditioning at home? No? She has air conditioning in the house. In the bedroom. So she can have sex with your boss in comfort. Lucky her, lucky him. It's always the way. The officer class enjoy themselves, and we are left on guard duty.'

'Jesus, Jesus, Jesus!' said Anna Maria Tancredi.

'You seem keener than usual,' he said, burying his face between her breasts, breathing in her sweetness. 'Is it the thought of all that money?'

She laughed.

'I think that is what turns you on,' she said. 'How much did you sink into Straits Limited?'

'Three.'

'Well, you have doubled your money. Now you have six. You will have to pay a lot of that back to the people who lent it to you, but you should have a good amount left over. It all depends what the price will be when the signal to dump comes. But it will be more than what it is now, that is for sure. You are going to be very rich. The collapse of Straits Limited will lead to a lot of people being left in debt and having to sell property and shares off cheaply. The whole market will be depressed. You can use your money to buy up a lot of things very cheaply. It will all be legal: apartment blocks, hotels, restaurants, shops, whatever you choose.'

'That sounds very agreeable. Are you promising to make me rich, as rich as you have made everyone else?'

'In my hands things grow,' she said.

Conversation ceased.

'Jesus, Jesus, Jesus!' Anna Maria screamed once more.

'You heard that?' said Traiano. 'I think it is the direction of the breeze. But that is the second time in half an hour. The boss is brilliant in everything he does.'

'I noticed,' said Muniddu. 'Where does he get those shoes from?'

They discussed the boss's shoes, all the time keeping one ear out for the sound of another orgasm from Anna Maria. It came eventually.

'Now they will have a shower,' said Muniddu. 'Then they will have a swim, then they will have drinks, and then they will have their dinner, all beautifully prepared for them earlier today, and then they may watch a film or something, and then do it again.'

'Is she always this randy?' asked Traiano.

'She is getting worse, or better, with age. I have not been working for her that long. But the other guys said there were sometimes men around who came to service her. There was the nephew. They used to do it out in the open by the pool. One of the guys who worked for her used to go to that side of the roof and catch sight of them, which you can do if you really lean over.'

'Holy Mary,' said Traiano.

'Well, she has no children, for her it is all a game,' said Muniddu. 'You and I know what it is like having children.'

Muniddu then spoke with great affection about his two children, a boy and a girl. The boy was called Riccardo, and was clever little chap, just starting at school. The girl was older and was called Rosalia, after the patron saint of Palermo. It struck Traiano that Muniddu felt for his son what he felt for Cristoforo and to a lesser extent for Salvatore; he felt a momentary stab of guilt at the thought that these children, through his agency, would soon be without a father. But he rapidly reassured himself with the thought of all the men that Muniddu had killed, all the orphans he had created, and how he had known the risks when he had embarked on the life he had chosen for himself. Anyway, according to Muniddu, they had two children, and that was enough; on this present job, he hardly ever got to spend any time with them. His wife complained when he was away, and she complained when he was there. Some people were never happy.

It was eleven when they finally went to their respective beds. Soon Muniddu was snoring. After an hour of tense waiting, Traiano went out into orange grove, and then into the garden. He stood underneath what he knew was the bedroom window. He had the phone that Volta had given with him, and he prepared to wait. He did not have to wait very long. The door of the air-conditioned bedroom opened, and Calogero stepped out onto the balcony. He threw down the phone, which Traiano caught with an expert catch. He then retreated to the pool house, which had a lavatory; he locked himself in, and switched on the light.

The copying of what they were looking for was very simple, and Volta had gone over it several times with him. He copied Anna Maria's list of contacts to the sim card; then he took the sim card out and put it in his phone, and copied the list of contacts to the phone; then he restored the sim

232

card to its original place. Both phones were identical Nokias, but he had been careful to mark his with a white sticker on the back in case of confusion. He then returned to the garden, where Calogero was waiting for him on the balcony. He threw the phone up to him, and Calogero caught it, then disappeared inside.

When he got back to his bed, Muniddu was awake.

'Where have you been?' he asked.

'I wasn't able to sleep as it was so hot. So I went out to the garden to get some fresh air. I did not want to wake you up,' he said apologetically. 'Sorry I woke you.'

'It's OK,' said Muniddu grudgingly.

A few moments later he was asleep once more.

At around half past ten the next morning, Anna Maria left the house to go to Mass, and as it was safe to do so, Muniddu emerged to use the pool, and this time Traiano came with him. Hearing their splashes, Calogero came down and jumped in. The water was a delight in the already building heat of the day.

'Muniddu,' said Calogero, 'has Traiano told you about his wedding?'

Calogero winked.

'No, don Calogero, what is there to tell?' asked Muniddu, sensing a joke in the offing, noticing how Traiano had suddenly adopted a look of embarrassment.

'His cock is green and his wife is not happy,' said Calogero.

'Don Calogero, shut up!' said Traiano.

Calogero explained the circumstances. Muniddu laughed uproariously. Then Calogero whispered something to Muniddu. Peace was restored. They swam quietly. Then suddenly Muniddu grabbed Traiano and pinioned him by the arms. Calogero then tried his best to pull down Traiano's bathing shorts. There was a terrible struggle. Traiano defended himself stoutly. The struggle went on, but it was two against one. Eventually, Traiano lost his shorts, and got out of the pool defeated, looking for a towel.

'Fuck you both,' he said angry and upset, and stomped off back to the garage.

The other two laughed.

But by the time that Muniddu got back to the garage, Traiano was smiling.

'The boss likes these jokes,' he said. 'I suppose that is the way he is. I ought to get used to it by now. But one day someone will give him a taste of his own medicine.'

'Is it really green?' said Muniddu.

'I am glad you did not see,' said Traiano. 'Yes, it is really green. I did it for a bet. Now it won't come off.'

'Holy Mary,' said Muniddu.

'Listen,' said Traiano, 'Next time we come here, let's jump on him and pull his shorts off, and see how he likes it.'

'He couldn't complain,' said Muniddu.

Later that evening, Traiano brought the car round, and Calogero got in. The gates opened and they were free.

Calogero sighed.

'You got the phone copied?' asked Calogero.

'No problems.'

'Volta showed you how?'

'He did. It is quite easy. A child could do it.'

'You would recognise Volta again?'

'Of course.'

'Excellent. One day we may have to kill him, you never know. A dangerous man. But for now we are using him. I am so tired.'

'I bet you are. Muniddu and I heard her orgasm at least six times. Then we lost count. Hard work for you, Uncle Calogero. Muniddu and I are going to tear your swimming trunks off you the next weekend.'

'Wonderful. We are invited for the first August. All going to plan.'

'You have insulted me,' said Captain Fabrizio Perraino.

It was Monday afternoon. The police car had come into the quarter early in the morning, and Alfio, Gino and Traiano, had been arrested while still in bed by a squad of police. They had not been allowed to dress, but hauled away with maximum fuss in their boxer shorts. In one case the front door had been broken down. In all cases their places of residence had been turned upside down. There had been impassioned screams from Alfio's mother and sisters and little brother; Ceccina and Cristoforo had outdone each other in crying and screaming. Gino, who lived alone, had been in bed with Catarina, who had made a similar outcry. By the time the three miscreants had been handcuffed and put in police cars, though it was still only six thirty in the morning, the whole of Purgatory was in uproar.

They had been taken to the police station, not the headquarters in Piazza Santa Nicolella, but to a quieter one further out of the city in Via Antonino Caruso, and then been locked in a cell without anything to eat or drink for several hours. It was only at mid-afternoon that Perraino came in to see them.

He addressed Gino and Alfio, the two older ones, by instinct, thinking the younger one was of less importance.

'You have insulted me,' he said, adding, 'this place smells of your piss. I will force you to clean it up before you are released, if you are ever released. I see that two of you were in Bicocca. You may well be going back there or somewhere worse.'

Perraino lit a cigarette to mask the smell of urine.

'Are you charging us with something?' said Alfio. 'Because if not, this is illegal. We want a lawyer.'

'Shut up or I will rearrange your teeth,' said Perraino. 'I can charge you with cruelty to animals, for torturing a poor innocent Chihuahua. Do you know how long you could do inside for that? And this time it would be Piazza Lanza, not the holiday camp that is Bicocca.'

Traiano coughed quietly, trying to suppress his laughter.

'We did nothing to that dog,' said Alfio angrily. 'We love animals.'

'The owner of that shooting club is a friend of mine; his daughter, who owns the dog, is a friend of mine; you went in there and insulted them, and so you insulted me.'

'Captain, captain,' said Gino. 'Please forgive my friend, he has a fierce temper, and he does not know what he is saying half the time. Shut up, Alfio. Look, Captain, if we had known that they were friends of yours, we would never have done anything to upset them or you. And as for the dog, well, the dog did not understand anything and seemed perfectly happy with things. We would never have hurt the dog. As for the gentleman, well, that was all a misunderstanding. We didn't have our identity cards on us, which was wrong, and we have driven all the way up from Catania, and we wanted to go in, and we didn't realise we had to be members. And the man on the door did not explain it well to us. Look, captain, we are a bit rough, I know. We are from Purgatory and Purgatory people are a little bit unrefined, you could say.'

'Your accent is different,' said Perraino suspiciously.

'I am from Agrigento,' said Gino. 'Originally. Maybe that makes me a little bit more aware of the respect we owe to the police. Captain, we do not want to get into trouble with our employer. We work for Calogero di Rienzi. He would be very angry if he knew we had been up to Nicolosi and upset people. He would be very angry if he knew we had upset you. Very angry indeed. It is the worst luck that we went to Nicolosi in the first place without realising that you had an interest up there. They are friends of yours and you are a friend, a very good friend, of Calogero. We apologise unreservedly, Captain.'

Alfio looked annoyed but resigned. Traiano stared penitently at the floor. The captain looked unimpressed. There was silence.

'Captain,' continued Gino, 'we are all just poor boys who do whatever we can in the quarter to make a bit of cash. We are not rich. I am the guy who puts the wood into the pizza oven. It is hard work, but at least it is work. Alfio here runs the door on one of the bars, and so does Traiano.'

'You have plenty of money, you scum,' said Perraino. 'I want two thousand.'

'That is more than all of us make in a month,' said Alfio in protest.

Traiano sighed in shock.

'Two thousand,' said Perraino. 'From each of you.'

He left the cell. The door slammed.

Two hours later, Perraino returned.

He stood in front of them, looking at the wet floor.

'Captain,' said Gino. 'We can pay. But we will need time. Six thousand at the end of the month; that is when we get paid. And just to show how sorry we are, if you come to the pizzeria when it is quiet on a Saturday evening, on the 31ˢᵗ of this month, Alfio's friend will do you the favour of giving you whatever you want.'

'She is a prostitute?'

'One of the best,' said Alfio. 'I guarantee you that she is gorgeous. She owes us a lot of favours and we will let you cash those favours in instead of us.'

Captain Perraino asked for the address of the pizzeria, and promised to be there, to collect the money and to see the girl. He fondly imagined that this would be the first of many collections and many girls.

On Tuesday evening, at the hour of the Angelus, Rosario knelt devoutly before the shrine of Saint Agatha. Even in late July, this was a darker corner of the Cathedral than others; and even in late July, when the heat in the square outside was unbearable even at six in the evening, the Cathedral was cool.

As the Angelus bell faded, and the Mass started at the side altar at the other side of the vast building, Volta appeared and sat next to him; Calogero knew they were meeting, and there was no need to meet in secret any more, but they had always met here and such habits were hard to break.

'What went wrong?' asked Volta. 'I was expecting you yesterday. With the phone. Have you got it?'

240

'Yes, here it is.' He handed over the Nokia. 'Goodness knows what you will find. Let us hope Traiano copied it successfully. The thing is that Traiano and two others were arrested on Monday morning first thing. They were hauled away in police cars, locked up all day and only released in the evening. It was the work of Perraino. They told me that. They have asked me questions about Perraino before now, and all this seems to be some sort of plan. I think they are going to kill Perraino.'

'They can't do that. Perraino is a policeman. You cannot kill policemen. It is one of the rules. It is one of the things that Palermo does not like or want. It causes endless trouble. To kill a policeman would be to shatter the peace of Palermo.'

'Put everything together, and that is what looks likely. What on earth is this Lotto person doing here? They said in my presence that Perraino deserved to die.'

'When del Monaco broke Perraino's jaw, look what happened then. If someone kills Perraino, all hell breaks loose.'

'Unless they kill Perraino in the midst of all hell breaking loose, so no one notices. Palermo may have other things on its mind soon.'

'But why would anyone want to kill Perraino? I know he is annoying, but what strategic advantage would there be in killing Perraino?'

'I have asked myself that question,' said Rosario. 'The answer is really very simple. Perraino has importance because…?'

'Of the aunt. If they are pulling the rug from under her, they may want to get rid of the nephew as well. But they would only be murdering him, if they were murdering her.'

There was silence.

'She needs to be warned. He needs to be warned,' said Rosario.

'How? Are you going to say to Perraino, please watch out, my brother is going to kill you? Are you going to say to Anna Maria Tancredi, watch out, my brother, your lover, is going to kill you, and then dump the shares? And with a precipitate dumping and the death of the person who constructed the whole scam, ruin the entire investment of every criminal and questionable person in Sicily? War will then break out…. If war did break out, who suffers the most? Not respectable people, not the honest people.'

'Even people like Perraino have a right to life, a right to legal protection.'

As he said this, Rosario realised how hollow it sounded.

'What could you do, write to them anonymously? They would ignore any such warning. If you went in person you would be putting yourself in danger; besides what exactly would you say? Perhaps you should speak to your brother, but what good would that do?'

'What do you know about Lotto?'

'I know that his name is not Michele Lotto; but apart from that we know nothing at all, which means one of two things. Either the man is a complete nonentity, or else he is someone very important indeed who has managed to do something very difficult, achieve complete anonymity.'

'We are sleepwalking into disaster,' said Rosario. 'God help us.'

'Perhaps, but if all the criminals in Sicily go to war with each other, is that so very bad a thing?'

'Yes, it is a very bad thing. It means that the rule of law is even more ignored than ever. And it means a world in which many people die, but my brother prospers. We may have been his dupes.'

Catarina, Gino's girlfriend, was not stupid. She had been shocked and horrified when the police had banged on the door and woken herself and Gino up very early on Monday morning, and more or less dragged him out of the squalid room in which he lived in Purgatory, and where she had been spending the night with him. But after the shock and the horror had worn off, she had reflected and reflected carefully.

Gino had, she had known from the start, very little to recommend him. He was from Agrigento, one of the most unattractive towns in Sicily, a place she knew only by repute, but about which she knew enough. He had been in Bicocca for the crime of stabbing someone. This fact gave him, in a certain way, an allure, and in another way, revealed that he was a bad bet. The sort of woman who ended up with the sort of man like Gino would spend a lot of her life fearing his imprisonment, waiting for his imprisonment to end, and dealing with the effects of his imprisonment. True, Gino, for a boy in his early twenties, had a lot of money, when you considered that his official job was loading and looking after the pizza oven in don Calogero's pizzeria. Like most boys of his age, he did not think of the future much, and was always eager to spend, which was nice; but again, which was a bad sign. He was broad-shouldered, strong and reasonably good-looking (something that no one could ever say about his friend Alfio, her cousin, the one with the teeth); his interest in the sexual act was strong, as one would expect, but short-lived. He snored in bed. Moreover, he did not seem to realise – but who of all these boys in Purgatory ever did? – that the sexual act was not something to be taken for granted, but to be conceded as a favour, something to be sought and won by long and arduous courtship.

But this, she knew, was her own fault. She had met Gino, when Alfio had introduced him, and given way to his invitation with very little persuasion. She had been disappointed by his lack of romance; or rather she had become used to it; but when she had met Rosario, it had thrown Gino into perspective.

Rosario was not handsome and not particularly charming. He was gauche, somewhat clumsy, not good at small talk with girls; he was what people would call shy. Yet his kiss had been gentle, tender and passionate, and at no time in their time together had he assumed anything, or made any real attempt to sleep with her, leaving her alone on the sofa, even offering her his bed, if she so desired, to have alone. And where had Gino been all that time, after the wedding, if not off and drinking with Alfio and the other boys? It was no way to treat a girl. Rosario was from Purgatory like the rest of them (bar Gino) but he was not like them; he was becoming a lawyer, he was educated, he wore a suit. If he married, his wife would have a good life.

It was unlikely that he would marry any time soon; and it was supremely unlikely that he would ever marry her. But if she were to have made a wise choice of companion, the boss's brother would surely be the man to choose. And they had spoken, they had conversed, they had kissed. She had established a foothold, a bridgehead in this new territory.

As for Gino, there was little conversation there. After the wedding, when he had found out that she had spent the rest of the night with Rosario, he had been furious. First of all he had accused her of sleeping with Rosario; then he had accused her of being with Rosario so others would find out (by which he meant don Calogero) and he would thereby be made to look foolish. Did he care about her, or about his own reputation? Was she just some sort of appurtenance for him, something adopted to boost his prestige?

A reconciliation had taken place and she had spent the night in his one room in Purgatory on the Sunday, only to have him arrested very early on the Monday morning by the police. The uproar was huge, and clearly deliberate. The police wanted to cause maximum fuss and alarm, by making so much noise, to try and tell everyone that they were the real masters of Purgatory, not don Calogero and his boys. The police had dragged Gino away, and they had given her the most disrespectful looks. Gino had been pulled out of bed wearing his boxer shorts, and she had had to follow him and the police down the stairs with the rest of his clothes and his shoes, pleading with them to let him put them on, which they had refused. The whole quarter had seen her standing there on the street clutching her boyfriend's clothes, wearing a few things she had hastily thrown on. The whole quarter had seen that she had spent the night with him, and this was not good. Her own parents were respectable people and had been under the impression (they might still be) that she had been spending the night at the home of a female friend. One had one's reputation to consider; one did not want to throw one's reputation away on a boy like Gino.

It was thus with considerable delight that on the Wednesday evening after the arrest, that she met Rosario at her place of work, one of the large shops on the via Etnea. She had quite a good job, in her own opinion, as a trainee salesgirl; and it had occurred to her that with these skills she could move somewhere to the north; but she was rearranging the swimwear on the rail when she saw him come in, and he saw her. He approached with the right amount of diffidence.

The usual conversation ensued. He was looking for a suit, another suit; they were to be found on the floor above, which was menswear. He hoped she had got home safely after the wedding. He was sorry he had not seen her since then. He then asked the important question: what time did she finish work? This evening, it was seven, which was mere twenty minutes away. If she liked, he would meet her outside the shop, and they could go for a drink or something. She consented. He nervously left her, looking back once or twice as he drew away, in search of his suit, as if the intervening twenty minutes would be sheer hell for him.

The next twenty minutes were in fact deeply uncomfortable for him. Having lied about needing a suit, he had felt the need to go and look at suits, but reassured himself he did not need to buy one, and could say that he had seen none that fitted or none that he liked. She too had been equally distracted during the interval, wondering whether he knew that she had spent the previous Sunday night in Gino's bed. If only she had not done so. That night of passion (which had not in truth been so very passionate, indeed been a mere ten minutes of writhing around followed by a long night of uncomfortable, cramped and intermittent sleep) might have cost her dearly. And why had he come? Did he like her? How much did he like her? How much did she like him? And why had he come now, why not sooner after the wedding?

They met on the pavement of the via Etnea and went to one of the better bars on the street, where he insisted they have their aperitifs sitting down at one of the tables, something she had never done. The terrible heat of the day was wearing off at last, and sitting outside they could see the crowd walking up and down the street, which was interesting. Conversation was not as difficult as he had feared.

'How's Gino?' he asked. 'I heard that he and Alfio and Traiano were all arrested on Monday morning. I know they have been released. But what was all that about? I ask because they are my friends – not close friends, but I have known Alfio all my life and Traiano since he was three years old. Gino is new to our quarter so he is a friend of a friend, but that is a friend too. But the reason I really ask is because I am a lawyer and it strikes me that what happened to them was illegal. You can't just arrest people, hold them for twelve hours and then release them without charge. Well, you can actually, but it could count as harassment, and they were not allowed lawyers or anything else when in custody. It was most irregular.'

Catarina told him what she had heard, which was identical to what he himself had already heard.

'But the man who questioned them, this Perraino, I know him. He is the worst,' said Rosario.

'That is what Gino and Alfio said. He is the very worst. And all because of a chihuahua.'

'I love dogs,' he said, swallowing his impatience, knowing he had to let her talk. 'It is a pity I live on my own and in such a small flat, otherwise I would have a dog. Chihuahuas are so small, and cute. I would like something a little bigger and more, well, masculine.'

'Like one of those horrible mastiffs?' she asked.

He made a face. 'No. Something medium sized. A labrador would be lovely.'

'They are so beautiful. But we all love dogs, I mean even Alfio and Gino and Traiano. The idea that they would be cruel to a chihuahua is ridiculous; and that they would be arrested for being cruel to a chihuahua is ridiculous too. And the owner himself, well, it was his daughter's, did not complain. It was this Perraino you mention. He thinks that this shooting club in Nicolosi belongs to him.'

'And does it?'

'No, of course not. But he thinks he has a proprietorial interest.'

'I would love to learn to shoot,' said Rosario. 'You know, clay pigeons.'

'But I think this is a different type of gun they use. Anyway, better guns than knives, I think. Everyone in Purgatory carries a knife, or so they say. Or more accurately, everyone male does.'

'I don't,' he said.

'You're nice,' she said.

There was silence between them. He felt that if there was a moment, this was it, this was when he should lean across the table and take her hand. But the moment passed.

'I am worried about Gino and Alfio wanting to get revenge against this Perraino. I am less worried about Traiano because though he's younger he is far more sensible. Your brother trusts him the most. But the others have these silly ideas about revenge. On Saturday, not this Saturday, but next Saturday, they are meeting up with him. That is when they are paid – the end of the month. Apparently they promised him some money in return for being released. Why? When they had done nothing wrong?'

'They should have called a lawyer.'

'Of course. Instead I think they are going to try something foolish. Ah, the end of the month. I get paid too, and then I am going away for a few days in August, not far, just up Mount Etna, with a few friends of mine who have got a house there. It will be cooler.'

'Is Gino going?' he asked.

'No. They are my friends not his. I am going with my parents. They do not know about Gino. He is not the sort of boy whom you can take to see your parents. They do not even like Alfio and he is their nephew. Well, they like him, they just disapprove of him. But I may see Gino up there because he says that every day possible in August, they are going up to Nicolosi to shoot at this shooting club. So, he will be nearby. Not that I care much,' she added with deliberation.

Now was the chance to take her hand. He did so. She smiled. Her face was ravishingly beautiful, with her dark hair, her dark eyes; he remembered the dress she had worn at the wedding, which had clung to her flesh. He remembered their kiss. For one tiny moment he felt as though he might pass out. He could not help smiling. He wanted to kiss her again. Then he regained his self-possession. What would Gino think? But he did not withdraw his hand.

'This Perraino is a nasty man, a very nasty man. I have met him. The worst sort of policeman. He's been mixed up with the wrong sort of people a long time. But what could Gino and Alfio ever do to harm him? Are they meeting him with Traiano?'

'It is Saturday night, and Traiano won't be there. I don't know where he is going. He is probably doing something with your brother. Saturday night is a dull night at the pizzeria. I mean, as it is closed on Sunday, that is the night that Gino has to work very late, as after the close of business he has to clean out the oven. Ah well. I never do anything on Saturday night. On Sundays, Gino has the day free; every other night he is working.'

Cleaning out the pizza oven could not be pleasant, Rosario imagined, not that he knew anything about the way pizza ovens worked; but he did know that the pizza oven in the pizzeria was one of the largest and most modern in the city, or so they had boasted at the time of its installation, and it had costs tens of thousands. No doubt being charged with its maintenance was a trusted job. But on Sundays Gino got the day off, and on Sunday nights he slept with Catarina. Lucky Gino, however hard he had to work. He felt a wild stab of jealousy. And then he realised that perhaps it was possible that he himself might sleep with Catarina. He felt a sudden fever not of lust, though that was present too, but of anxiety. He felt the need to withdraw his hand.

'Do you ever talk to don Calogero about his work?' she was now asking him.

He reflected. He had wanted to meet up with her to pump her for information; now she was pumping him, he thought, or about to. How clever was she?

'This is a new thing, people calling him don Calogero,' said Rosario. 'Until very recently it was just Caloriu or Calogero. Once he wore jeans like anyone else, now he wears very expensive clothes; people like Traiano worship him and think he is a huge success and want to emulate him. I suppose Gino does too, and so does Alfio. We do talk about work. I am going to be a fully qualified property lawyer, and one day take over from the lawyer Rossi who works in our office, looking after the properties, looking after the contracts. Calogero has borrowed immense amount of money and invested in lots of falling down buildings which he is gradually doing up. He has extended himself a great deal but he will make a fortune in due course.'

'I meant the other sort of work, the non-legal work.'

'You mean the illegal work,' he said flatly. 'If only it were that simple. Some of the illegal work is very illegal. I mean the drug selling. That goes on in one of the bars. Traiano is in charge of that. He is a drug dealer. Then there is the prostitution; that's on the edge of legality, and the girls and boys who do that do not work for Calogero, though he gets a cut by providing the places where they sell themselves. But the really illegal stuff they have stopped, the things like stealing. When Calogero started out as a little boy, he specialised in stealing car radios. I don't think he would stoop to that nowadays.'

'Holy Mary,' she said.

'These people are criminals, as I told you. You need to get away from them. You need to get away from me. You don't want to end up like my sister-in-law, do you?'

'Stefania? Why not?'

He sighed.

'I suppose Stefania is one of the girls of Purgatory who has done well. But they probably thought the same of my mother once.'

'Why don't you live with your mother, Saro?'

'It is very hard to explain,' he said. 'But that is our predicament. There are so many things we find hard to confront, so we pretend they are not there. My mother shut herself away from the truth about my father and about Calogero. She preferred not to know. The same was true of Assunta and Elena, my sisters. It was too hard for them to confront, so they looked away.'

This pained her, he could see. For he was not just talking about the women of his own family, he was talking about all the women of Purgatory.

'But what can we do?' she said, releasing his hand.

'Nothing. Except go away. Go to the other side of the straits of Messina. Escape.'

'You are right. I should get rid of Gino. He is nice, but he is not good. He is violent. Not with me, of course, but his mind is violent, and his actions.'

'Is he going to kill Perraino?' he asked.

'I am surprised you ask me,' she said. 'But the fact you ask me, means that you think it possible; and when it is possible, it is somehow also probable. He told me to go away that weekend, to the friends in Nicolosi. Well, that is what he planned, but he was very keen that I kept to the plan. Perhaps he will come to Nicolosi on the Sunday. I have told you too much. I think they are planning just to beat him up when he comes into the quarter.'

'Perhaps,' said Rosario.

It was an odd thing to hope for, but he hoped it was just that. But he felt in his heart a certain dread. They left the bar, their aperitif over, and she declared that she had to go home to her mother and father. He would accompany her to her door, he said, sensing that this was expected of him. As they crossed the University square, their hands joined once more, and they walked holding hands up the via Etnea, through the evening crowd, and then turned right towards Purgatory. They crossed the square outside the Church of the Holy Souls in Purgatory, still joined at the hand, and then disappeared down one of the narrow claustrophobic alleys which led to the street door of the building she lived in. There at the door they paused. The doorway was a secluded and dark spot; it was here, on several occasions, late at night, that Gino had made love to her. Now she and Rosario met in an embrace. They kissed. The kiss made him for a moment forget everything; it snatched him away from Purgatory, from the difficult present. It transported him to another world, a world where everything was perfect. They kissed once, they kissed again; her hands caressed his back. He held her tight, for a moment unembarrassed by his arousal, thinking only of the arousal; certainly not thinking that they had been seen by one of Calogero's 'pigeons' crossing the square hand in hand, and who now watched them wide-eyed from a distance of about ten metres.

'I must go,' he said at last.

The pigeon in question was the same boy, Tonino Grassi, that Calogero had used to find Alfio and Gino the time he had had lunch with his brother and Volta. That time he had given the boy fifty euros. Naturally the boy was back, knowing that rewards were on offer, knowing that don Calogero wanted to know everything that happened in the quarter. As the boy had hoped, he was very interested to hear about his brother and Catarina. It seemed that they had crossed the University square hand in hand, walked down the Etnea hand in hand, and crossed the square in front of the Church of the Holy Souls in Purgatory hand in hand. And then in the doorway...

'Have you seen people having sex?' asked Calogero.

'Yes,' said the boy with decision.

One did, after all, see everything on the streets of Purgatory.

'Was he having sex with her?' asked Calogero.

The boy looked thoughtful.

'Was he pressed up against her?'

'Yes. They were holding each other and kissing.'

'Was he pushing back and forth?'

'No, he was still. She was rubbing his bottom.'

'Was she?'

It sounded to Calogero that if they were not having sex then – and that alleyway was notorious for such encounters – they would soon be having sex, and indeed might have done so already. This event had been on Wednesday night. The boy Tonino, now sent away with his reward, had had to wait until Friday when he had finally caught don Calogero crossing the square outside the Church of the Holy Souls in Purgatory. Knowledge was power, and Calogero was glad to know what he knew, and wondered when and if he would have to use it.

Chapter Eight

The weekend passed, and on Monday evening, the 26th July, Rosario wearily climbed the stairs to his flat. He put the key in the door and stepped into the living room. There in the chair facing the door was Calogero.

'Hi,' he said.

'Hi,' replied Calogero.

Rosario sank into the unoccupied chair.

'So, you have found yourself a girl at long last,' said Calogero. 'I wish I could say congratulations, but I can't. You are very close to a nasty awakening. She is the wrong girl, not just for you, she is the wrong girl altogether. I cannot believe your dunderheaded stupidity. You were warned. Her cousin and her boyfriend warned you. They came to see me first, naturally, as you are my brother, and I told them they could speak to you, but no more. So they spoke to you; and you should have listened. Any sensible man would have listened. Any man with a sense of self-preservation should have listened. Anyone who knows what is good for him. But not you. You are impervious to common sense. What is the next thing I hear? You are seen walking hand in hand with the girl along the Via Etnea; and then you are seen kissing her in her parents' doorway, while she fondled your backside. If Gino comes to me again, to complain of you stealing his girl, what am I to say to him? And if I let him do what he wants to you, can you guess what he will do? Do you know why he was in

Bicocca? He stabbed a man. In such a place that that man now needs a colostomy bag for the rest of his life. Is that what you want? That would put an abrupt end to your sex life.'

'None of this is your business,' said Rosario coldly. 'She does not belong to Gino. I don't belong to you. I can do as I please. So can she.'

'Really? So if Gino attacks you with a knife, you will not look to me for protection, will you? But this is my affair as much as yours. If you want a girlfriend, by all means get one, but not one who belongs to one of my men. I do not want my men upset or frustrated or angered by you or anyone else. Understood? I value them. Gino and Alfio have important work to do for me.'

'What work?'

This question riled Calogero, he could tell.

'It is none of your business what they do for me,' said Calogero quietly and calmly.

'They are your thugs. So is Traiano. So are they all.'

'You are trying to provoke me,' said Calogero. 'When are you going to get it into your thick skull that that girl Catarina would not let you screw her or whatever you did to her, if you were not my brother? Petrocchi only gave you a job because you are my brother. If you were not my brother, you would be no one. You would not even have this flat. All the respect you enjoy comes from that relationship. And if I cut you loose, you are dead. Gino would kill you tomorrow. Indeed tonight. But I will not let him kill you; I will kill you myself.'

'Gino is thug and a murderer. Traiano is thug and a murderer; you are a thug and a murderer.'

'So you keep on reminding me. And you forget to add that so was our father. Money, power, position, all of it comes from the ability to inflict pain and the ability to shed blood. Gino has that girl because he has a more powerful fist than you. Gino has that girl because he is prepared to stab and maim and even kill in order to keep her. Do you want that girl? Do you want me to get her for you, by killing Gino? Is that what you want? You know what, if you wanted me to, I would do it, only not this week. I would do anything for you. You know that. You know how I treat the people I love. Just tell me, and I will kill Gino. But I want something in return – your gratitude.'

'You know I do not want you to kill Gino, Caloriu. I do not want you to kill anyone. I wish that Vitale, that Turiddu and that del Monaco were all still alive. And Ino. I wish all the people our father killed were still alive.'

'The dead do not return, ever,' said Calogero. 'Stop mourning them. Why not be grateful for what you have? A loving family.'

There was silence between them. Rosario felt the sting of the charge of ingratitude, and the charge of hypocrisy that underlay it.

'Why couldn't you kill Gino this week?' he asked at last.

'Because I need him. Just as I need you. This weekend is the moment that turns me into a big-time crook not just a small-time crook. Or something. You have your part. At 9am on Monday morning, you must dump the shares that we have bought, mine, yours, and get Petrocchi to dump the Confraternity's. The price will still be rising on Monday first thing. But not for much longer. By Tuesday all the people who invested are going to be running for cover. Their scheme will explode in their faces. Then there will be a lot of recriminations and a rearranging of the pieces on the board.'

'And some pieces will no longer be on the board at all,' observed Rosario.

'Don't ask about that,' said Calogero. 'Because if I tell you, you become complicit; and then one day you might be asked about it in court. Not a happy prospect for a lawyer. This girl, are you in love with her?'

'Catarina? No.'

'Good. Did you spend the weekend with her?'

'No. I was in the parish of Acireale.'

'Ah, innocent Catholic activities.'

'Are you in love with Tancredi?'

'Of course not. She is a business associate. But she is an attractive woman and if she wants me, I am not going to hold back. She is forty-five. But I do not particularly enjoy her company, I have to say. We are from different worlds. One has to remember that. One cannot ever really cross over from our world to theirs. I belong here. She belongs there. Of course, she thinks I can be useful to her; and I think she can be useful to me.'

He stood up to go.

'Stefania will be waiting for me, the children will be waiting for me. Why don't you come over too? They love their uncle. Stefania likes you too.'

'I will come with you,' said Rosario. He stood up. 'I am full of foreboding,' he said.

'You will feel better by Monday, once those shares have gone,' said Calogero. 'I will feel better by Monday too, perhaps, when all sorts of complications are gone.'

As they crossed the square walking towards where Calogero lived, the light of the evening sun was shining directly through the door of the Church of the Holy Souls in Purgatory, for like, say, the Cathedral of Catania, the Church of the Holy Souls in Purgatory was built with its main altar facing east, and its main door open to the west. The level of the sun's rays meant that at this hour of evening, and in summer only, the picture of the Spanish Madonna and its surrounding lapis lazuli and gilded decoration was directly illuminated by the rays of the sun. The Madonna was in the centre of a baroque sunburst, and that sunburst was now complemented by the

261

real sun. Both of them knew this, and knew that this phenomenon of the sun shining directly through the open door occurred only at this time of year, and so were drawn to enter the Church and look at the picture.

The masterpiece of Velasquez, the only Velasquez in Sicily, the picture that all the guidebooks said every visitor to Catania should see, glowed in the evening sunlight. Rosario knelt down and stared at the picture for a moment, and then shut his eyes. Calogero sat down next to him, looking up at the picture, remembering how he had stolen it as a teenager, and then cleverly given it back. To think that this cult object was the protectress of the quarter! To think that since the picture's return (though it had never left the quarter, only spending the years of captivity in a storeroom belonging to Turiddu's father) the quarter had prospered! To think that the Virgin of Nazareth presided over a quarter famous for crime, violence, drugs, theft and prostitution! What did she make of all that? And what did all the people who loved her, who passed her church every day, make of the contrast between purity and light and the squalor of the everyday?

He looked around the church, examined its curves, its broken pediments, and its graceful dome. All the work of the great Stefano Ittar, or so it was assumed. The dates fitted, but the original paperwork and plans were lost. But the curves, the lightness of the composition, the way air and stone assumed the same consistency, all that was, he was sure, the work of Ittar, the greatest of Catania's architects. It was nice to think that the Viceroy's wife had donated the picture to the original church in an unimportant quarter, and then Ittar, inspired by the painting, has created a fitting frame for it. The whole building led you to that one spot: the compassionate face of the Spanish Madonna, she who interceded for all the souls in Purgatory; she who gave hope to those bathing in a lake of fire.

His brother now sat next to him and spoke.

'On Monday, Caloriu, I will sell the shares. But why don't you sell everything you own, all the properties, all the businesses, and go away, go somewhere else, with Stefania and the children, and live comfortably in Rome, or Milan or Florence or Turin?'

'They say Turin is beautiful,' said Calogero. 'That is very tempting. I would love to live in Turin and look at beautiful architecture all day, every day. I would prefer Turin to Florence. They say the food is better. But if I were to go away, to retreat, to withdraw, they would say I was a coward, and they would come after me. All the people who do not like me, the police but the others as well, they would sense that I was on the run and that they had an advantage. And I would be walking across the square outside the royal palace in Turin one day, and get a dagger between the ribs or a bullet in the head. When one starts fighting, one cannot stop. And there are other reasons too: when one starts fighting, and I started early, one does not want to stop. You want to go on until you have beaten all your enemies; and there are always fresh enemies to beat. But I appreciate your sentiments, yet I decline your temptation, which is not from my perspective very tempting.' He looked at his brother. 'And you, Saro, are you not ever tempted? Can't I tempt you? Let me get Catarina for you. Give up being alone. Do what you are meant to do. Breed!'

'If you kill Gino, I will never forgive you, and I would never look at Catarina again. And what would she think?'

'You assume that murder comes easily to me,' said Calogero. 'I like Gino. Everyone does. A nice boy. I could have him sent away; I could have him killed. But it would be a special favour to you. Depends on how badly you want to have Catarina.'

'Of course I want her,' he could not help saying.

They both stood up. Rosario thought that this was a diabolical conversation to be having in church. His cheeks were red.

'I thought so,' said Calogero. 'So there is some blood in your veins after all. Don't look so ashamed.'

Stefania was glad to see her brother-in-law, who always had that sheepish look about him; the food was good, and the two little girls, Isabella and Natalia, and the baby boy Renato were all glad to see their uncle. Afterwards, Rosario helped put the children to bed, while Calogero made his excuses and left to make his usual nocturnal round of the quarter. Rosario stayed and had a beer with Stefania.

'He's planning something. Everything is tense. I sense it somehow. No one says anything concrete, but you can sense an atmosphere even without words,' he said.

Stefania smiled.

'Yes,' she said. 'You can. The children cannot. They are too young. But I can, you can. The children are so innocent. They take everything at face value. They do not understand that everything needs to be interpreted. You are tense, I see it.'

He nodded.

'On Monday I have to dump all these worthless shares on my own behalf, on his behalf and on behalf of the Confraternity. Several millions worth. So, not worthless. The price is rising. But one is on edge, because what if something goes wrong?'

'You do not make money without risk,' she said. 'Caloriu thinks he is going to be a very rich man sometime soon. He is confident. Not, I hope, overconfident. Traiano, who perhaps knows less of the world of high finance, is less confident. Traiano likes old fashioned crime, not this new stuff. What do you know of this woman Tancredi?'

'I have never seen her.'

'I wasn't asking about her appearance, but about her reputation as a banker and a businesswoman,' said Stefania.

'She is eminent in her field,' said Rosario. 'She is highly respectable. But she is a crook. She masks her real activities by all sorts of legal stuff, in particular work for the Church and various Catholic charities and foundations. But she works for Palermo, laundering cash, and she has important contacts in Rome, I believe.'

'Is she competent?'

'She has been so far. But it does not follow that she will always be.'

'And what does she look like?'

'I have never seen her, as I said.'

'Of course, I know,' said Stefania. 'There is no need to be squeamish.'

'She is forty-five and said to be attractive. Twenty years his senior. The policeman Perraino used to be her lover. He is also her nephew. I believe she collects men, and then throws them aside when she has finished with them.'

'Good for her,' remarked Stefania. 'When I am forty-five, I might take that up.'

'How do you know?' he asked, curious.

'I won't claim that a woman always does. But he has been odd ever since he had to go away to Noto in January. And when he came back, he was not very forthcoming with details. I thought at first he was going to Syracuse to see Anna the Romanian prostitute. He has always had a soft spot, if one can call it that, considering he has no affections, for her. But no. He does go to Syracuse but he always goes on to somewhere else from there. Noto was the first place, then more recently Donnafugata. He is not good at keeping secrets. I mean he is good, but he keeps them in such a way that you know he has a secret. Tancredi is his secret. There is an elasticity to his step that indicates he is sleeping with her. But of course it is much more than that. Anna has been speaking to Traiano and passing things on to me. But as you say, there is something afoot, some huge plot. No one wants to talk about it, and I do not want to know. Better that way. It is the only way. But one day something will happen and the great don Calogero will find himself either dead or in jail. That is the way it ends; that is the way it always ends. He thinks he is clever, and he is clever, but gambling is never wise. Careful people do not gamble with their own lives. But gamblers never think of the odds, they just think of the thrill of the game. Right now he is excited. That is a bad sign. It means someone is going to suffer, and suffer badly.'

'Aren't you worried about Tancredi?'

'Worried? No. Annoyed? Not even. Jealous? Not a bit. Your brother has never been one for the bedroom.'

Rosario laughed.

'Didn't Turiddu say that?'

'The Turiddu he killed? Yes. Which shows how true it is. But I am the one who knows it is true. If Tancredi is the exacting woman you suggest she is, I feel sorry for Caloriu. He will be made to work in a department in which he is terribly lazy. But I get the impression that after Monday things will be different. If it all goes to plan. I am taking the children away for the weekend. We are going to Cefalù. I have never been, but it is supposed to be a wonderful place. Then we will come back on Monday, and by then everything will have been settled, whatever the everything is. It will be nice to be away from here, away from this terrible heat, away from this oppressive atmosphere. He has not been his usual self since January. That I attribute to Tancredi. She has ignited his ambitions; she has fired him up with a love of money.'

There was silence between them.

'Have you been to Cefalù?' she asked.

'Never,' he said. 'I would love to.'

'Then you should come with me. The children would be delighted, and you would be a help. I have hired an apartment on the sea. Right on the sea, in the old town. It looks lovely. Giuseppina is coming too.'

Giuseppina was her younger sister, a nice girl, who often helped out with the children. Giuseppina was, as far as he knew, single, and he had always had a suspicion that Stefania would like to throw them together. Perhaps this was just such an occasion.

'And I would be back at work on Monday?' he asked.

'You would have to leave early, but yes.'

'Then I shall come,' he said.

The week in Purgatory dragged on as everyone waited for the end of torrid July and the start of liberating August, when the quarter would empty out, some to the slopes of Etna, to Nicolosi, to Bronte, to Randazzo; others to the beaches of the Cyclopean coast or further afield; some to the west of the island, to breezier places like Agrigento, Erice, Trapani and Marsala; and some further afield still, to the Italian mainland, to visit relatives in exile. In truth, the majority would stay, to live on in sweaty and tiny apartments without airconditioning, to emerge into the cool of the evening when the sun went down; but the few who went away, and the increased heat, would give Purgatory the appearance of a ghost town for three weeks at least.

As the week ground on, the last eternal week before the holidays, he spoke to his boss, the lawyer Petrocchi, about the sale of the shares.

'I never liked those shares and I never wanted to buy them,' said Petrocchi.

'It was the same with me,' said Rosario.

'Then why did you buy them?' asked Petrocchi curiously, wondering what means of persuasion had been used. In his own case, Trajan Antonescu had held a gun to his head while Calogero di Rienzi had looked on.

'My brother sent round one of his people, the one called Traiano, and he shot me through the calf.'

'Holy Mary. You never told me. Did it hurt? Did you tell the police?'

'It didn't hurt much. It was a bit of a shock. But they choose a part of the leg where a bullet passes through and does little harm. It heals quite well very quickly. And yes, of course I told the police: and nothing happened. The police captain who came to take my statement in hospital lost it. He was someone my brother knows. It was all planned. They have all eventualities covered.'

'The sooner we are out of this bridge project the better. The price will be still going up on Monday?'

'Everyone says so. But they also say not beyond Monday.'

'I wonder what they know? Forget that. I did not ask. I do not want to know. Are you going somewhere nice this summer?'

'Cefalù for the weekend with my sister-in-law and the children and her sister. Then back on Monday to sell the shares at 9am precisely.'

Petrocchi noted the reference to the sister.

'The office will be quiet in August and there will be little to do,' he said conversationally. 'I am going to Zafferana Etnea. We have a house there. It is quite a nice house. On the second Sunday each August they have the feast of the Madonna of Divine Providence. This year that is the 8th August, the week after next. My daughter will be back from University and staying with us. She is a very good girl but a bit shy, our youngest. Perhaps you would like to come up and stay. From Zafferana, you can go on long hikes up the slopes of the volcano. It is very pretty. You would like it.'

'I would be delighted.'

'Good, come midweek, on the Wednesday. It is all very relaxed. I will tell my wife. I am sure she will be delighted. She has heard me talk of you. I will send you an email with the details. By the way, make sure you spend time with the lawyer Rossi. He wanted to speak to you, he told me. In fact, go to him now.'

The lawyer Rossi, being one of the least regarded persons in the office, and indeed the whole building, occupied an office of his own where the air conditioning worked only intermittently. Now was one of those times when it was not working. It was something to do with the facts of supply and demand: when it was hot, the air conditioning usually failed as it had to work too hard, but in the winter months it functioned perfectly. There had been long discussions between Rossi and the building's maintenance staff, none of which had reached a satisfactory conclusion. These discussions had been going on for several years.

He found Rossi soaked with sweat, his jacket hanging off the back of his chair, and surrounded by papers.

'Your brother,' said Rossi, as soon as he saw Rosario, 'has given me lots of work to do. Lots. And all just before the holidays begin. The day after tomorrow I have to fly to Novara, to visit my wife's relatives. Have you been there? Trust me, you do not want to go. Freezing in winter and boiling in summer. Horrible place. But that is where her parents live. Anyway, I have done everything Calogero di Rienzi asked me to do. Indeed, when did I not?' They both knew that Rossi had posthumously forged his father's will. That fact hung between them. 'Your brother has drawn up a new will. No, not quite. He has drawn up a will. Before this he had no will. Do you want to see it? So when the time comes there will be no nasty surprises?'

'I am sure you are not supposed to show it to me,' said Rosario.

'I am sure I am not,' said Rossi. 'He leaves everything to his wife, and not a penny to you or your sisters. I presume he trusts her to look after the interests of her children. I think he has drawn up the will at her suggestion. Perhaps he feels or she feels that it may be needed. Who knows? Anyway, there is more business. He has given a bit to your married sister, a bit more to your unmarried sister, and he has given quite a bit to you.'

'What do you mean, given?'

'Exactly what I say. He has executed a deed passing over to you several bits of property. First of all the flat you live in. I gather that is quite small so not worth much. But still, quite nice. Not to be sniffed at. Secondly, he has given you ownership of the pizzeria. Not ownership of the business, that he has given to signor Antonescu; you get the property itself and presumably signor Antonescu pays you rent. The same goes for the bar, you own the building, a tall narrow building, and signor Antonescu owns the business. They both make a fortune so you should get a very decent rent.'

Rossi smiled triumphantly.

'That was another thing that has kept me busy. Trajan Antonescu has made a will as well, leaving everything to his wife, Francesca, known as Ceccina. One has the impression that these people are tying up loose ends, as if they feared the worst. Perhaps they do. It is wise to hope for the best and prepare for the worst. There are also two other gifts of small flats, one to Luigi Fisichella, known as Gino, and one to Alfio Camilleri.'

'Should you be telling me all this?' asked Rosario. 'And why wasn't I told? I mean told by my brother?'

'You don't want all these nice things? I think it was meant to be a surprise for you.' Rossi was exasperated. 'Look, you take all the paperwork and the deeds and if you decided that you want to give it back, that will mean doing everything again in reverse. Just make sure you save it until the holidays are over. OK? Not that it bothers me, as I will get yet another fee. Your brother has always been most generous to me,' he said with meaning.

Another person charging him with ingratitude, Rosario reasoned.

'You think they are fearing the worst? I too fear the worst, all the time. Don't you?'

The lawyer Rossi looked at him.

'I wish I had never met your brother,' he said. 'Perhaps you wish the same. His tentacles are everywhere. He is like a sea urchin that you step on, and one of the spines gets in your foot and stays there forever. You know, when I think of it, where my wife's family moved to, Novara, perhaps it is not such a bad place after all.' He looked at Rosario directly. 'Ah, Saro, you are a nice boy, and now you own a drug den and a brothel. What a fate. That is why your brother did not tell you. He knew you would refuse. It is a left-handed gift. One with strings attached. He has the gift of making us all complicit and all dishonest. I am sorry for you. But most of all, I am sorry for myself.'

After work, he walked down the Via Etnea to the department store where Catarina worked, in order to buy himself a pair of swimming trunks. This was a perfectly legitimate thing to do, he reasoned to himself, but as he put one foot in front of the other he realised that he was walking to his doom. He had promised himself to stay away. He had been warned to stay away. He had been threatened with consequences if he did not stay away – and yet though he knew he ought to stay away, he could not, and was prepared to risk it. He entered the shop and went upstairs to the department he had seen her in the last time. There she was. At the sight of her, his heart pounded and his cheeks burned. Eventually, after he hung around trying to look interested in his surroundings for longer than seemed plausible, she looked towards him. She smiled. She approached.

'I was hoping to see you again.'

'I didn't want to call, in case….'

'I know. I understand. Don't worry about Gino. He is very busy right now.'

'I am worried about Gino,' he said, realising that this sounded cowardly. Well, he was a coward.

'Go into that changing cubicle,' she said. 'Just take something with you, and go in there and wait.'

He did as he was told, and did not have to wait long. The curtain rustled and she was with him. Their kiss was immediate, guilty, urgent.

'I'll come to your flat this evening, when I can get away from home,' she said, and then was suddenly gone.

When he had recovered from this, he walked back along the via Etnea and back into Purgatory with his head reeling. He had made a vow to God and the Madonna that he would never fall into fornication and never ever marry. And now? What had seemed so inevitable a moment ago now seemed a dreadful prospect. He did not go home; he did not go to Church; rather he went and did something that he had not done for months. He went to see his mother.

His younger sister, Elena, opened the door.

'Thank goodness you have come,' she said, something she had never said before now. 'I suppose you have heard?'

'Heard what?'

'About Caloriu making this distribution of the property and making a new will?'

'Oh, that, yes,' he said.

He followed her into the sitting room. His mother was there, in tears; she paid no attention to his arrival. His other sister, Assunta, was there, looking angry, with her fat new husband, who merely looked embarrassed.

'Caloriu is not going to die,' said Assunta to the weeping and sobbing mother. 'If he makes a will, it is simply a precaution. And this division of the property is not a sign that he is going to die either. It is just his way of arranging things. The wrong way, as it turns out. You,' she said, looking at Rosario, 'seem to have done well for yourself.'

He was taken aback by her tone. But Elena sprang to his defence.

'Caloriu is only giving Saro a bit of what should have been his originally, if our father had left a proper will. And he has given me a bit too. And if he has given you next to nothing now it is because he gave you a fortune when you got married, you may remember. You and Federico' (this was the fat brother-in-law) 'were given half a million. If you chose to spend so much of it on your wedding, that was your choice.'

Federico opened his mouth to contradict her, but what could he say? Assunta realised too that there was no counter argument, so she merely contented herself with bursting into tears.

'Caloriu will die and we will be left with nothing,' she wailed, while her mother set up an antiphonal cry.

Rosario sat next to his mother on the sofa and tried to take her hand.

'If Caloriu stepped into this room right now, how would he feel?' he asked. 'You are all imagining his death and the loss of his money.'

'Are you saying I am greedy, you little snake?' shot back Assunta.

Federico tried to calm her. Elena giggled.

The mother then spoke: 'God took away my husband, and now he is going to take away my eldest son.'

This declaration was greeted in profound silence.

'God had nothing to do with it,' said Assunta stoutly.

'Maybe He did,' said Rosario. 'Maybe our father's accident was divine justice for all the murders he committed.'

'Nothing was ever proved,' said Elena, now shifting sides.

Federico looked profoundly embarrassed.

'I think I am going to go,' said Rosario.

'I never want to see you again!' screamed Assunta. (He had had no idea she had ever disliked him so much. It was slightly surprising, rather like waking up after sleepwalking and finding oneself on a cliff edge.) 'You are in league with that grasping bitch Stefania,' she accused. 'I would not be surprised if you were screwing her, the amount of time you spend together.'

'What?' asked Rosario, genuinely amazed.

'It's what they say,' remarked Elena with a smirk, unable to resist sticking her little knife in.

'You think I am having an affair with Stefania? You are all mad.'

He looked at his brother-in-law, in a mute appeal to some statement of male sanity, but Federico looked away. He left the room and the apartment. As he walked down the stairs, he heard someone following him. It was fat Federico, out of breath.

'Look, Saro,' he said. 'They are all upset. This will of his has upset them. You know he cheated them when your father died. Well, now that he has made partial restitution, they none of them think it is enough. Assunta is not being reasonable, I know, and Elena neither, and though they have always been close, there have been tensions. So, I hope you will forgive....'

'Federico, do you think I have been having an affair with Stefania?'

Federico looked embarrassed once more.

'Saro, how can I say who is having an affair with whom? All I can say is what I have heard. People say she is neglected, and that he has someone else, and that she has got her revenge... They say that the child Renato is yours. But I don't think even Assunta believes that really.'

'Holy Mary,' said Rosario. 'Did my mother say anything?'

'She never says anything, as you know.'

'Well, she could at least have contradicted this. She knows Stefania and she knows me. Well, good bye, Federico. Assunta never wants to see me again, not that she ever saw me much, so we shall not meet perhaps for some time. Well, you married her and you must stick with your choice. No hard feelings.'

'She will change, you see.'

'Maybe. But I may not be around to see it. She may change and it will be too late. As for my mother, this is unforgivable.'

He walked out the street door. He went home, depressed and angry and hurt. Some twenty minutes later, Catarina, whom he had forgotten about, rang his door bell. He heard the street door open, and heard her come up the stairs. His heart pounded. She entered the room, and he could resist her no longer.

Later that evening, Calogero was having a meeting with his men.

'Everything is prepared. If things are well prepared, and you know what to do, then nothing can go wrong. And if it does go wrong, we have made our wills and left our affairs in order. Gino and Alfio, you know what do on Saturday night late, when Perraino comes to the quarter. When all is done you can ring up Traiano with a cheerful message about something completely unrelated. The tone of the message will convey your success. If something goes wrong, though I do not know what could, you run and you hide. You look after yourselves. But I trust you and nothing will go wrong. Traiano and I will be in Donnafugata. At midmorning we take out Muniddu, and when the other person gets back from Mass, we take that person out too. Then we stay in Donnafugata, pretending all is normal until the evening. We will not be lounging by the pool. We will be doing our best to clean up after ourselves. We will be planting Muniddu's DNA all over her house. Then on Sunday evening, when everyone is relaxing, at 7pm precisely, all over Sicily, Michele Lotto will unleash the dogs of war, and take out the important people who are blocking his backers. He has an extensive shopping list, and his men have been watching them for ages. I do not know how many are on the list, but it is a lot. At this point all of you, including our other men, need to be very vigilant. It will be August so we can shut all our businesses and keep off the streets. Hunker down. When they are all dead, then it will be safe to come out. Perhaps by Wednesday. But until then the maximum vigilance. Remember that we do not have mobile phones for a very good reason. If you do call up on the landline, keep the conversation innocent. If you do use a pigeon to send a message, likewise. The question to ask is about the weather. A nice innocent question. Too hot to go out, you will understand what that means. We will all meet again next week.'

Chapter Nine

On Saturday morning he woke up with a start, alone in bed, remembering that Stefania had gone the previous day to Cefalù, taking the children. The flat was quiet and he instinctively made the sign of the cross, having a premonition of death, whether his own, or the death of others, he was not sure. Certainly this weekend would see the death of many, perhaps even of himself. But what would be, would be.

He went into the kitchen to make himself some coffee. He had slept well, very well, and it was late. He knew that Traiano would soon be round as arranged, and as the coffee bubbled, he heard the sound of the doorbell and admitted him. He met him at the door. He was carrying his overnight bag.

'You have your knife? You have your gun?'

'Both,' answered Traiano, accepting some coffee.

'Not that we will use them,' he observed.

'I would not feel safe without them,' said Traiano. 'I have been practising all week up at Nicolosi.'

'Good. How is Ceccina, and Cristoforo?'

'They are fine. It felt funny making my will the other day. But they are fine. I did not tell her, naturally. I did not say I am going away and may never be back. I said I was going away and that I would be back later in the week. It did not seem to occur to her that there was anything wrong. I was very nice to her last night. She is very keen. I think the pregnancy has affected her. It's made her more passionate.'

'Good,' said Calogero. 'They say that can happen. Any worries?'

'None. We can handle Muniddu.'

'We can,' said Calogero. 'You just have to put your mind to it. And that wild Romanian will handle Palermo, or Palermo him; whichever way, we come out in a better position. Just don't lose your nerve.'

At noon they left the quarter, Traiano driving the car, and headed south to Syracuse for their last meeting with the wild Romanian as Calogero called him. Once more they walked along the seafront. Calogero and Michele Lotto went first while Traiano and his mother and half-brother Salvatore trailed behind.

Michele Lotto explained what would happen on Sunday evening, if everything went to plan, which Calogero assured him it would. He had sixty men from Romania on the island, and they had thirty targets. They knew where each of these targets would be: some on beaches, some in the mountains, some on boats at sea, some in the depths of the countryside. Each one was marked. The thirty pairs of men were all handpicked. He himself was going to Castelvetrano to take on Antonio Santucci. Calogero remembered Antonio Santucci, the one who had come to the quarter and indeed spoken to him about Lotto. Also marked for destruction were Santucci's father, Lorenzo, and his uncle, Domenico, in fact every male relative of the immediate family, including Antonio Santucci's two teenage sons. He would be travelling to Castelvetrano by car and taking out Antonio who was staying there in his country house on this first weekend of August, along with the others. He knew where they all were, because he had a traitor in their midst. Antonio Santucci had become arrogant. People didn't like him. Slights were remembered. He had an eye in Castelvetrano, and he had eyes on the other twenty-seven victims as well. His men had been lying in wait for weeks; like careful racegoers, they had been studying the form; they had been memorising things, learning their quarries' habits. All was prepared. Once the signal was given, then the massacre began and the peace of Palermo ended.

The signal was the clock sounding seven in the evening. Michele Lotto talked through the list of those to die, and Calogero listened carefully. He detected that Lotto was out to impress him with his ruthless display of power. Thirty victims in all was a huge amount, and the thirty included Tancredi and Muniddu, for whom he was responsible. But one thing occurred to Calogero. Thirty was a large number, but what about the others who were not on the list? Lotto explained his decapitation strategy; some were not high up enough the chain to be decapitated, men like Muniddu would only die because it was convenient. But there were others further up the chain who would step into the dead men's shoes, and these others were the ones who knew that they would eventually do business with Lotto and the people he represented, even though these others had no idea of what exactly was coming.

There was going to be a general purification, was the way Lotto put it. The thirty would die and the survivors might well fall to quarrelling murderously amongst themselves. That was the idea, that the massacre would look like the result of an internal fissure. Then, when Palermo was weakened, Bucharest would move its people in.

'What are you doing for the rest of the day?' asked Anna of her son.

'We are going to Donnafugata, and he will be screwing her, while I sit above the garage on the other side of the orange grove with her bodyguard.'

'He likes her?'

'I don't think he does. I think she likes him. You know what he is like. Who does he like, really? He has very few friends, real friends. He loves his children, he loves his brother Saro, even if he got me to shoot him in the leg, and of course he loves me.'

'And do you have any friends?'

'Only him. He is a full-time occupation, as I am sure you understand. After all, he dominates your every thought, doesn't he?'

She sniffed with annoyance.

'It is perfectly natural, he dominates mine,' said Traiano with a mischievous smile.

'It is not healthy and it is not natural,' said Anna.

'I never got a chance at either of those occupations, being healthy or natural. Killing people is neither, beating them up is neither. Enjoying stuff like that is neither. Unnatural acts are second nature to me. But I have settled down in one regard. I am happy with my wife and my children. I have been blessed in that. Ceccina and I are very happy. Another baby soon, if I live to see it, which I have every intention of doing so. Are you happy with him?'

'No,' said Anna. 'I put up with him because Calogero makes me.'

Traiano sighed.

'When I first heard of him, I wanted to kill him. When I met him, I wanted to kill him even more. But then we had to go into business with him. But who knows, one day we may get to kill him. I do not like him. He is a brute. He reminds me of Romania, a country I cannot remember at all, a country I want to forget I ever knew. Damn him. It won't be forever.'

'Your promises are worthless,' she said.

'But you do not see him often, do you?'

'He comes on Saturday nights. Tonight is his night. He is a curious man. What he does the rest of the time, I have no idea. He spends his time plotting horrible things. But on Saturday he comes, he takes his pleasure, he eats, he sleeps and he wakes in the morning. Regular habits.'

'He must trust you. A man like that has many enemies. You could strangle him in his sleep. It doesn't take much strength. He would be dead before he woke up.'

She shot him a look of disgust. Her child's father, little Salvatore's father Turiddu, had died that way. She had, Traiano could see, barely forgiven him still.

'One day, I will kill Lotto,' promised Traiano, knowing he had a great deal to make up to her.

'May that day come soon,' she said ironically.

Before they left Syracuse, when they were still in the underground car park on the island of Ortygia, before Traiano started the car, Calogero found a piece of paper and a pen and began writing down names as fast as he could. He had a good memory. Then he passed the list to Traiano and asked him to count the names. They came to twenty-seven. He took the list again, wracked his brains, and came up with another name. But it was till only twenty-eight. He thought once more. Then he remembered. Muniddu and Anna Maria made thirty.

'These are all the people that evil bastard is planning to have killed,' he told Traiano. 'These are the names he mentioned. Luckily, I have an excellent memory for names. Five are members of the Santucci family: Antonio, Lorenzo, Domenico, Sandro and Beppe. Remember that Antonio?

287

I never liked him much. Lorenzo and Domenico are the father and uncle; the other two are his sons.'

'How old are they?' asked Traiano.

'No idea. Young, younger than you, perhaps. Who knows? All hell is going to break loose. They may kill most of the people on this list, but a few will get away and their revenge will be terrible.'

'But revenge against who?'

'That is what Lotto is banking on, that they will assume it is some other historical enemy in Sicily and not a foreign takeover bid by the Romanians. But these things cannot be kept secret forever. They will find out in the end. Though by the time they find out they may not be in a position to do anything about it. They will all be dead or in hiding. It is an ambitious plan, Lotto's. It could just work. Who dares wins.'

'Who said that?'

'Who dares wins? It's just a saying. Now drive the car.'

'I don't like Lotto.'

'Neither do I.'

'Neither does Anna. I told her, as a good son ought, that one day I would kill him.'

'May that day come soon.'

'That is exactly what she said.'

At 4pm they arrived at the house outside Donnafugata. They waited for the gates to open.

'Just be natural,' said Calogero.

He was dropped off at the front door, and entered the dark cool house. She was standing at the top of the stairs as she had been last time. This time he left his bag at the bottom of the stairs with his clothes as well.

Traiano drove round to the garage. Muniddu had heard the car and had come down to greet him, opening the door for him as he parked. His smile was broad. Within ten minutes they were sitting on the balcony with cokes, looking out over the tops of the orange trees.

'Jesus, Jesus, Jesus,' came the distant cry of Anna Maria Tancredi, invoking the sacred name.

Both men giggled.

'That was quick,' said Muniddu.

'He is getting more practiced at what she needs,' said Traiano. 'That's my boss for you. A quick learner.'

They then fell to talking about wives and children. Traiano felt he was getting to like Muniddu; he thought though only of the present, and not the immediate future, which his wife and his children would find very different.

In the house, Calogero leaned back on the pillows.

'You are absolutely sure?' he asked.

'I saw a doctor in Palermo last week. I wanted to make sure it was not something else. But it is what it is. Three months.'

'And he is a reputable doctor?' he asked, wondering if he were a doctor like Doctor Moro, or a proper doctor.

'Of course.'

'I didn't think it was possible,' said Calogero.

'Neither did I,' she said. 'I long ago gave up taking steps against it happening because I did not think it could happen. It really is a surprise. I am forty-five. But the doctor says it is all fine and there will be no complications.'

'I am delighted,' said Calogero.

'I have always wanted a child,' she said. 'To inherit all this.'

'Not just a child, a son, I hope,' he said. 'I am delighted,' he repeated. 'This changes everything. Now, listen. Before coming here, we passed through Syracuse. I have some very important things to tell don Antonio Santucci. Can you get him on the phone?'

'Can't it wait?'

'It has waited long enough. I planned to bring this up as soon as I came into the house, but you distracted me. Never mind, it was a pleasant distraction, and it was over quickly. There will be time for more distractions later. But now I have to speak to Antonio Santucci. Put on some clothes, go downstairs and get hold of him. You may have to phone around. He may not be in Palermo; he may be on holiday. But get hold of him. Now go.'

She understood. She rose, got her dressing gown and disappeared. Calogero went to the bedroom balcony, and whistled. This was a whistle that he had used to summon Traiano as a little boy. He would remember its urgent tones. He then went in search of his clothes which were scattered in the hallway downstairs. Traiano found him there doing up his shirt.

'Boss?' he asked.

'Everything has changed,' he said, keeping his voice low, gesturing to the next room where Anna Maria was on the phone. 'She is pregnant. Don't ask questions. So, we are doing an emergency handbrake turn while there is time.'

Anna Maria emerged for a moment.

'I have got him,' she said.

'Excellent,' said Calogero. He tucked in his shirt. They went into the room where the phone was, Traiano following.

'Put him on loudspeaker,' said Calogero. 'Don Antonio, I am sorry for disturbing your weekend and the start of your holiday perhaps.'

'I am sure you must have a reason,' said Santucci's voice, with a touch of coldness.

'You told me to keep an eye on Michele Lotto. I did just that. In fact I asked Anna the Romanian prostitute to do just that. She is a clever woman. She has been observing the man, who comes to see her every week, and she has heard what he is up to. Zero hour is tomorrow at 7pm. That is when Lotto with a team of sixty Romanians comes after thirty of your top people. Anna compiled the list and I have it here. I will read it to you. You may like to take down the names.'

He read the names, after which there was silence.

'That makes twenty-eight,' said Antonio Santucci. 'You said thirty.'

'The twenty-ninth is Anna Maria Tancredi and the thirtieth is her bodyguard Muniddu.'

'How did she get these names?' asked Antonio Santucci.

'Anna has been overhearing his telephone conversations. He trusts her. He does not trust mobile phones. But he uses the landline in her house. She has been listening as it unfolded. Only yesterday did she realise that zero hour was tomorrow evening. Only this morning did she give me the names. Lotto speaks in a Romanian dialect she does not fully understand. She is from Iasi, he is from Bucharest; it is like the difference between Sicilian and Romanesco.'

'Yes, OK, OK,' said Santucci impatiently. 'Have we no way of finding out who these Romanians are, this army of sixty?'

'We looked into that, or rather she did. It was all number withheld whenever she tried redial.'

'Our phone system is crap,' said Antonio with resignation. 'Now listen. This is important. Are you sure that the following people are not on the list?'

He recited some names.

'They are not names Anna heard.'

'If it is a decapitation strategy, that is very interesting indeed,' said Santucci. 'As soon as this call is over, the twenty-eight names I have are going to be instructed to move position, so to speak, so when our Romanian friends turn up, they will find no one at home. And everyone else in our organisation is to take maximum precautions. You are at Donnafugata? Tell Muniddu what to do. And you, do what you know you must do. Can I trust you to do that?'

'Absolutely,' said Calogero.

The call ended. Anna Maria, Calogero noticed, was pale.

'I told you it was important,' he said with a wan smile. 'Don't be alarmed, everything is going to be fine. You can stay here and Muniddu will look after you, and nothing will happen, I guarantee that. You will both be safe.'

He emphasised the 'both'. He turned to Traiano and told him to fetch Muniddu.

'He had better sleep in the house while I am not here,' said Calogero.

'Where are you going?' she asked.

'Didn't you hear? Syracuse. At some time tonight I will ring you here and after I have rung you, I want you to ring Santucci.'

'And say what?'

'Nothing. Just that I am well and send my regards. Nothing, just in case someone is listening. He will understand.'

'Then you are coming back?'

'No. With those Romanians roaming the island, I would make you a target. They may well be after me too. You will be safe here with Muniddu. I will go to ground somewhere with Traiano, and sit this out. We will ring you, on the landline. But remember, innocent conversations.'

She nodded.

Muniddu entered. Calogero outlined the situation to him briefly.

'Anna Maria will give you a bedroom in the house,' said Calogero. 'We all trust you. The Romanian gang are after your masters, but your masters have been warned, and the Romanians are going to get a shock. Now, Traiano come with me.'

They went into the garden and then into the orange grove.

'Jesus, boss,' said Traiano.

'Thinking on your feet; a quick change of plan. Go into the house and get Anna on the phone.'

He hurried off to do what he was told. Calogero wandered through the trees as he did so. Then he returned to Traiano.

'We need to go back to Syracuse at once,' he said.

After the most hurried of goodbyes, they left.

'You are different, somehow,' observed Stefania.

She was wearing a hat and dark glasses as she said this, so it was hard to interpret what she was saying. They were on the beach; the sun was bright; the three children were enjoying themselves; the wide long bay was a delight and behind them was the town of Cefalù and the huge mountain behind it. He had not been to a more lovely place. Stefania was extended on a sun lounger, wearing her latest bathing costume, an elegant one piece in modest dark blue, which had cost a fortune, but which was, she judged, worth every cent. She was easily the most beautiful woman on the beach in her own eyes; and, she detected, in the eyes of her brother-in-law Rosario. He had nothing of his brother's charisma of course; he was tall, thin, angular, even more so than usual, as he was now dressed in just a pair of bathing shorts; but he was not as unattractive as she usually considered him. Perhaps everyone looked better in the sunshine.

Giuseppina had not come, after all. In fact, when she had heard that Stefania had invited Rosario to join them, she had said she was not coming. Some people, thought Stefania, took umbrage too easily, and did not know what was good for them. Or perhaps Giuseppina resented the implication that her elder sister was throwing her together with her brother-in-law too obviously. Well, she was only trying to help, and this was the thanks she got.

If Rosario was disappointed by the absence of Giuseppina, he did not show it. He was far too busy, in her absence, with the children. Little Renato was now covered in sun cream and wearing a large hat; his uncle had just taken him into the water, and the boy was devotedly sitting next to him on the sand. It was nice to see how the child loved his uncle. She remembered what Calogero had once said to her; that if anything happened to him, Rosario would look after her and the children, and have care of the legal part of the business; the less than legal would fall into the hands of Traiano. If anything happened to Calogero... that was a constant, not worry, but factor. She had stopped worrying about it a long time ago. What would be, would be. If it happened, she was prepared for it. Because she had thought about it, and thought about it more than ever this weekend, she was curious about the moment, should it ever come. How would she react to the news? How would she carry herself as a widow with the eyes of the world on her? How would the children react? What would she feel if they told her her husband was not coming home, that he was dead, and dead through violence?

'What did you feel,' she asked her brother-in-law, 'when they told you your father was dead?'

Rosario considered.

'I was twelve. I don't think I felt very much. I was dismayed by the way my mother was so upset. It was not nice to see. But he was away so often that I did not really miss him. Then they told me about all the things he had done, and I felt a grim satisfaction. I felt he deserved it. And he did. He blew himself up and got a taste of his own medicine. Hoist with his own petard, as Shakespeare says.'

She reflected that if Calogero were killed, the same judgement would apply.

'Were you glad to be an orphan?'

'Yes,' said Rosario. 'Do you think...?'

'That Calogero will be killed? One day, perhaps. This weekend, who knows? How can we tell? What I would like to know is how I would feel if it happened. When it happens.'

'I would feel liberated,' confessed Rosario. 'It would be the end of a very sad story. A sad story needs a quick end.'

'I suppose it does,' she said. 'He senses it too. He has made his will, he has divided the properties up. Your elder sister was furious. She phoned me up and screamed down the phone.'

'What exactly did she say?'

'The usual. Assunta was never imaginative. That I was a grasping scheming bitch. Well, that was no surprise. I do not mean that I am, I just mean I always thought that that was her estimation of me. She has been thinking that for years, and now she has said it. Unwise of her, as it means I do not need to be polite to her anymore. Or her fat husband. Though he is not so bad, and I feel sorry for him. Poor Assunta, she wants her share of the pie, and she thinks she has been cheated. Poor Caloriu having such an unloving sister. Oh yes, and she called me a whore. And said that Renato was not Caloriu's son.'

'She said the same to me,' said Rosario. 'I think she got this idea from something Calogero said to me when he was drunk; that if ever he died, I would have to marry you. Mind you, he said that to me, and Traiano was there, so how it got back to Assunta, I do not know.'

'Perhaps Assunta has got an imagination after all,' observed Stefania. 'But if I were to marry anyone it would surely be Traiano. He is so beautiful. Just like his mother. There is something Caravaggesque about both of them. When I was in Rome with Caloriu we went to see the Madonna of the Pilgrims; you know the one, you lived in Rome; the model Caravaggio used was a prostitute too; and Traiano looks like the Bacchus in the painting in the Uffizi. I saw that too, on my own. Caloriu has never been to Florence. Too busy. Sad. Yes, I should marry our version of the Bacchus.'

'He is already married.'

'I had forgotten. Yes, of course. From which you can tell that my search for a second husband is in the very early stages. Why don't you get married?'

'I am only twenty-two,' he said.

'Caloriu and I were seventeen; Ceccina and Traiano just sixteen,' said Stefania. 'Perhaps not the best examples. There is no hurry. What one looks for is companionship, but one does not often find it, alas. My goodness, Anna is ringing me. What on earth can she want.' She picked up her phone. 'Hi,' she said. Then: 'OK.... OK.... OK... I will tell him.' All the time she looked at Rosario.

'A message for me?' he asked.

'Yes. It wasn't Anna. It was Calogero. They must be in Syracuse. The message is for both of us. We are to stay here till Wednesday or whenever he tells us to go; then we can go back. Let's hope the flat is free till then. And you are not to sell the shares on Monday. I wonder what is happening? But of course, I do not like asking questions. Or more accurately, he does not like answering questions.'

They were back in the underground car park on the island of Ortygia. It was getting close to six o'clock. Frustratingly it took some time to find a parking place. The minutes passed. Anna had told her son that Lotto came round at seven, and that he was always very punctual, though, sometimes he turned up early. Calogero very much hoped that this would not be one of these days. The plan was very simple. They knew Lotto's habits; they knew the plan of Anna's place. They had their weapons. Everything else could stay in the car. They walked across the island to the house overlooking the Arethusa Fountain where Anna lived. Luckily, because it was a guest house, and because at the height of summer it was full, there were lots of comings and goings, and the entry of two unfamiliar men was not remarkable. She was at the desk, in the entrance hall, and immediately led them to the door behind the desk and her private quarters. Calogero at once went to the phone and called his wife. The others waited for him to finish his instructions to Stefania. They stood together in the sitting room. It was about twenty-five minutes past six. There were footsteps above.

'The guests,' she explained. 'They are all coming in, having their showers, then going out again.'

He did not have to tell her why they had come back so suddenly and so hurriedly. She knew. She knew him. She had her instincts. They were never wrong.

'Just do everything as you normally do,' said Calogero evenly. 'After it is over there will be more instructions, but they can wait till then. Right, where can we hide our clothes in this room?'

She indicated a cupboard. The two men quietly stripped themselves naked. Then they went through to the bedroom at the back, with its neat white counterpane on the double bed, and then into the bathroom, where they stood behind the door, facing the shower. Each held his knife. Calogero took in the details, which were just as he had remembered them from his previous cursory visit which had been for no deadly purpose. The small high window was glazed with opaque glass. The walls were tiled. The shower had no curtain and there was a drain in the centre of the floor, as laid down by Italian law. The whole place could not be better designed as an abattoir.

They stood in silence leaning against the wall behind the door. It was a hot day, but the place was cold. There were various ambient noises from around the building: muffled talk, the sound of water running, feet on tiles and doors closing.

'Look at your toes,' said Calogero very quietly. 'Imagine each toe is a person.'

He did as he was told: his son Cristoforo; the child yet to be born, perhaps another boy; his wife Ceccina; his boss Caloriu, standing next to him; his mother, now preparing to receive Lotto; Lotto himself; don Antonio Santucci whom Lotto wanted to kill; Alfio, with his terrible teeth; Saro, whom he had shot through the leg; Gino, from Agrigento; don Giorgio, the best priest in the world – but he had run out of toes and was working through them a second time.

Calogero thought of just one person: the new child. At the age of forty-five, who could have thought it? What an utter surprise. What a great blessing. He would do anything to protect that child and his mother. What a reversal. How lucky for Anna Maria, how unlucky for Lotto. How lucky for Antonio Santucci and his clan.

'What is the time?' whispered Traiano.

'Nowhere near seven,' he whispered back. 'Think of the names you are going to give the new child.'

Traiano thought: if it was a girl, perhaps Maria, but not just Maria. It could not be Maria Assunta as that was Caloriu's sister who was not very nice. Maria Immaculata? Maria Regina? That was a little more original. Maria Vittoria? He couldn't think of anyone called Maria Vittoria and the child might be born some time around the feast of Our Lady of Victories in October. But he also liked the Greek names, Sophia and Irene, wisdom and peace, though he wanted the child to be Sicilian not Romanian and those names did have a hint of the east about them. Perhaps his daughter would be Maria Vittoria Antonescu. And if it were another boy? Francesco would be nice, Franco, Ciccio. Saint Francis was his favourite saint. He must ask Caloriu who his favourite saint was. He had never asked. Thinking of the saints, he said a prayer to Saint Francis that his children would not grow up without a father.

Calogero was going through names too. He hoped naturally for a boy, and the name Giorgio, though it was that of the priest who so heartily loathed him, was one that appealed. Saint George was a soldier and a saint, and that was good, and he was the patron of Ragusa the nearest city to Donnafugata, as far as he could remember. But he had met Anna Maria in Noto, and the patron there was Saint Nicholas, but not the famous Saint Nicholas, some minor character of the same name. He tried to work out when the child would be born – six months from now – February. What feast days were there in February? Did he like the name Nicola?

A door opened. But it was from the wrong direction surely? False alarm. Surely to God it must be seven o'clock by now. Please, dear God, let him not be late on this day of all days, the day of his much-deserved death. The same thought flew through both their heads.

Suddenly there were voices. Anna's voice, speaking what seemed like from a distance Italian, but must be Romanian, and another voice, indistinct, his voice. They were in the sitting room. God forbid Lotto should go near the cupboard. Now they were in the bedroom. The voices were distinct, low. Was Anna going to betray them? What a crazy thought. Her own son? She hated Lotto, anyway. One heard the pressure of someone sitting on the side of the bed; one could almost feel it. Then more low voices, then the sound of clothing being removed. More voices, more sound of pressure on a mattress. They were lying down. Calogero looked at Traiano. It was all going to plan. But it was very quiet. At last there came the sound of snatched breaths, and then, at long last, the reassurance of the regular creaking of the bedsprings. Once more Calogero looked at Traiano. Then came Anna calling on the Lord by name, and a noise rather like a cough, which was Lotto's vocal contribution. Then, for what seemed like an eternity, nothing. Then a voice, someone getting up, and finally, the bathroom door opening.

Confronted with the naked hairy back of Lotto, Calogero put an arm round his neck and drove his knife into his back, aiming for the heart. He swung him round, and Traiano put his knife into the man's chest. There was no struggle, and they gently let the body reach the floor without making any noise. There had been no sound either, just a sort of cough that rather resembled the sound that the man had made a few minutes earlier. But he

304

was undoubtedly dead. Calogero put his fingers to the man's neck to feel for a pulse. There was lots of blood, more blood than Traiano had imagined possible. The body of Lotto had turned the colour of putty. The bowel had opened as well. The smell was intolerable. Calogero opened the window a crack, and turned on the shower, so that the clear fresh water would carry away the vileness of murder.

As the water thundered from the shower, they pushed the body to one side; each one stood over the lavatory bowl and relieved the pressure on their bladder; they both tried their best to wash way the blood that had turned the paleness of their own flesh dark red; then they squatted side by side against the wall, and spoke under the noise of the shower.

'Easy, wasn't it?' said Calogero.

'Yes,' said Traiano.

They settled down to wait until dark.

In Castelvetrano, where he had been hoping to enjoy a few happy and carefree days with his wife and children, Antonio Santucci was working on the three lists. For just as Calogero had seen that one list implied another, Antonio had seen the possibility of another list as well.

Before him was the shopping list of Lotto: all the people he intended to kill, with his name, Antonio Santucci at the top, along with his uncle, Domenico, his father, Lorenzo, and his two sons, Sandro and Beppe, though not, he noticed, his brother-in-law. He had asked Calogero about this omission. It was perfectly possible that Anna the Romanian prostitute had heard the name but not noted it down; this would mean that the omission was accidental and not deliberate. But it was hard to tell. He was very annoyed that they had bugged the flat where Lotto was living, and bugged the phone where he was living; they should have bugged the phone and flat of Anna the Romanian prostitute, though God knew, it was tedious going through hours of recordings of creaking bedsprings. But if the woman was as good an eavesdropper as Calogero thought she was, then this human intelligence was of better value than any electronically harvested information.

So, his brother-in-law, whom he had never liked, clearly headed up the second list, the list of notable omissions. Was this a sign that his brother-in-law had been in league with Lotto and the Romanians? Had he been hoping to step into dead men's shoes? Had he been using the Romanians? But one thing he was sure of: his brother-in-law was not a man confident or strong enough to work alone. So, who were the other notable omissions? Gradually he assembled a list of men whom you would include in any decapitation strategy, if that was what you were planning, but who were not on Lotto's list. He wrote down, after careful thought, five names, and looked for a pattern. And after a time, a pattern emerged. These five men all knew each other – well, that was obvious enough. He remembered seeing them laughing together, whispering together, not all five at once but in pairs, on the edge of meetings, at weddings, at funerals. For years these five important men had formed a cabal. Perhaps it was time to get rid of them? They formed a counterweight to his own position, and he remembered times when one, some, or even all of them had opposed him, or at least not enthusiastically run with his suggestions.

Then there was the third list to consider. There were some men on Lotto's list, who if Lotto's men were to kill them, he would not particularly miss. Some were old, dead wood, who needed pruning. Some were younger but too ambitious. He looked at the twenty-eight names, and felt that there were at least six that he could leave to take their chances with Lotto's men come tomorrow evening. That left twenty-two who would need to be warned. His father and his uncle he would now phone and tell to move at once, for they were surely being watched by Lotto's army. They would have to move discreetly, without fuss, and swiftly. They would want to take wives with them. He picked up the phone and began to work through the names, calling each one and speaking of the need to break off the holiday and go somewhere else because bad weather was approaching. Of course, once Lotto's men knew their master was dead, would they still act? He wondered. It might take them some time to realise it. So, he worked through the list, all twenty-two of them, leaving the six aside to take their chances. He looked at the clock. It was past eight. By now, surely, Lotto would be dead. He trusted Calogero di Rienzi to do his work well.

Rosario and Stefania and the three children were in a pizzeria facing the sea in Cefalù. The waiter was enchanted with the three children, particularly the little boy. He seemed to think that Rosario and Stefania were married and these were their children. Stefania was amused by this, Rosario slightly embarrassed. He wondered if he should explain to the waiter that he was her brother-in-law, not her husband, the children's uncle not their father. But it occurred to him that one day he could be sitting in just such a restaurant, in just such a place, with a wife, with children, and he should try and not get used to it, but see if he liked the situation. To be tied to someone for life was of course not a novel idea. He was tied to his family for life. To his mother, whom he hardly ever saw, but who was always there; to his sisters, with whom there had just been such a spectacular breach, and in relation to whom he would now live in anything but indifference; to Calogero, the most important person, the one who, like his dead father, had shaped his life. To take on new attachments, new commitments, to new people, to take the risk of creating new people, people who did not yet exist, children. He looked at his two nieces and at the young Renato. They were innocent; they did not know; but they would one day come to know, just as he had, in that police station when Volta had told him his father had been a mass murderer.

He thought about what had happened between him and Catarina in his flat. It did not, technically, count as sexual intercourse, he was sure. Though it was probably enough to make Gino want to kill him. He reflected on what had happened; the way they had both fallen on each other, and how proceedings had reached an abrupt and early conclusion with his words of 'Oh God, I think I am dying!' He really had said that. He had thought it, he had felt it. And then afterwards, an empty feeling of total aloneness, as she had left him to retreat into himself. There had been no possibility of her calling on the Holy Name. He smiled.

'What are you thinking about?' asked Stefania.

'About the way Sicilian women call on the Holy Name when, you know....'

Isabella and Natalia suddenly looked up from their pizzas and paid attention.

'Oh that,' she said. 'Everyone is different, and in some ways, everyone is the same.'

She looked at him. He felt for a moment that she might offer herself there and then, ask him to join her in her bedroom after the children were in bed. He imagined the scene. Behind her, he could see the floodlit town of Cefalù and the massive bulk of its Norman cathedral. Tomorrow they would go to Church. Tomorrow he would renew his desire to serve God. Living in the world was too hard. He would be a priest after all.

The corpse lay silently on the bathroom floor. In whispered voices they had done everything they could possibly do to clean themselves and the place up; they had then waited to dry naturally in the heat of the evening, and then emerged into the bedroom, with dry feet, and into the sitting room, where they put on their clothes. They had cleaned their knives and these they put away. Then they sat down on the sofa, where, some hours later, Anna, returning, found them both fast asleep.

After one last phone call, to his most trusted man, summoning him to Castelvetrano – he was in Erice, about an hour away at most – Antonio Santucci went in search of his wife and supper. The children were there too. The conversation was as it usually was, though a seasoned observer, and his wife was certainly such, would have noticed an unusual level of preoccupation and taciturnity about him.

'Where is Carlo this weekend?' he asked, above the chatter of the children.

Carlo was her brother. He was also her husband's second cousin, as she was herself.

'He is on a boat with some of his friends. You remember, I told you. Five of them, all men. They have left the wives and children behind. Well, it is quite a small boat. I think they were going to the islands.'

'I wouldn't want to be stuck on a boat with your brother,' he said.

'Darling,' she remonstrated. 'I wish you would be kinder to Carlo.'

'I think I remember you telling me. The others with him, are they….' He reeled off a list of names.

'You have a good memory,' she said. 'Five of them. They felt the need to get away together, to sail, to drink, to chat. You should do something similar, go away with your best friends.'

He looked at her, examining her expression for some hint of irony. He had no friends. She surely knew that.

'Tomorrow evening, let us go and see your mother,' he said amiably. 'Don't look surprised. You always say we should go to see her more than we do. She will be delighted. Let's aim to get there by seven. Children, we are going to see Granny tomorrow night.'

There was a general moan round the table. His wife did not know whether to be annoyed or delighted. Her husband had spent their entire married life being hostile to her family, which of course was his family too, as they were second cousins, and encouraging the children to dislike them too; now he was proposing they drive all the way to Palermo to visit her mother, which was a welcome, if sudden change.

As supper ended, Antonio was called away by the arrival of his trusted lieutenant. They had a quiet conversation in the garden. He explained the Romanian threat, and what was to be done about it. He explained that his brother-in-law and his friends had betrayed them. The man nodded vigorously. He had never liked Carlo.

'The last time we went shopping in Moldova, or Belarus or Transdniestria, or wherever it was….'

'I think it was the latter, boss.'

'Wherever. You remember they sold us what we wanted but they also forced us to buy a whole lot of stuff that I thought we would never ever get to use. I was annoyed at the time. You remember?'

'Are you talking about the rocket-propelled grenades, boss?'

'Yes. Real white elephants. I presume we still have them?'

'Of course, boss.'

'And you can use them?'

'Of course, boss.'

'Good,' said Antonio. 'Now let me explain.'

Gino and Alfio were waiting in the pizzeria. Catarina was waiting at Gino's place. She had not liked the idea in the least, but Gino had told her that her collaboration was essential, and it would be brief, if unpleasant. The clients were fading away, as it was eleven o'clock, and though Saturday was the busiest night, it was August tomorrow, and as this was the first proper day of the holidays, the quarter and the city were emptying out. Tomorrow they would be closed. The pizza that Perraino would eat would be the last to be cooked in the huge, expensive, up to date oven that Gino had care of.

The two men sat at the table, watching, and waiting. Catarina was to come over when they called her. Perraino arrived at 11pm, and joined them.

'Do you have the money?' was his first question.

'Yes, boss,' said Alfio with real penitence, and took out a thick large envelope. 'It is all there,' he said, handing it over.

Perraino glanced at the contents briefly, remarking that if it were not all there, he would make them pay for it. Then he put the envelope in the pocket of his jeans, which was uncomfortable, but he was not wearing a jacket in this hot weather. Gino signalled to the pizza chef, when Perraino indicated what pizza he would eat. Three bottles of Peroni came over. When the pizza came, Gino told the chef and the waiters that they could all go and that he would lock up along with Alfio. Soon they were alone. He went to the phone and rang for Catarina.

Perraino greedily consumed his pizza. He was hungry. He had heard the pizza here was good, and so it proved.

'We are really really sorry, boss,' Alfio was saying. 'We didn't know the people at Nicolosi were your friends. It will never happen again.'

'Yeah,' said Gino.

'It had better not,' said Perraino.

'And the thing is that we love dogs,' said Gino.

'Where is that Romanian boy?' asked Perraino.

But at this point Catarina entered.

'Hi,' she said, with a smile, taking a seat next to Perraino.

He smiled back. She was wearing a very short skirt, and her eyes were inviting. This was more like it, though Perraino. There had been a time, before his jaw had been broken, when he had often encountered such inviting glances from girls. His hand rested on her knee, and inched its way towards the hem of her skirt. Her smile became radiant. Glancing toward the ceiling of the room, her hand inched towards the buttons of his jeans, and with expert fingers began to open them.

'I will get you a room,' said Alfio. 'I just need to check.'

Perraino grunted.

Gino rose to pull down the pizzeria shutters.

Perraino's hand was completely up her skirt, exploring her underwear, when the plastic bag came down over his head. While Alfio did this, Gino wrestled him to the ground. Catarina, her job done, scarpered. Gino banged Perraino's head against the floor several times with extreme force, while Alfio tightened the bag around his neck with a leather shoelace. They extracted the envelope from his pocket, careful to avoid contact with his open buttons. When it was clear the man was unconscious, they half-dragged and half-carried him to the pizza oven and put him in. Gino closed the metal door, and then put the gas on the highest setting, the setting one used to clean it. By morning, they hoped, Perraino would be charred bones. They settled down to wait.

Anna woke them up at a little before one in the morning. They stirred, refreshed by their sleep. But the lethargy was soon dispelled by the realisation that the most important part of the operation, the moment that required the maximum daring, was still ahead. This was the moment when all could go wrong. But of course Anna had a plan, which they were sure, bold as it was, would work.

Anna was wearing her make-up and her dressing-gown. She watched them take up the cheap Chinese mat that lay on the sitting room floor and take it to the bathroom. They placed the washed and dried corpse on it, and rolled it up. Then they lightly tied the roll. The bathroom was clean, but she had instructions to clean it again, and to dispose of Lotto's clothes, and of course to buy a new identical carpet. They waited. At just past one in the morning a knock came at the door.

'Hello, gorgeous,' said the photographer. 'You look great. Thanks for giving me this chance. I have been so looking forward to it, ever since I saw you. The pictures will be wonderful.'

Anna said something, then the voices faded away. Calogero and Traiano went to the front door and saw what was happening. The photographer was setting up several lights, looking for the right background. He had been pestering Anna ever since they had met for the opportunity to photograph her; he was not a young man, nearly fifty, and they had met in the bar in the Cathedral Square after Mass one Sunday. It turned out that his father was one of Anna's old gentlemen. He had been surprised when just this

315

evening she had phoned and suggested a nocturnal appointment. He
wondered what rush of excitement had made her give way.

'Right,' he said. 'Stand there. I want you to put your weight on your left
foot and draw your right foot up slightly behind. Yes, that is right. OK.
You can take off the dressing gown. That is wonderful. Really wonderful.
Shoulders a little back, please.'

It was one in the morning, and there was no one around. But if there were,
their eyes would have been drawn to the magnificent spectacle of Anna the
naked Romanian prostitute posing in front of the Fountain of Arethusa.
And no one would have paid even the slightest attention to two men
carrying away a rolled-up carpet, and making their way down to the
water's edge.

After they had dumped their load into the sea with a gentle splash,
releasing it from the mat, and thrown the mat into the water at a different
place, Calogero and Traiano walked back to the car. In the distance they
could see the brightly lit figure of Anna, posing against the night sky. A
small but deeply appreciative crowd had gathered at a respectful distance.
All eyes were fixed on her. It was as if the nymph Arethusa had returned to
Syracuse after many centuries of absence.

Away they drove. At the first petrol station, there was a public phone.
Traiano called Muniddu.

'Hi, handsome,' he said. 'Just checking you are OK. They say the weather
is going to be lovely tomorrow.'

Their conversation was brief and inconsequential.

Muniddu walked along the corridor to Anna Maria's bedroom, and knocked on the door.

'All well, signora,' he called.

At the petrol station, Traiano made another call, this time to the pizzeria.

'Hi, handsome,' he said. 'I am just calling to say that the weather tomorrow is going to be really good.'

'Guess what?' said Gino. 'Alfio just got laid. Can you believe it?'

After that conversation, he returned to Calogero, who was waiting in the car.

'You forgot to call off the Perraino operation,' he said, as he settled into his seat.

'Did I?' said Calogero, as the car sped away into the night along deserted roads.

Chapter Ten

Sunday was a day of tension and waiting. At Donnafugata, Anna Maria Tancredi stayed at home and Muniddu did not let her out of his sight; his shotgun was always to hand. In Syracuse, after going to Mass in the Cathedral, Anna walked with little Salvatore along the harbour edge, scanning it for the sight of her old mat and the murdered body of Lotto, though, thankfully, there was no sign of either. In Palermo, after a long drive, Antonio Santucci sat down to a late lunch with his wife, his children and his ecstatic and talkative mother-in-law, keeping one eye on the clock. In Cefalù, Rosario, Stefania and the children embarked on another day of carefree enjoyment, after attending Mass in the Norman cathedral. In the Purgatory quarter of Catania, having dozed all night by the pizza oven, Gino and Alfio finally switched it off, let it cool, and then began to grind to dust the charred remains of the late Captain Perraino with a hammer, preparatory to flushing the ashes down the loo. In the small hotel in Noto, where they had stayed in January, and where they had been lucky enough to find a room in the early hours, Traiano slept on one bed, while Calogero read a book on another, a hefty tome he had borrowed from Anna Maria, another book about Caravaggio. He too looked at the clock from time to time. The hour of maximum danger was approaching.

While Antonio and his wife and mother-in-law began to recover from their huge late lunch, out to sea, Carlo Santucci, brother-in-law and second cousin of Antonio was relaxing on his yacht with five close friends. They were in the lee of Favignana, a pleasant spot to anchor after a long day of sailing. As seven in the evening approached, they opened bottles of beer, and settled down to enjoy the cooler air and the coming sunset. Carlo looked towards the land, as if expecting something to happen. An anxiety had come upon him. He surveyed the distant scene. There were numerous boats in the water, as the spot was a popular anchorage, though none were particularly near. Later the police were to establish that at least six rocket propelled grenades had been aimed at the yacht, the last of which hit the fuel tank and caused the entire craft to explode. By that time, though, most aboard were dead.

Rosario and Stefania were walking along the seafront at Cefalù with the children, hoping to see the sunset. They had reached the end of the bay, and were turning back towards the town, enjoying the view that lay before them. The children were not yet tired. The two little girls, Isabella and Natalia, ran in front of them, and little Renato rode on his uncle's shoulders. A few hundred metres in front of them were a group of convivial bathers, settling down to opening a cooler full of drinks; two men were walking by, not really dressed for the beach, Rosario noticed out of the corner of his eye. He took in the way the sunlight was hitting the bulk of the Norman cathedral and the mass of the mountain behind it. He turned to Stefania to draw her attention to this. There was a sound, a popping sound, like a distant opening of a bottle of prosecco, repeated three or four times; a woman screamed; he received the sense that Stefania was paying him no attention. She was running towards the girls. The two men were now running towards them. Stefania caught hold of the girls and held them tight. The two men ran towards Rosario and Renato. Rosario noticed that they were slowing down now, and one of them had a gun in his hand. Stupidly, he could not move. He watched the men walk past him, one of them putting the gun into the waistband of his trousers, and then carrying on. Everything had stopped for a moment. It was as if he were now deaf.

319

Gradually he focussed on the crowd gathering on the beach below, people watching with their hands held to their mouths, people screaming into mobile phones. He saw Stefania clutching the two girls, who looked puzzled. He walked towards her, took her arm, and steered her away from the scene, back towards their flat.

It was necessary to get something to eat. They were not on the list, and it was most unlikely that the Romanian gang even knew that Lotto was dead. Even if they did, they would not automatically jump to the conclusion that he and Traiano had killed him. They would assume that that was the work of Palermo. In fact the Romanians, if they thought anything about his disappearance would assume that Palermo may have killed him too, or so Calogero reasoned. Besides, without their leader, the Romanians were an army without a general, a useless rabble who would, sooner or later, go back to Romania and report their huge failure. Whatever way, it was necessary to get something to eat; and if possible in a bar with a television.

They arrived at a bar along the Corso Vittorio Emanuele in time for the nine o'clock news on RAI Uno. They sat outside, just by the gracious façade of the Church of Saint Dominic, but at a place where they could see and hear the television. Traiano had his usual coke, and Calogero had a Peroni. There were desultory negotiations about food. It was Sunday night, and there was an atmosphere of tiredness and fatalism about the place. A yacht had been blown up near Favignana. It had been attacked with rocket propelled grenades. All six people aboard had been killed. They were thought to be members of the San Lorenzo crime family.

'Who?' asked Traiano.

Calogero shrugged.

A reporter was already peddling the usual line. An internal settling of accounts in the world of Sicilian crime. But then came another talking head; they both paid attention. It was Volta.

'This cannot be put down to business as usual,' Volta was saying. 'The use of rocket propelled grenades is a dolorous first for Sicily. These were bought somewhere in the Middle East or eastern Europe. There is a message in the weapons used, and a clue. The violence in Sicily is showing an international dimension.'

Then the television news did a tour of what it was calling the Sunday of Violence. A restaurant in Taormina, sprayed with bullets, but no casualties; a stabbing in Mondello, one dead; two killed in a raid on a country house near Corleone; a prominent Palermo businessman, a leading figure in the construction industry, shot dead on the beach at Cefalù while picnicking with his family.

'Call Saro,' commanded Calogero.

Traiano at once went into the bar and called up Rosario's mobile.

'Hi, handsome,' he said. 'Are you having a nice time at the beach?'

'Hi, handsome,' replied Rosario. 'Yes, fine. The children are enjoying themselves and so is Stefania. We had pizza last night for supper, but tonight we all stayed in.'

'OK, have fun,' said Traiano, ringing off. He went back to Calogero. 'They are fine,' he said.

Calogero nodded. He was filled with admiration for what Antonio Santucci had done. He had got the Romanians to do his dirty work for him, and he had hidden his own murders in the massacre. But most of the Romanians would have found their targets gone; they would be angry and confused, and wondering where their leader was. Sixty murderous Romanians on the loose. It was not a good thing to contemplate. Santucci would put his people on the ground too. In the meantime, it was necessary to lie low. The peace of Palermo was, for the moment, shattered.

Rosario had been watching the scene on the beach from the balcony of their flat when the call had come though. The children were in bed. Stefania came out to him.

'Was that him?'

'No, it was Traiano. I just spoke to Traiano. They were checking we were OK, that is all.'

'Did he say where he was?'

'No.'

'A deliberate omission. He is hiding somewhere. He knew that this was going to happen, and he left us exposed to it.'

'He can't have known it was going to happen here. That was coincidence. We could have been somewhere else. We could have been looking out to sea at Favignana.'

'Don't defend him,' said Stefania shortly. 'I know you don't,' she said. They both stood looking down at the beach, at the police cars, at the area taped off, at the little tent put over the body, at the milling curious crowd at a distance. She sighed. 'Come to bed,' she said.

'It is still early,' he replied.

'I did not say it was time to go to sleep,' she said. He had been sleeping on the sofa. 'Come to bed.'

Her meaning was unmistakeable. She left him to stand on the balcony alone.

Calogero was reading his book. Caravaggio was clearly a very great artist and a very bad man. He had committed murder, or so it was thought. The evidence was not quite clear. Only a fool, reflected Calogero, would leave a trail of evidence linking him to a crime. Caravaggio had not been one of them. He reflected on the body of Lotto, somewhere in the harbour at

Syracuse, perhaps now floating out to sea, and being nibbled by the fish. He hoped it would never be recovered, and was reasonably confident that the currents in the harbour would carry it to some unfrequented spot where it would rapidly decay. He wondered how long that would take. He shut his book with a snap.

'So, Uncle Caloriu,' said Traiano, who had been waiting for him to finish reading, 'Are you going to have two wives from now on?'

'Not two wives, but certainly two families.'

'When we were waiting for Lotto to come in, I was thinking of names for my next child. Either Maria Vittoria or Sebastiano.'

'I was thinking of Giorgio or Nicola,' said Calogero. 'I haven't given girls' names a thought. I have two daughters already. I think this might be a boy.'

'Well, I am glad. I am glad we did not have to drown Muniddu. I quite like him. I did not like Lotto and neither did Anna. But all these crazy Romanians that came over to finish off the people in Palermo. A lot of them missed their targets; will they just go home when they realise Lotto is dead?'

'Let's hope so, though I have a funny feeling that quite a few of them are going to turn up dead in the next few days. Antonio Santucci will release his men to hunt them down. The Romanians, if they have any sense, will head to the ferries or to the airport and go back home. But they must be panicking. Their targets were not there; Lotto has vanished; someone betrayed them. But they have no way of finding us. Anna Maria is safe. Ring Muniddu.'

He reached for the phone by the bed.

'Hi, handsome,' he said.

After a moment he passed the phone to Calogero. Calogero listened to Muniddu with great attention.

'A message,' he said. 'On the 10th August they expect me in Palermo.'

'The men with guns running towards us, and running towards the children,' said Stefania, not for the first time. 'That is what remains with me. Did you see their faces?'

'No. I mean, I saw their faces, but it was as if I wasn't seeing anything. I could not recognise them again. Yet I won't ever forget it. The way they had the guns in their hands, the way they moved,' said Rosario. 'But I don't think the children saw anything. They didn't notice. They are in a world of their own. They went to bed quietly. They didn't seem traumatised. We are traumatised, not them.'

'I am not traumatised, though I suppose I am. I am angry. Caloriu knew that something was happening this weekend and he allowed us to walk straight into it. I blame him. Very much.'

He shifted slightly in the bed. She was leaning against his arm which had become numb, but he was not quite sure of how he could ask her to move her weight, or even if he should do so. Nor should he question the guilt of his brother. After all, her sleeping with him was her revenge; not an expression of love, but an expression of anger. Not love for him, but anger against Calogero.

'He just rang you, or rather Traiano rang you. No word of enquiry from him about how we are feeling.'

'Feelings were never his strong point. With him it is always power.'

It struck him that perhaps she had never seen a gun before now, never witnessed a shooting, and that perhaps she like so many others had assumed that such things happened in another world. Of course, in Purgatory they used knives. But now they had all joined the gun club in Nicolosi, perhaps there would now be more shootings in Purgatory, and fewer beatings and knifings. Violence was everywhere; it was what underpinned Calogero's fortune, his work, his world; but when one saw it close up, or even witnessed a clean surgical execution at a short distance, then one did not like it.

His mobile phone rang. The number was one he did not recognise, but he knew, and so did she, that it would be Traiano.

'Take it,' she whispered.

'Hi, handsome,' said Traiano. 'Are you in bed with a beautiful lady?'

'If I were I would not be answering the phone, would I?' he replied.

He squirmed. Stefania's slender fingers were groping him.

'Tell Stefania when you see her tomorrow that on 10th August, she and Caloriu are invited to Palermo. It is very important. Caloriu thinks she might want to come. He will have meetings, she will be free to see the sights.'

'I heard,' she said, as he put the phone aside.

He was at last able to free his arm.

Somewhere, far out to sea in the warm Mediterranean, curious fish were beginning to nibble the mortal remains of the man who had called himself Michele Lotto.

'So, what happened?' asked Rosario.

It was the 9th August, a Monday. Catania was empty. He and Volta were sitting down to lunch together.

What indeed had happened, reflected Volta. It was so hard to work it all out. Several members of the San Lorenzo crime family had been killed on a yacht off Favignana. A few other men, who were also associated with the same crime family in one way or another, had been assassinated. And then the next week, a load of dead Romanians had turned up in various unexpected places. The rocket propelled grenades and the Romanians both pointed to some eastern connection. That was what the police thought. The Romanians had tried a hostile takeover bid and had failed. And their leader, who had been rumoured to have been hiding in Syracuse, had disappeared. Now, it seemed, the Romanians had gone. But they would be back. He was sure of that – for revenge if nothing else. As for the bridge project, there had been no significant moves on the market at all. The dumping of the shares had been cancelled, quite why, he was not sure. What had made Calogero di Rienzi change his mind, and change his mind at the last minute? The price was still rising, but the coming of August, and the holidays, and the spate of very public murders, had distracted the public from the bridge project. The government was furious, he knew that. Having someone shot dead on the beach in Cefalù was bad for tourism. Having a restaurant in Taormina sprayed with bullets was bad for tourism too. So was the incident with the yacht near Favignana. It went further than that: spectacular public assassinations were bad for the government, because they called into question their ability to govern. The government would limp on to the spring, when Brussels would pull the plug, by refusing to lend any more money. They would replace the Prime Minister with some banker of their choice. That was certain; but that would only be possible because of, among other things, the severe denting of its credibility that the government had received this summer. What was the point of the government telling people that they were in charge and all was well when bullets flew over beautiful Cefalù and Taormina, and when yachts exploded off Favignana?

What had happened, indeed, reflected Rosario? His brother was on his way to Palermo, with Stefania in tow. There while she went shopping Calogero would get what he wanted too – an entry into the upper circles of criminality. The whole thing had been a disaster from that point of view. Calogero's rise was proving to be unstoppable. And he had given Anna Maria Tancredi a child. Traiano had told him. He had said that he was bound to find out in years to come anyway, so he would tell him now. In six months of so he would have a new nephew or a niece. It was all a big surprise, to Anna Maria and to Calogero. He was telling him this as a favour, asking him not to tell anyone, certainly not Calogero, and asking him, when he was told by anyone else, to act surprised. But he mentioned this now to Volta, who furrowed his brow.

'I would have thought she was too old,' said Volta.

'That is what I thought,' said Rosario. 'That is probably what he thought. And she too. That child will be important one day. Of course no one knows. I wonder what my sister-in-law will say when she finds out, as she undoubtedly will do? By the way, what was in Tancredi's phone, the one that Traiano got for you?'

'The telephone number of her hairdresser, the telephone number of her gynaecologist, her maid, her sister, her nephew... Oh by the way, Captain Perraino has disappeared, have you heard? They are thinking that the Romanians might have killed him. But where and when, no one is sure. And there is no body. The car was found in Nicolosi, funnily enough. Burned out. So he must have met a bad end. So, the phone: all the numbers you would expect.'

'So, all that effort for nothing? A waste of time?' asked Rosario.

'One number was interesting.'

'Rome?'

'No, Brussels. It is another mobile in Brussels, and pretty hard to find out who it belongs to. But that may be significant. Isn't that where the real power is? And you, what about you? How have the holidays been?'

He had mentioned witnessing the killing on the beach at Cefalù. How indeed had the holidays been? He had made love, if that was what it had been, with Gino's girlfriend, Catarina, and satisfied a brief but powerful lust with her. He had made love to his sister-in-law, whom he had long found attractive, but a little forbidding, spending three successive nights with her in Cefalù, which he saw as an essential part of his education.

'I have got a girlfriend,' he said. 'So the holidays have been good so far.'

Volta's raised eyebrows led to an explanation. After Cefalù he had returned to Catania and then immediately gone to Zafferana Etnea where the lawyer Petrocchi had his house. There he had spent the best part of a week. There had been walks across the lava fields of Mount Etna, indeed right up to the summit; there had been long talks with Petrocchi, mainly about the shares in Straits Limited and about his brother's involvement with Tancredi, a person whom the lawyer Petrocchi held in the greatest, if wary, respect. At some point he had come to the realisation that Petrocchi saw his connection to Calogero and Tancredi as a not altogether bad thing. And while all this went on, he had become friendly with Petrocchi's youngest daughter, Carolina. They were the same age, she was a very good Catholic who went to Mass every day. She was a student in Rome, as he had been, and after the summer was over, he was planning, at her invitation, to spend time in Rome with her.

'I thought you wanted to be a priest,' said Volta.

'A good Catholic wife might be better for me,' said Rosario. After all, one could only risk so much.

A rich Catholic wife, your boss's daughter, thought Volta grimly.

They were in the best suite in the best hotel in Palermo. The air conditioning worked: everything was splendidly cold. Even the sheets on the bed were cool to the touch, and the marble of the bathroom made you shiver. A bottle of champagne had been waiting for them, in a bucket full of ice. The man who carried up their bags, to whom Calogero gave the extravagant tip of fifty euros, whispered that signor Santucci would be in the bar that evening at six. In such luxurious surroundings, and left alone at last, he had felt it incumbent on him to do his duty as a husband, which she was pleased about, in case her nights in Cefalù had left her in an interesting condition. Then he had had a shower, put on his silk boxer shorts, his linen shirt, and his linen suit, and gone downstairs, leaving her to luxuriate on her own in bed. The children had been left behind in Catania with their Aunt Giuseppina to look after them.

Santucci was waiting for him. He looked at the waiter, who brought two perfect negronis, a drink Calogero did not really like, but was too polite to refuse. They raised their glasses slightly before the first sip, wishing each other health and prosperity.

'My sympathy on the passing of your brother-in-law,' murmured Calogero.

'My poor wife is inconsolable; she was so close to her brother; and my mother-in-law is devastated. Her only son. But what can you do? I myself never liked him much. We were second cousins, as perhaps you know. Those awful Romanians. And the awful incident on the beach in Cefalù. Your wife was there? Holy Mary! What a world we live in. But I can assure you, we have sent all the Romanians back to where they came from, or to Hell, whichever was the closer. I assured our friends in Rome of that. They were nervous as you can imagine. They thought it might derail the bridge project. Talking of which, Anna Maria is well? She told me the good news. Congratulations! And as for Lotto, or whatever he was called, any sign of him?'

'I spoke to Anna the Romanian prostitute and she has been scanning the horizon every day – not a sign.'

'Wonderful news. Brilliant work. Wonderful woman that Anna. I would very much like to meet her. Of course, we must expect the Romanians to come back at some stage, but not just yet. They are still licking their wounds. They may be expecting Lotto to turn up. In which case, he would have some explaining to do, wouldn't he? How things went so badly wrong. He should not have spoken in the presence of a prostitute with sharp ears and a good memory. Unlike so professional a man to make so obvious an error. But who cares how the ending comes about, as long as it is the right ending?' His smile was seraphic. 'We have lost a few good men, but most of us have survived, and we have come out of this stronger, I feel. The peace of Palermo has been saved. And a large part of that is to your credit. We are very grateful. We know how to reward our friends. For you, we have two rewards, both of which are commensurate with your great abilities. For a start, we give you Catania. It is yours. Do with it what you like. It is true that we have never been so very interested in our second city, so this may seem an easy gift to make. The whole province of Catania is yours. You have our blessing, and people will co-operate with you, I am confident. And one can add Syracuse and its province as well, as I know that you love the place. It is a valuable little fiefdom. Doors will open for you from now on. The prospects of investment are huge, and the bridge project will be bring you a fortune, thanks to our clever Anna Maria. I am glad she has you. By the way, that nasty little skunk, Perraino, has disappeared. Into thin air! Who would have thought it? The Romanians must have done it. Why I cannot think. Mistaken identity? Maybe he offended them somehow or another? But as I said earlier, who cares about what really happened as long as the final result is one we all wanted? And who would not want Perraino out of the picture? But to move on to your other reward, the real reason we have invited you here. Tomorrow is the 10th August, the feast of Saint Lawrence. We always have a big family party on that day. A car will come and collect you at noon. It will take you up to my father's house; it is his name day; my uncle Domenico will be there, my other relatives, well, lots of people. You remember the list? So many people whose lives you saved. They will want to meet you and greet you, and make you a member of the family. Initiate you, if you like, explain the rules, explain how things work. And then we will eat and drink and get to know you. Though I feel, dearest Calogero, that I know you already.'

He put down his glass, and then stood. So did Calogero.

'Until tomorrow,' said Antonio Santucci.

'Until tomorrow,' echoed Calogero.

He watched Santucci go. He wondered if he should have another drink, or go upstairs and fetch Stefania and take her out to dinner. What would he tell her? Best nothing. Best to keep silent. By this time tomorrow, he would be initiated; by this time tomorrow, he reflected, he would be a member of the Mafia.

Printed in Great Britain
by Amazon